I KNOW WHAT YOU'RE THINKING

I KNOW WHAT YOU'RE THINKING

PHILL FEATHERSTONE

Cover by Park Designs.

Typeset in Fanwood by Opitus Books.

ISBN 9781838003562

First published by Opitus Books, United Kingdom, 2022.
www.opitus.net

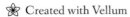 Created with Vellum

BY PHILL FEATHERSTONE

amazon.co.uk®

A gift from **Phill Featherstone**

I hope you enjoy reading my book. Thank you for being part of the tour. Best wishes. From Phill Featherstone

Gift note included with **I Know What You're Thinking**

CONTENTS

1

Beth was lying on her back with Cameron beside her. She adjusted her blindfold. Cameron felt claustrophobic when he wore a blindfold so he didn't have one, but Beth found it helped. They had agreed that it was better if they didn't touch, so they'd left a space between them. It wasn't a very big space but it was there.

'Ready?' Cameron said.

'Yes,' said Beth, in a voice not much louder than a whisper.

'Okay. We've not done it before, at least not like this, so be prepared for it not to work.'

'It will work, I know it will. There's no point trying if we're not positive.'

'If you say so. Okay, let's go.'

Cameron closed his eyes and took a deep breath. Beth started to go through her relaxation procedure.

long, straight lane between snowy fields. The lane was lined with fir trees, and as they'd passed them melting snow had sluttered from the branches. She remembered what she and Cameron had been wearing. She heard the crisp crunch beneath their boots. She concentrated as hard as she could, holding her breath, not moving, until she could keep it up no longer. She took off the blindfold and rolled onto her side. Cameron was on his back, eyes closed.

'Anything?' she said.

'Not really. I mean I kept trying. I kept thinking what it might be that you'd want to send me, but there were so many things and nothing came clear.'

Beth was disappointed. 'I don't think you should be trying to think of anything,' she said. 'The idea is that you empty your head and make your mind a blank. If you're expecting a particular image it will push what I'm actually trying to send you out of the way.'

'Mm.' Cameron was doubtful.

'Look,' said Beth, sitting up again. 'I know you're not sure that this works but let's give it another go. When I was the receiver what you were thinking of got through to me, didn't it.'

'Sort of,' said Cameron.

'It did. When I remember what I saw, it could have been a dagger. It's just that I mistook what it was. Give it another go, okay? Send me something.'

They lay down, and Beth again covered her eyes. Cameron took hold of her hand. She tried to clear her head but this time it was harder. She couldn't shift the image of the lane in the snow that she'd been attempting to send to Cameron. Every time she tried to recreate the velvet room and the blackness, the frosted trees and the frozen ruts pushed their way in. She sat up, took off her blindfold and dropped it beside the bed.

'What's up?' said Cameron.

'It's no good. I can't get out of my head what I was trying to send to you.' She slid her legs off the bed. 'I think I need to take a break.'

'What was it that you were trying to send me?'

'You remember when we walked along that lane in the snow, last year, you know, when you told me I was the only girl you'd really loved? Well it was that.'

'Holy shit!'

'What?'

'That's what I was trying just now to send to you.'

Beth was lost. 'You mean you were thinking of the lane?'

'Yes. And the snow, and when we stopped under the trees and a great lump of it came off a branch and just missed us. All that.'

'Why? What made you think of that? Why remember it now, so much later?'

Cameron shook his head. 'I don't know. It just came into my head.'

'But that's what I was trying to send to you. Just now. When you were the receiver but said you didn't get it.'

They both looked at each other.

'Oh my God,' said Beth. She was so excited that the words caught in her throat and she could barely get them out. 'Don't you see? You did get it. It worked. You knew what I was thinking.'

2

THE UNCANNY ABILITY TO share each other's thoughts wasn't new. For as long as they'd known each other, which was the year they both started school, Beth and Cameron had been aware of a curious link between them. It showed itself in lots of small ways. For example, they'd both start to speak at the same time and be saying the same thing. Or they would turn up to a friend's birthday party each with an identical gift. At meals they'd nearly always make identical choices. Beth would know what Cameron wanted for Christmas before he'd said anything to anyone about it. Cameron would know what bedtime story Beth had had the night before.

At first they themselves didn't think it was anything unusual. It had always been like that. Then adults started to notice. 'Anyone would think you were twins,' Beth's Gran said. It was often treated as a joke. Archy, Cameron's friend, said it wasn't surprising that they both thought the same thing because they'd only got one brain between them. Some of their other friends treated it with the same amused indulgence, the rest ignored it. Most of the adults reckoned it was just coincidence. Gran thought it was cute. So did Molly, Cameron's mother. Zak, his step-dad looked for ways to explain it.

That was when they were younger, but not long after they moved to secondary school it became an issue. At the end of their first term they were hauled before their head of year. They were puzzled to know why, and were astonished when they were told that the answers they'd given in a history test the day before were virtually identical. The teacher put their work side by side and demanded to know which of them had copied from the other and how they'd managed to do it. Beth and Cameron were bewildered and denied they'd cheated. The teacher didn't believe them. She pointed to their answers; not quite the same and just different enough, she said, to hide their deception.

They were interviewed independently and each insisted that the work was their own. They were put in detention; it was not for copying, the head of year explained, but for failing to own up to it and tell the truth. Cameron was moved to another group which did different work and so the problem didn't arise again, but they'd acquired a reputation which it took them some time to shake off.

Beth was convinced that they had a special gift, Cameron not so much. He believed that what was going on was mostly fluke with a lacing of coincidence, and that it wasn't surprising because they spent so much time together. He told her that telepathy was a load of rubbish, and he dug up online articles debunking it. Beth challenged him to give another explanation for what they experienced. He couldn't. She also pointed out that many scientists agreed that there was a lot about the mind that was still not fully understood, and she talked about reports she'd found in her own explorations of the internet that dealt with aspects of the brain outside the five recognised senses: for example, the functioning of mirror neurons, and the work sponsored by Elon Musk on 'neuralinks'. They never had a full blown row about it but they had some vigorous discussions.

Cameron said he'd prove once and for all that telepathy was nonsense. He persuaded Beth to carry out a test which he'd found online. It used a pack of 'Zener' cards, five sets of five cards, each set bearing a different symbol – a circle, a square, a cross, a star, and wavy lines.

'What do we have to do?' said Beth.

'One of us is the sender and the other the receiver. We sit back to back. The sender puts the pack of cards face down and turns them over one by one. They concentrate on the card and try to transmit that symbol to the receiver.'

'And the receiver writes down what they think it is.'

'Yes. We do that for all the cards in the pack. Then we check and see how many are right.'

'How many times do we do it?' said Beth.

Cameron consulted the instructions. 'It says here you should go through the pack five times. It will take a while.'

'All right,' said Beth. She didn't believe the experiment would tell them anything; she knew that they had a connection but she'd decided Cameron should be humoured.

For their first run Cameron was sender and Beth receiver. When they were done they went through Cameron's pile of cards and checked them against the list Beth had made. They were astounded. Ten of the twenty-five cards on Beth's list were correct.

Beth was exultant and even Cameron was impressed. 'Unbelievable!' she gushed. 'Let's do it again. I'll send, you receive.'

On this second run the score was two.

'Oh,' said Beth, disappointed. Perhaps she was a more effective receiver than Cameron and he was a better sender. It could be that it was more successful that way round. She handed him the cards. 'Again. Really concentrate now.'

'Yes, miss.'

They repeated the test and this time the score was three.

'Well at least it's going up,' said Cameron.

'Yes, but it's not even average,' said Beth. 'With five of each symbol you've got a one in five chance of being right.'

They did it again, and scored another two. Then four. Then they gave up.

'Useless,' said Cameron. He checked their results on the ready reckoner that had come with the cards. 'Twenty-one correct out of a hundred attempts. It says that's "insignificant". Pathetic!'

Cameron felt vindicated. Fond as he was of Beth, there was no mysterious mental link between them. She didn't know what was happening in his head, and he confessed to himself that sometimes that was a good thing. He certainly had no idea what was going on in hers. Then something happened that changed his mind.

He was with Beth on a patch of waste ground. It was the site of an old factory where there was a concrete pan that was good for skateboarding. At the edge of the site was a huge mound of earth and rubble, and some lads were on top of it messing about with an old tyre they'd found. The tyre was huge, perhaps from a tractor, and they were having trouble handling it. Cameron climbed up to join them, Beth stayed at the bottom with her Gran's dog. She bent down to rub the animal's head, and just then the boys lost control of the tyre and it started down the mound. Beth had her back to it and it was obvious she was directly in its path. Cameron tried to shout but no sound came, he couldn't utter. It was as if his throat was paralysed, but inside his head he screamed at her to move. Beth felt a sudden lunge, like a hand in her back pushing her aside. She staggered and the tyre bounced past, missing her by inches.

She swung around and saw Cameron and a couple of his friends scrambling down towards her.

'Shit, that was lucky,' one of them said.

'Sorry,' said the boy who'd let go of it. 'I didn't realise it would go like that. Good job you got out of the way.'

'Yes, it would have flattened you if it had hit.'

Beth could see it had been a near miss. The tyre was big and heavy; if it had struck her it would have done her harm. She also knew that her escape wasn't down to chance. When they were alone she and Cameron talked about it.

'Thank you,' she said.

Cameron was shaken by what had so nearly happened. 'What for?' he said. 'I didn't do anything. I tried to shout but something stuck in my throat and I couldn't.'

'You didn't need to. I felt you helping me. It wasn't a voice in my head or anything like that. It was like you were shoving me out of the way.'

Less than a week later it happened again. This time they were going for a bus to take them into town. Cameron saw it coming. 'Come on,' he shouted, and made to run across the road. Beth was behind him and she froze; he was about to career into the path of a car. At that same instant Cameron felt something hold him. It was like a fist grabbing his shirt so he couldn't step off the kerb, and the car brushed past him. Beth stood open mouthed. She hadn't actually done anything but she knew that somehow she had protected him.

Beth needed no more evidence that their minds sometimes connected. She didn't know how or why, but these things couldn't be just coincidence. She wanted to challenge Cameron's scepticism and prove to him once and for all that they really had an extrasensory link. So they set up the experiment in her bedroom, and Cameron was at last convinced. He had to accept that for reasons neither of them could fathom one was able to reach into the mind of the other. However, it wasn't something they could rely on being able to do; it just happened sometimes. 'Pity,' Cameron said. 'If we could manage it all the time we could make some money out of it.'

Cameron bought a bottle of wine, they found a quiet corner of the park to drink it, and they talked. They agreed that the favoured tests of telepathy, like trying to reproduce sequences of cards or find objects that had been hidden in a room, were a waste of time. What connected the two of them wasn't something mathematical or scientific: it was emotional and beyond understanding. The only sensible way to handle it was to talk frequently about what they were doing and what they were planning to do, so that they could avoid being labelled freaks – obviously what some of their friends thought.

As they went through their teens they grew closer, and their relationship progressed from friendship into something more. And as they developed a physical attachment the mental bond between them became even stronger. Not always but often each would know what the other wanted, or didn't want, without putting it into words. When a year ago Cameron got set on by a gang of hooligans and his mobile was taken, Beth knew something had happened to him and went to find him. When Beth took her Grade 8 piano exam Cameron was scarcely able to sleep the night before, and when he did drop off the dream he had was very like the one Beth had in her own bed in another part of the town.

They realised that they were privileged; they had an astonishing gift. They didn't know that one day it would save Cameron's life, and almost cost Beth hers.

3

DR HANS FOLKEN was at his home in London. His house was secluded, on the St John's Gardens side of Ladbroke Grove. It was like all the others in that neighbourhood – large, detached, luxurious, and anonymous. It was guarded by a high wall topped with razor wire, and fronted by a metal electric gate, wide and solid. That made Hans Folken feel very safe.

His wife, Anita, was in Brussels and it was his housekeeper's night off. However, he wasn't alone. Somewhere in the house his butler-cum-assistant, Simon, also awaited the visitor who was expected that evening. Folken was filling the time by realigning the framed photographs on the wall of his study. His housekeeper was a good woman but she had no eye for straightness and every time she dusted, as she had that day, she left his photo gallery askew. When he grumbled about it to Anita she said he should get somebody in to fix the frames to the wall with screws, like they do in an art gallery, but that wasn't the point. The point was that the housekeeper should take more trouble.

The collection recorded milestones in Folken's life, some of the achievements of which he was most proud. They were placed so that they could be easily appreciated from the chairs on which he would sit his visitors. There was a picture of him as a freshman at Oxford, one of a row of impossibly young looking faces lined up in the quadrangle of an ancient college. Next to it was one taken three years later, of his graduation. There was another, this time of him receiving his Ph.D, and next to that a snap taken with a few colleagues in Regent's Park. It had been his birthday and they'd walked the short distance from University College, where he'd had his first job. He tutted as he levelled it.

He looked at the clock on his desk. His visitor was late. He'd expected as much. Until a few weeks ago he'd never heard of the man who was coming to see him, but after his first approach he had looked him up online and discovered that Mikael Dimitri Ivanovitch was, according to accounts, the fifth richest man in Russia. In Folken's experience such people lived in a different time frame from ordinary people. He called it "BT", or billionaire's time. Its characteristic was that it paid scant attention to the progress of the clock and focussed almost entirely on the needs and fancies of the individual at its centre. It had been arranged that Ivanovitch would meet him at eight o'clock; that might have meant a known time for the rest of the world but for the Russian it merely meant when it was convenient to him.

Folken moved along the wall and stood before a large frame containing a newspaper cutting and a photograph. The cutting was about the award of the contract for constructing the National Human Genome Database, the NHGD, to the company he'd founded, Aurora Healthcare. Folken had kept the cutting, even though the report spelt his name like the bird, with an 'a', a 'c', and an 'o'. The photograph showed him welcoming the Prime Minister to the Aurora building on completion of the project two years later. It wasn't quite the completion. The job was never done, because not only did it need constant updating, but as each individual reached the age of eighteen they had to be tested and their genetic profile entered. However, it had marked a milestone; the DNA of 99% of the adult population of England, Wales and Northern Ireland was now on file and accessible to those who had a right to it. Beside it was an official portrait of him at Buckingham Palace receiving his OBE from a member of the Royal Family. This trio of achievements was positioned so that they were the most prominent objects in the collection.

An alarm sounded on his computer. It indicated that one of the security cameras had picked up activity outside. A window in the corner of the screen showed a man illuminated by the spotlight on the gate. He had slavic features and his hair was close cropped. His dark suit was cut to show his impressive body shape. Folken pressed a key and a mechanical voice asked the man if he needed help.

He stepped towards the grill and leant forward. 'Mr Ivanovitch, he wishes to have entrance.' The voice was heavily accented.

Folken pressed a another key and the gate slid back. A large black car came through and the barrier closed behind it. The camera tracked the car circling the flower bed in front of the house and stopping at the portico.

'Simon,' Folken said into the intercom. 'Our visitors are here.' Simon would already have known that because he, too, would have heard the warning, but Folken liked creating the impression that he was in control.

In the distance he heard the door chime. He adjusted his tie, flicked his shoulders for dandruff, arranged the coloured promotional leaflets on the coffee table in front of his desk into a tasteful fan, and tweaked the light level. Then he sat down at his desk, took a folder of documents from a drawer and pretended to look through it. He heard movement and voices in the hall, then there was a gentle tap on the door.

Simon appeared. 'Mr Ivanovitch, sir,' he said.

'Thank you, Simon.'

Simon held the door open and a heavily built man with silver hair came in. Folken had seen Mikael Dimitri Ivanovitch before but only in a zoom call. He'd seemed slimmer and younger then, clearly the result of careful make-up and lighting. In the flesh he looked pretty close to Folken's own age, and somewhat heavier. He wore a dark grey suit with a maroon waistcoat and a tie in turquoise silk, a peacock display which Folken hadn't expected.

Folken rose and came from behind his desk. He held out his hand and adopted a warm smile. 'Mr Ivanovitch, my name is Hans Folken. It's good to meet you in person. You are welcome.'

Ivanovitch took Folken's hand and held it for a moment. He didn't smile. He didn't apologise for being late.

The next few minutes were taken up by the two men settling and sizing each other up. Folken's people had told him that Ivanovitch was partial to Scottish single malt whisky. He himself had a wide range of them and he'd selected a special one. Ivanovitch accepted, chose water rather than ice, and held the amber liquid to the light. Meanwhile Folken gave an introduction to the small, very exclusive Speyside distillery where it had been produced.

Ivanovitch responded to the chat with an impatience he didn't try to conceal. They were meeting to finalise a deal, and he could never understand the convention that negotiations and transactions had to be bracketed by pointless babble. They both knew why he was there, and his time was precious. His private plane was waiting. So was his daughter. He had watched her on dialysis the previous afternoon and experienced the confused mix of emotions he always felt when he saw her submit to this trial – anxiety, anguish, sorrow, rage. The sooner the matter he had come to arrange could be concluded the sooner he would be able to free her not only from dependence on the machine, but also from the itching, nausea, cramps and interminable fatigue that accompanied her condition.

'Your flight was comfortable?' Folken asked.

The Russian grunted. 'Comfortable enough.' Why would it not be? It was his own jet, so his comfort was its business. If he were not comfortable he would replace the plane, the crew, or both.

'And the room service. To your taste?'

The Russian had sent away the attractive young woman who had appeared the night before at the door of his hotel room. 'Thank you, I had other plans.' The Russian's foot began to tap.

Folken found the tapping irritating but understood that it was a signal for him to move to business. 'Perhaps I might explain to you the advantages of obtaining the service you seek from a provider based in this country,' he began.

Ivanovitch sighed. He had no need of any further sales pitch. The zoom presentation had been very thorough. It had started with a video. Over a lush soundtrack a well-known actor delivered a smooth narration emphasising tradition and quality. It was mostly old stuff: rolling images of green fields, and unspoilt villages of the like that by now it was hard to find outside a national park. There were drone views of London – Buckingham Palace, the Houses of

Parliament, and the City – shot from too high to show that many of the shiny office buildings were now mostly empty. This was followed by Constable and Hockney country landscapes and views of the Thames by Turner, Manet and Canaletto. They were accompanied by lines from Shakespeare: "This royal throne of kings, this sceptred isle". Then there had been a slow pan along a low, modern building with lots of stainless steel and glass. The camera zoomed in and there was a dissolve into a bright, clean hospital suite and a state of the art operating theatre staffed by young female nurses with model complexions and bodies, and handsome, distinguished looking male doctors. Finally there had been Folken himself, sitting behind his desk in this same room and speaking in reassuring tones of the exceptional service offered by Aurora New Life. The implication was that Alexandra Christina Ivanovitch would be uniquely privileged in receiving not only the best possible care but also an organ from a native of this demi-paradise. She would ingest the tradition, history, talents and values that had been displayed in the video. Ivanovitch didn't buy that; anyway, why would he want it? Alexandra Christina was Russian. She had a heritage richer by far than what this tired little country offered. What he did want was for her to be well again.

'When can the procedure be done?' he asked.

'Very soon,' Folken replied. 'As you know, this country is a world leader in the mass recording of genetic information. We at Aurora are proud of the pioneering work we have done in this sphere. We are still the only nation that can claim to have on file the individual genetic map of almost all its adult citizens. What that means is that in effect we have in our population the world's biggest bank of potential organ donors. Because of the database we are able to quickly locate them and select the most suitable. As soon as we have your authorisation to proceed we can have a donor ready within hours.'

Both men knew what Folken meant by "authorisation".

'The fee you are asking is considerable,' Ivanovitch said.

Folken nodded sympathetically. 'It is indeed a large sum, but this is an expensive procedure. Our facilities are second to none and our people have exceptional skills.' He treated Ivanovitch to his best, most sanctimonious smile. 'And how can we put a value on the health and the quality of life of your daughter?'

Ivanovitch frowned. It was the answer he'd expected. He sipped his single malt.

'We can guarantee, absolutely guarantee, the closest possible match,' said Folken. 'Your daughter will receive a kidney which will be almost identical to her own, except,' and he permitted himself a little smile, 'this one will function. It will be from a fit, young person close to her own age. It will be perfect in every way.'

'Whose will it be?'

'We have a shortlist of possibilities. We will narrow

these down when we've carried out some final tests. However, it is our policy not to reveal the identity of the donor.'

'In that case, how do I know that it is what you say? You could be giving my daughter a kidney from some drunken old hag.'

Folken looked pained. 'We could, of course we could. But ask yourself, would we? Aurora is a reputable company. You are a powerful man and you have influential friends. Would it be sensible for us to provide you with anything less than the very best?'

Ivanovitch smiled grimly. It would certainly not be sensible. It might also be fatal, and he was not referring to the life of his daughter. 'Will they know?' he asked.

'Will who know? The donor?' Folken laughed softly. 'They will know that they have donated a kidney, naturally, but no more than that. They will not know who has received it. Our watchword is discretion. By entrusting Aurora with this work you can be assured that the whole operation will be carried out in the utmost secrecy. Your daughter and the donor will be in adjacent operating theatres but they will not see each other. The transfer will be immediate. There will be no delays, no possibility for the organ to deteriorate in transit, which could well happen in other environments and with other providers.'

Ivanovitch drained his whisky and held out his glass for it to be refilled. 'How long will Alexandra Christina be here? How soon before she is able to go home?'

Folken put on his best professional frown and spoke earnestly. 'The final answer to that question will depend on the assessment of the medical experts I shall assign to the task. I understand that you want your own personal physician to be in attendance throughout. We have no objection to that, although it must be understood that during the actual procedure he can be an observer only. However, we shall welcome his input in assisting with your daughter's preparation and in monitoring her recovery, and of course he will be involved in making the recommendation for her discharge.'

The Russian sighed. Why did these people always take so long to say anything? 'Yes, but how long?'

'You will be using your own transport?'

'My jet will bring us over and it will wait at Aberdeen airport until my daughter is ready to come home.'

Folken was momentarily taken off guard. He had mentioned in the zoom call that the site of the transplant facility was in the newly independent Kingdom of Scotland, but its precise location had not been revealed. How had Ivanovitch discovered that Aberdeen was the nearest airport? He suppressed his surprise and carried on.

'Your daughter will need a little time to recover from her journey, and of course there are the final tests. However, if everything goes well these things won't take long and we should be ready to go ahead the following day. The operation will take up to three hours, and we will need to observe her closely for the next twenty-four. She should be able to leave, attended by your physician and a nurse and in your own plane, within a few days, provided we are satisfied with the after care arrangements you have made.'

Ivanovitch felt a surge of resentment, the old, peasant anger which had sustained his grandfather and father through hard times and had propelled his family to a position of wealth and power they could never have imagined. What right do these people think they have to judge the arrangements he has made for his own daughter? Who do they think they are? However, the diplomatic part of him, the part that enabled him to walk with presidents and monarchs, the part that directed a multi-billion dollar business, told him that the only thing that mattered was his daughter's welfare, and he was reassured by the importance that was being given to that.

'She will of course still be weak,' Folken continued. 'She will need a high level of care. The final decision will have to be made by the medical people, but three or four days is usual.'

The Russian grunted. 'And the guarantee?'

Folken was puzzled. 'Guarantee?'

'What guarantee do I have, what guarantee does Alexandra Christina have, that what you are doing will work? That it won't go wrong, that I won't end up a couple of million dollars down and my daughter no better?'

Folken fixed the Russian with a well practised look

meant to convey transparent honesty tinged with a little disappointment. 'There are many unpredictables in medicine. Every transplant carries risks. However, we have the best surgeons, the best equipment and the best support staff in the world. And of course, we have the best data and can locate *the* most appropriate donor. It is impossible to give an absolute guarantee, no one can, but we have done these procedures before. All have been successful. I have every confidence in a satisfactory outcome.'

'And the price...'

'...is as has been quoted to you. I am afraid that in a situation like this we do not bargain.'

Ivanovitch thought for a moment. He was making a fuss about the fee because he was a businessman and dealing was what he did. The sum was more than a lifetime's income for some people, but to him it was negligible. 'Very well,' he said.

'Payable in advance, of course,' said Folken. 'As soon as the funds have been received all that remains is for your daughter's physician to contact us to make the arrangements. We shall then bring the donor to our clinic and have them ready.'

The Russian nodded. He stood up and took something from his document case, which he held out to Folken. It was a CD. On the cover was a photograph of a young woman playing a cello. She was bent over the instrument, her hair falling forward and hiding her face. Folken was familiar enough with the Russian

alphabet to be able to read the name: Александра
Кристина Иванович.

'This is your daughter?' Folken said.

'Yes. It is a recording of Dvorak's Cello Concerto
she made with our National Orchestra. It won the
Golden Gramophone Award, our equivalent of your
Grammy. It was her first recording and so far the only
one, because soon after she made it she became too ill
to manage the intensive practicing required of a top
soloist, and she certainly can't travel easily.'

He read Folken's puzzled expression; why had he
been given this?

'Play it,' said Ivanovich. 'It will help you to
understand the talent you will be giving back to the
world.'

'Thank you,' said Folken. 'I will.' The two men shook
hands. 'If you have any questions, if you or Alexandra
Christina would like to talk over any aspect of the
procedure, if there is anything at all you wish to know or
seek reassurance on, do not hesitate to contact me.'

The Russian nodded. He wouldn't.

Folken summoned Simon to show his visitor out.
When he'd gone he smiled to himself, picked up his
phone and touched a number. It was answered at once.

'McIntyre, you have been watching the subject we
identified?'

'Yes, Doctor.'

'And everything checks out?'

'Yes, Doctor.'

'Very good. Go ahead with the seizure.'

'Yes, Doctor.'

'And do we have a back-up?'

'Aye, Doctor.'

The system was foolproof; the primary donor had been chosen and they had a substitute if there were problems. The transplant would be straightforward. It would be simple, and highly profitable. It would be like all the others. Or so Folken thought.

4

MOLLY SAT on the bed and rubbed her legs. They ached almost constantly now, and her varicose veins were getting worse. She bent forward to pick up her magazine from the floor and gave an involuntary gasp. It was becoming increasingly hard to move without discomfort. As well as the distorted veins, she had arthritis in her hands, knees and shoulders, her skin was blotchy, her hair dry and brittle, and a lot of the time she felt weak and nauseous. Oh, and her jaw hurt from the tooth implants. Apart from that, she would tell people, she was just fine. She unwrapped another calcium tablet and dissolved it on her tongue. It tasted awful; bloody chalk!

Molly was pregnant for the thirteenth time in eighteen years. She had successfully brought eleven gestations to full term. There had been one miscarriage, back in the early days before the antenatal treatments were as effective as they are now, and one termination at the parents' request following an in-utero diagnosis of spina bifida. One of the births had been premature, delivered after thirty two weeks, but the baby had survived and, as far as she knew, thrived. Eleven live children, eleven different fathers, eleven different mothers. Although in a way she was mother to them all.

Now once again she was into the second trimester, and recently back from the routine battery of tests, injections and scans. All was well, she had been told, but she had known it would be. Her body was good at growing babies. So far she hadn't felt too bad but she knew that things would only get worse from now on. A hot summer had been forecast and she was not looking forward to struggling towards a fetid June in her final month.

She had vowed she would stop after baby number five, but then had been persuaded to do just one more. Then another one after that. And another. The truth was, it was the only thing she was good at. There was nothing else she knew how to do, and she had come to rely on the money. This one would be the last, though. The procession of hostings had destroyed her body and it had been touch and go whether the medical assessor, a grim, dark haired woman (Dr Salazar, was she called?) who seemed to have taken an immediate dislike to Molly, would approve her for this one. In the end she had agreed, although with obvious reluctance.

'It really is against my better judgement,' she had

said in her clipped, austere voice. 'However, the biological parents are desperate and you do have a first class record. More important, the tissue matches are excellent. Therefore I'll authorise it, but I shall make a note on your file that in my opinion this should be your last time.'

It was a judgement Molly had heard with a mixture of relief and dread. She was looking forward to stopping, to no longer having to suffer the regular bloating of her body, but her joy was dampened by the prospect of losing her earning power. She had a little put aside but nowhere near enough. How would she manage?

She rummaged under the settee and pulled out a flowery tin. Inside was a Victoria sponge, a yellow heaven filled with jam and cream. She had always craved Victoria sponges when she was pregnant, every time. They were strictly forbidden but she knew a woman who baked them and she had an arrangement with her. This was a new one today, freshly delivered only an hour ago. She cut herself a slice and started to eat it. There was no plate and she balanced it on the flat of her hand, letting the crumbs fall back into the tin. She felt guilty as a schoolgirl taking a quiet spliff behind the bike sheds. If she were to be found out there would be trouble. She would be told off and a portion of her fee would be docked. But no one would know, certainly not the baby's parents who were a long way away. She licked her hand and wiped it on her stomach. 'There you are, little guy,' she said. 'Victoria sponge, from your host mum.'

Following her assessment Molly had gone to the clinic for the fertilised ovum to be implanted in her womb. It was routine and she was used to it, but it was unpleasant. This time it felt different. For a start, there had been more people around. The dark haired doctor – Salamar, that was the name – had been there, and an important looking man with an elegant, blond woman. She had looked bored, but the man had followed everything intently. She'd got the impression that he was some sort of physician, but his interest hadn't been medical, that side of it had been left to Salamar. From the way the others behaved towards this couple there seemed to be something special about them.

She'd asked one of the nurses who the man was, and she'd whispered, 'He's the boss.' And then, looking around to make sure she wasn't being watched or overheard, 'He's the daddy.'

'Who is he?'

The nurse held a finger to her lips and with her other hand gave Molly's wrist a playful slap. 'You know I can't tell you that,' she said.

Molly had been kept under observation a little longer than usual before she was allowed home. At first she'd thought that was because she was getting on, but now she'd come to the conclusion that there was something different about this pregnancy. There were more screenings scheduled this time, and the important looking man who'd been at the implant had taken to calling her regularly. As well as this, she'd been given some additional food vouchers and there were incremental additions to her personal credit account after each satisfactory check up. Her regular doctor said it was to ensure she was able to maintain a healthy diet but she thought it was more than that. All foetuses were special, but there was something extra special about this one.

She flipped open her datapad and keyed in her bank access code. Yes, there it was, in her account already. Besides receiving the credits promptly, the payments for this one were particularly good, and on top of them there'd been an unexpected bonus.

Two women had turned up at her home a few days before. She'd thought they were from the clinic but they showed some official looking ID and said they were doing research on teenage leisure for the national database.

'I don't know anything about teenagers,' she'd said.

The one who seemed to be taking the lead smiled and said, 'But you have a teenage son.'

'Oh, Cameron. Yes. But he doesn't live here. He lives with his step-father, Zak Lawless. I can give you his address.'

'Thank you, we already have it and we'll call there later. While we're with you would you answer a few questions?' It was framed as a request but it was obvious to Molly that she had no choice; what Zak called "a rhetorical imperative" – he used terms like that.

The questions had been simple and seemed innocent enough. Like where Cameron would go to hang out, what he did in his spare time, who his friends were. She told them he spent most of his time with Zak and with Zak's other stepson, Archy, and when he wasn't there he was with his girlfriend, Beth. They seemed particularly interested in that.

'Where does Beth live?'

She told them.

'And how often does Cameron come to see you?'

'Every week. Sometimes more, but always on a Friday afternoon.'

'Does he come on his own?'

'Mostly. Sometimes Beth comes with him. She's his girlfriend. A lovely girl, I'm very fond of her.'

'And what do you do during these visits?'

'Beth and me talk. Cameron watches the TV.'

'How long do they stay?'

'An hour or two.'

She was made uneasy by the number of questions, but she told herself that nothing she told them could do any harm. And if they didn't learn it from her they could easily get the information in some other way. But she did wonder why they wanted to know so much about Cameron.

When they'd finished they asked for her life card and one of them put it in a portable reader. 'To acknowledge your help with our project and to thank you,' she said, handing the card back and smiling.

Molly didn't check it until after they'd gone, but she'd been surprised at the amount they'd transferred. Before they'd left they told her not to tell anyone about their visit and their questions. She'd been puzzled as to why not, but they said it was necessary to maintain confidentiality in order to ensure the integrity of the data. They also told her that if she co-operated she would receive another payment when their research was complete.

The baby inside her moved slightly. It was barely perceptible, just a flutter of its three inch form, but she'd felt that sensation before and she knew what it meant. It meant that the foetus was growing. Already it would have eyelids and fingerprints. It was not yet a person, but it soon would be. All she had to do was wait. Wait and keep herself healthy. That meant no alcohol, no drugs, no smoking, and no sex. Unlike the biological mother, Molly thought ruefully, who was probably enjoying all those things in spades. Oh, and no cake either. Molly cut herself another slice. Eat well, take the supplements, go for the check ups and wait. And hide the cake.

The baby stirred again and she found herself thinking about the labour. It was routine for her now and quick, a few hours at the most. Experience would alert her to its heralds well before the actual process began. At those first signs she would call a medicar and be taken to the clinic, where a delivery room would be waiting. When she was judged ready she'd be told to take up her position on the couch and a structure like a small tent would screen the lower half of her body. Molly would see nothing of what was going on below her waist. Speakers would relay tranquil music, what the team leader had once, when Molly had been told not to push, light-heartedly referred to as 'music on hold'. However, such humour was rare. Usually the only sounds, apart from her own breathing and occasional cries, were the exchanges of the birthing team and their instructions, conveyed by a nurse at her head. Most of the biological parents stipulated no drugs because there had been social media gossip that they could get into the baby's bloodstream and cause autism. That was ridiculous, but it meant that painkillers were off the menu, even epidurals.

She never saw the babies and rarely heard them cry. The tent hid them from her view and they were removed immediately. She'd always assumed that they were taken to their rich parents for a brief examination, probably photographs, she hoped a cuddle, before being handed over to their carers. She felt no attachment to the children she'd carried around for so long and she rarely thought about them again. Only once had that been different.

After the birth she would remain in the clinic, eating the junk food which was off limits during gestation, watching TV, and expressing her milk. Then, after a few days and, she assumes, when whatever further tests they run on the baby have yielded satisfactory results, she will get a message confirming the transfer of the final credits to her account and she'll go home.

Always in the past she had taken a few months to recover before re-registering and starting the whole process again. Not this time, though. This one would be the last.

5

Jonas Eze came out of the side entrance of the club his father owned. He pulled the heavy door shut behind him and felt it lock with a solid clunk. The club was closed until the late evening; then a long line of teenagers would form a restless queue outside, their entry controlled by two huge doormen.

Jonas had spent a long morning at the club and at last had been let out for what he considered to be a well-earned and much overdue lunch. Would he go back afterwards? It was a close call. His father would be furious if he didn't, but he'd gone out and Jonas reckoned he could probably stay out of his way until he'd calmed down. And there was no doubt that he had worked hard.

It was not the sort of work that Jonas enjoyed. In fact, there was no work that Jonas enjoyed, unless you count playing online games and stalking the net. Why his father, Solomon, insisted on him working in the club was a mystery to Jonas. It had been explained to him like this: 'Some day you'll own this place so you'd better learn how to run it, or sure as shit you're gonna be broke in a heartbeat.' Jonas didn't buy that. The club made a lot of money, and so when his time came to take it over he'd just put in a manager, somebody who knew what they were doing. The manager would do the work and Jonas would rake it in. And occasionally when he felt like it he'd be the DJ.

Learning 'how to run it' as Solomon understood it meant Jonas should start where he himself had, at the very bottom. That meant drudgery and boredom. His presence was clearly an irritation to the staff, who filled his time with whatever no one else wanted to do: mopping floors, cleaning the washrooms, arranging furniture. Or maybe, he thought in his sourest moments, his father had instructed them to give him all the crap jobs. They certainly didn't pay him the respect he thought should be due to the owner's son and somebody who would one day be their boss.

That morning had been better than some. He'd changed kegs and filled shelves in the bars, thrown out a couple of chairs that had been broken the night before, and fixed a UV tube that kept flickering. Then he'd played with the sound equipment until the regular DJ turned up and told him to piss off. He was relieved when his father had left for a meeting and he'd been able to sneak out.

It was only a few steps from the club to his car.

He'd left it in a space further along the street and been lucky to find the spot, but as he approached it he saw that fate now required him to pay for his good fortune. He'd been boxed in; the two vehicles parked front and back were much too close to let him out. The one behind, a black Porsche, was his father's. When Jonas had arrived he'd only been able to squeeze into the tight space by reversing right up to it. Now a white van had done the same in front of him. The vehicle was solid and stubborn-looking, an impression reinforced by its dented rear panel. There was no name or phone number on it, just a notice saying that no tools were left inside it overnight. It was almost touching his front bumper. He was well and truly stuck.

'Shit!' he said aloud, swinging a kick at the van's back tyre.

'Somebody did that to me yesterday,' said a voice behind him. 'Doesn't it make you want to throttle them?' He picked up a slight Scottish accent.

Jonas turned. The speaker was a woman, about his height and not much older. He took in a pleasant face, hair bunched on top of her head and falling in curls around her face. Neat brows, big lashes, red lips. She was dressed in casual business style in a dark jacket and trousers, and a white shirt that showed off her full breasts. She had an expensive looking bag in soft, green leather slung over her shoulder. The overall impression was of somebody successful, sharp, competent. Jonas liked the look of her.

She gave him a sympathetic smile. 'What is it with

these morons?' She said. She shook her head and her curls bobbed. 'Look, there's a gap over there you could park a truck in.' She came closer to point out the space across the road and Jonas caught a whiff of her perfume, sweet and clean with a subtle allure. 'All that room and he – or she – has to park right here and block you in. Would you believe it?' She looked at the car behind Jonas. 'Do you know whose that is?'

'Yeah, that's my dad's.'

'Ah.' She smiled again. Jonas registered a pretty mouth and very white teeth. 'Your problem is solved, then.'

'Not really,' Jonas mumbled. 'He's not here. He's gone to meet some people. I don't know where he is or how long he'll be.'

'Call him.'

It was a good idea. His father wouldn't like being disturbed, but he was on foot so he couldn't be far away. Jonas could go to where he was and get his car key. He took out his phone. 'Siri, call dad,' he said into it. The phone rang. Jonas clamped it to his ear and waited. And waited.

'No answer?' said the woman.

'No.' Jonas gave a weary shrug. 'I'm not surprised. He often turns the ringer off when he's with people, and he doesn't do voicemail. Looks like I'm stuck.'

It was annoying and frustrating. Jonas could see his plans for an afternoon doing his own thing going up in flames. If he couldn't get away before his father returned he'd be made to go back inside and he'd have lost the opportunity to skive off. He leant against the club wall beneath a poster advertising the next live event. The woman was watching him. The wait might not be too bad if he could fill the time in her company. She'd stopped to talk to him so she couldn't be in a hurry. They'd only just met and that meant he was pushing it, but she might. There was no harm in asking her.

'I'm going to have to wait till my dad gets back, or the guy in front of me moves,' he said. 'How are you fixed for time? Do you fancy getting a coffee somewhere?'

The woman smiled again. She had a great smile; coffee with her would be good.

'I'd love to, I really would,' she said, 'but I'm due to meet somebody and I can't.' Jonas was disappointed, but at least she'd seemed keen on the idea; it was just that she was busy.

She walked to the front of the van. 'What about this one?' She looked inside. 'I think you might be in luck,' she said, looking back at Jonas. 'The driver's here. He looks to be asleep. If you wake him up you can ask him to pull forward and let you out. He only needs to move a couple of feet and you'll be all right.'

Jonas joined the woman and peered into the vehicle. She was right. There was a man behind the wheel. He was slumped back in his seat, his eyes shut and his mouth open. Jonas was about to tap on the window when the man suddenly opened his eyes and turned towards him. At the same time he felt a sharp jab in the back of his thigh.

He thought he'd been stung and he slapped his jeans in case something had got in there. Wasp? Ant? He looked up. A man in a dark suit had now joined the woman, who was still smiling. It was a vision that blurred and began to spin as his head swam. He felt dizzy. He put out an arm to steady himself, and his knees gave way. The suited man caught him before he hit the ground and pushed him towards the van. A side door opened. There was another man in there, who grabbed the unconscious Jonas under his arms and the two of them heaved him inside. The suited man climbed in after him and closed the door. The woman got in the front.

'Anybody see?' said the man.

'No,' said the woman. 'Nobody around in these streets at this time of day.'

One of the men got some zip ties from the seat pocket and tightened them around Jonas' wrists first, then his ankles. The woman watched. 'Don't pull them too tight,' she said.

'Why not? We don't want the wee fucker getting free, do we,' said the man.

'He won't. There was plenty in that shot I gave him.'

The suited man reached into Jonas' jacket, found his wallet and took out a plastic card which he gave to the woman. She reached into her bag for a hand-held reader and inserted the card. She waited while the machine compared the information on the card with the National Database. After a moment Jonas's photo came up on the small screen.

'Jonas Eze,' she said, reading the description underneath. 'Age 21, height 5 feet 7 inches, weight 195 pounds. That's him all right. Good looking boy. He could do to lose a few pounds, though.'

'You can say that again,' said the man. 'I nearly did myself a mischief getting him into the van.'

'He'll be losing weight soon enough,' said the driver. 'This time next week he'll be a lot lighter.'

The three men laughed. The driver put the vehicle into forward and moved away from the kerb.

'Better get him into the box,' said the suited man.

'No hurry,' said the woman, putting the card reader back. 'He's not going to be waking up for some time.'

'Yeah, but we don't want any bother at the border.'

'We'll put him in the box long before we get to the border,' said the woman. 'For now just leave him be.' She nodded to the driver. 'Turn as if we're heading south. When we get to the edge of the city find a quiet side street, stop the van, change the plates and dump the old ones. The cameras outside the club will have recorded us and we don't want to be picked up by others. That would help anyone who wanted to track our route. When we've got the new plates on we'll turn around and head north.'

'Yes boss, anything you say boss,' said the driver.

The woman gave him a sideways glance. 'You know

it makes sense,' she said. She turned to look at their prisoner. He was sleeping soundly, his eyes closed and his face relaxed. He seemed a nice boy. She would have liked to have gone for that coffee. They might have got on.

She took a phone from her bag. It was old fashioned and battered. She popped in a SIM card and keyed a number. It was answered on the second ring.

'We have the target,' she said.

'You've checked the ID?' came the answering voice.

'Yes, of course. It's the correct one.'

'Were you seen?'

'There was a camera outside the club but it won't have got much.'

'Good. Where are you now?'

'We're on our way out of the city towards the M1. We're just doing a detour to change the plates.'

'Good. So you should be here, what, about nine?'

'Maybe, if the traffic's kind.'

'I'll tell Dr Salamar to get everything ready. The recipient is cleared, we'll just have to do the final tests on the donor when you get him here.' There was a moment's pause, then the voice went on. 'Oh, and Jeannie.'

'Yes?'

'Good snatch. Tell your team well done.'

'Thank you, Dr Folken.' She smiled to herself. Usually Aurora's Head of Security, Jock McIntyre, supervised the snatches. This was her first, and it had gone well.

Jeannie took the SIM card out of the phone, snapped it in half and threw it from the car window. The vehicle's route information system said it would take them two and a half hours to reach Carlisle. She settled back in her seat and closed her eyes.

6

MOLLY SOMETIMES WISHED that Cameron lived with her and not with Zak because she got lonely, but she knew that wouldn't work. There were things about the boy that would drive her mad: his untidiness, the hours he kept, his casual attitude, the way he spent almost every waking minute looking at his phone screen, even when she was talking to him. Beth was different. When Beth came they chatted like friends. Molly often wished she had a daughter. It wasn't just the company of another woman. She knew very well that because of the way she'd used her body she was likely to age prematurely. Dr Salamar had told her as much. At some stage she would need help, she would need care. She couldn't see Cameron doing that. Or Zak, for that matter, although they were still legally married.

Zak was a conundrum. He had been and in some ways still was the love of her life. At times when she was under stress or just wanted to cheer herself up –

like when she was going into labour – she would recall the day they met; it was like re-running a favourite movie.

She'd been in a supermarket, bending over one of the chiller cabinets, and had stepped back. She hadn't known that Zak was immediately behind her. She'd trodden on his foot, lost her balance, dropped her basket, and they'd both ended up on the floor.

Zak brushed aside the staff who came running over to assist. 'I'm really sorry,' he said, helping her up. 'Are you all right?'

'I'm fine thanks,' she said. 'It's me who should be sorry. I backed into you.'

'No, I was too close. I should have left you more room.'

'No, honestly, it was me.'

They caught each other's eye and both burst out laughing.

'Okay, fifty-fifty,' he said. 'I was just going to get some lunch. I don't suppose you'd join me, would you?'

It was a bit soon, they'd only just met, but he seemed nice, and they were in public. And it was a supermarket caff, not a posh restaurant.

'Why not?' she said. 'But we've agreed we were equally to blame for the collision, so we go Dutch.'

'Fair enough,' he said. 'I'll buy the paninis, you get the coffees.'

He stood back so she could go to the counter ahead of him and she thanked whatever gods cared for her that she wasn't pregnant. Three months before she had been, but she was taking a break and had been putting in some time at the gym. She felt good, and she thought she looked good too.

Zak was like no one she'd met before. Talking to him was easy. He listened, and followed where she wanted to go rather than always dragging things back to himself. And when she'd finished and was thinking what to say next he'd gently take the conversation in a new direction. He seemed to have an unusual angle on almost all the things they discussed. Physically he wasn't really her type: he was dark and she preferred men who were fair. His hair was long and she liked short. He had tattoos and she wasn't keen on those, and his ears were pierced more times than hers. But there was something about him. He looked like he was famous, the sort of face you night see on the cover of a rock album, or on the Pyramid Stage at Glastonbury wringing chords from a Fender Stratocaster.

She asked him what he did and he told her he had his own business. She said nothing, hoping he'd go on.

'I'm an ethical hacker,' he said.

'What's that?'

'I specialise in capital liberation.' Molly looked blank. 'I find scammers and hackers and I scam and hack them back. Then I donate what I wring out of them to good causes.'

It seemed to Molly both virtuous and romantic, like a medieval knight riding out to right wrongs. When he asked her about her work she said she was between jobs, which actually was true. They spent an hour and a half in the café, while the frozen items in their baskets slowly thawed. It was, she realised afterwards, their first date.

Two days later they met again, and this time it was the posh restaurant. Zak turned up in an open necked white shirt, a maroon Tuxedo, faded denims, and trainers. The head waiter clearly knew him because he greeted him warmly by name – Mr Lawless – and led them to a prime table.

'Is that really your name? Lawless?'

'Yes,' he said. 'Why are you smiling?'

'I'm not, it's just that Zak Lawless is a great name.'

'Thanks. I like it.'

'It's unusual, though. I've never met anyone called that before.'

'No, there aren't many of us. It's a very ancient name. It's from the old English word for outlaw, although it didn't in those days mean a sort of bandit. It was just somebody with an independent outlook. Some of us were quite well-to-do. There was a Thomas Lagheles who was a Freeman of the city of York in the 1300s.'

'So it means kind of a free spirit.'

'I like to think so.'

The wine came and the starters, and they talked about more personal things than they had in the supermarket café. It turned out that Zak had a son, Archy, who was within a couple of months the same age as Cameron. Not that night but later she learnt that Archy was really Zak's stepson, his former wife's child but not his. Zak and Archy lived in Windwood, which was an area of big houses near the edge of the city and not too far from the home she and Cameron had recently moved into.

She wondered why Archy wasn't with his mother. 'And Mrs Lawless?' It was pushy she thought, but she had to ask.

He didn't seem to mind. 'No longer with us.'

Molly felt embarrassed. 'Oh, I'm sorry.'

'She was killed in a car smash three years ago, two days after Archy's second birthday.'

'Oh, how awful, for both of you.'

'Yes.' Zak smiled ruefully, 'it was. Drunk driving, I'm afraid.'

'That's terrible. I hope they caught the idiot responsible.'

There was a long pause. 'The drunk driver was her,' said Zak. 'Nobody else was involved.'

The conversation stalled a bit after that, but it picked up later and she ended up back at his place. Had she planned it? she asked herself as she looked at Zak sleeping beside her, his hair fanned out over the pillow. She didn't think she had, although she'd had the foresight to arrange for Cameron to spend the night at his new friend Beth's, so maybe this outcome had been in her mind all along.

Three weeks later she and Cameron moved in with Zak and Archy. The four of them got on spectacularly well. Zak was kind, thoughtful, clever, considerate, funny. The only time they argued was over money, and then not seriously. It was just that Zak insisted on paying for everything. The two boys were immediately like brothers. Molly was surprised because they shared a passion for video games but apart from that they were completely different. Cameron was sturdy and strong, Archy was what his step-dad called 'a skinny rabbit.' Cameron was sporty and into football, Archy was clumsy and uncoordinated and not the least bit interested in sport of any kind. He was studious, an inventor and excellent with machinery; Cameron was into superheroes, rushing about, and elaborate pictures of alien worlds, painstakingly illustrated in coloured felt-tips. Despite their differences they were seldom apart and at the end of Molly and Zak's first week of living together Cameron sidled up to her and said that Archy was his best friend.

'What, better than Beth?'

'Beth's different.'

And she was.

Molly married Zak later that year. Beth was her bridesmaid.

Zak was an unusual character who brought together several contradictions. One of these was between his outside and his inside. On the outside he was stuck in a phase he'd probably entered in his teens. It was a mesh of hippie-beatnik and heavy metal, with a dash of goth: long hair, beard, mainly black clothing, and of course the piercings and tattoos. On the inside were the laid-back liberal values you'd expect, but there was also a razor sharp intellect, which you perhaps wouldn't. He spoke several languages. He could hold forth fluently on economics, politics, philosophy, sociology, the environment. He had an encyclopaedic knowledge of history and geography. He solved Maths problems for fun. He was able to explain relativity and string theory to Cameron and Archy, and to anyone else who was interested. Rumour was that he had higher degrees from both Cambridge and Harvard, although Zak himself would neither confirm nor deny this. He was a better than average guitar player, classical as well as rock. He needed very little sleep and would work throughout the night.

Most impressive, however, were his computing skills. He could read and write code as if it were his mother tongue. He knew what a blockchain was. He could find his way around the world wide web, including the dark web, as deftly as Theseus in the Minotaur's lair. He was able to hack into most sites; or as he put it 'get under their bonnets'. He enjoyed seeking out malware, quarantining it, reshaping it and returning it to the originator so it devoured their system. He worked from home, standing, in an office with several large computers on huge shelves. In the basement below were more of them. They were housed in sleek racks, winking their red lights and humming saucily to each other. Molly asked what they were for and Zak said that they were his staff.

Molly didn't really understand exactly what Zak did. It was partly that he wasn't very forthcoming, but it was mainly because when he did try to explain his work to her she couldn't grasp it. Truncated backtraces, overwrite traps, kernels, blocked threads – he might as well have been speaking Greek. One of the things he did that Molly could follow was investigating hashtags. It seemed that there were people who hired him to find out where in social media a particular idea came from and who was involved in distributing it. For example, misleading information, right wing propaganda, climate change denial, racist or homophobic memes. His clients wanted to discover who was originating and spreading the stuff so they knew where to go to choke it. Zak found out and told them.

One of the things Molly found most endearing was what Zak referred to as his levelling up work. He would identify a target – a corporation that wasn't paying all the tax it should or an individual with hidden offshore investments, especially someone in the public eye. Then, and Molly had no idea how, he would get into their accounts. Once in he would make a transfer to one of the half dozen charities he favoured, and at the same time make a public announcement of the donation.

'But don't they know that their money has gone?'

'Of course they do,' he said. 'But I never take more than a few thousand, and these are businesses and people for whom that's nothing.'

'Couldn't they ask the charity to give them the money back?'

'Yes, they could, but how would that look? One day a nice juicy announcement that they've made a generous donation to a good cause, and the next day news that they've changed their mind and asked for it to be returned. Who would do that?'

He had a point, because as far as she knew nobody did ask for their gift to be cancelled.

'Sort of Robin Hood,' she said.

'I like to think so,' he said.

Archy was keen on the computers. He would sit at Zak's elbow watching his fingers flash over the keys and the changing data on screen.

'He's going to follow in your footsteps,' she said.

'I surely hope so,' said Zak.

Their first year together was out of this world. Molly was happier than she'd ever been. However, after a while she began to get restless. Zak would spend hours on his work, seven days and nights a week. Molly would read, go shopping, watch TV, go shopping, watch TV, read, meet friends. It wasn't enough. She was bored; she needed something else.

'You could get a job,' Zak said.

'I don't want a job. Besides, what could I do. I have no qualifications. The sort of thing I could get I'd be even more bored than I am doing nothing.'

She'd been hoping that he would find her a niche, something she could do to help him with what he did, but no offer came. It was then that she told him about her surrogacy.

He didn't believe her. 'What, really? You're a gussy,' he said, employing the disdainful, off-colour, slang insult some people used when talking about surrogates.

She explained that it was what she did, that she was good at it, and that it helped people who otherwise wouldn't have the fulfilment and enjoyment of bringing up a child.

'You mean the fulfilment and enjoyment of watching a nanny bring it up.'

That had about summed up Zak's attitude. They didn't row; the discussions were cool, not hot, but there was no doubt that he couldn't get his head around it. He wasn't openly disapproving but it was obvious he didn't want anything to do with it. And he didn't want his wife to do it either, although he said all along that it was her choice.

A few weeks later Molly moved out, back to her own apartment and was thankful that she'd kept it on. Three weeks after that she went to the clinic and started the process of being impregnated again.

She and Zak remained close. They went for walks, visited the theatre and cinema, took holidays together. Sometimes they were even lovers – when Molly was 'between assignments' as Zak put it.

Cameron was given the choice of staying with Zak and Archy or leaving with Molly; he opted for Archy and Zak. He went to see his mother often. Usually Zak would take him, sometimes with Archy and sometimes picking up Beth on the way. These visits were highlights for Molly; mostly she was on her own.

7

Jonas was dragged out of the van and made to stand. It was difficult; his wrists were strapped together and so were his ankles. He'd been shaken about for hours, and at one stage he'd been crammed into a tiny, stifling space under the van's floor. His whole body was stiff, his legs were weak, and there was a throbbing pain behind his eyes. He had a raging thirst and a foul taste in his mouth. Tape across his lips made breathing difficult, and a black fabric bag covering his head prevented him from seeing anything. Cotton wads had been stuffed into his ears and they had been covered in tape, too, so that sounds were faint. He tried to make sense of the muffled mutterings that came through but it was all too confused to be clear.

He had only the vaguest notion of what had happened to him. He remembered leaving the club, and he had an image of talking to an attractive black woman. There had been a white van obstructing his car, and a big man in a suit; then nothing. He came round in total darkness. He wasn't bound but the box or whatever it was he was in made it difficult to move and impossible to stretch out. It was stiflingly hot. For a terrible few seconds he thought it was a coffin and that the movement of the vehicle meant he was in a hearse. He had a moment's panic as he recalled a movie he'd seen where someone had been buried alive. He shouted and banged as best he could on the sides of the box but there wasn't enough space to make much impact. The top, only centimetres above him, had opened and an angry face looked down and shouted at him to shut up. He felt the spray of the man's spittle.

'If there's a border inspection and he goes off like that we're fucked,' somebody said.

'Better wrap him up.' That was a woman's voice, he thought the same one who'd spoken to him outside the club. How could it be? She'd seemed so friendly and cute.

The ear plugs and the gag came then. The filthy bag wasn't put over his head until he was let out of the box and spent the last few miles of the journey on the van floor.

He was aware of somebody cutting the wrist ties, but before he could rub any life back into them they were seized again and retied, this time to another wrist on each side. He heard a snip and felt release as his legs were freed.

His two anonymous guards walked forward, pulling Jonas with them. Sandwiched between them, helpless and blind, he had no choice, he had to go where they went. No one said anything but he felt himself being propelled across a hard surface. Wind and driven rain found gaps in his clothing. Then he was aware of being led inside; at least he was now out of the weather. The building was warm and smelt of antiseptic. Was it a hospital? Why was he being taken into a hospital?

His minders stopped. There was more mumbling and a sudden burst of laughter. Then they were off again, through several sets of doors, along passageways, and finally into a room. He heard a door shut firmly behind him. It was only then that the black bag, the itchy, clammy, disgusting sweatbag that had been over his head and face since he'd woken up, was removed.

At first the light stung his eyes and he could see nothing. When he could bear to open them he saw that he was in a high, white, square room. It was spartan in the extreme. There was an iron bedstead with unbearably white sheets and covers, a gleaming steel washbasin with shiny taps, and a table and chair. There were sandwiches on a paper plate on the table, covered in film. The light came from a fluorescent fitting let into the ceiling. It flickered slightly. There was a shiny black dome the size of a large bowl on the ceiling. Cctv? There were two doors. One had no handle and was faced in stainless steel. The other was painted white and the top third was taken up by a mirror that Jonas recognised as one-way glass.

One of the men who'd been part of his human

anchor pulled a pair of cutters from his pocket and clipped the plastic tying him and his companion to Jonas. At last he was able to rub his aching wrists and hands, wincing from the pain as the circulation came back. The other man ripped the tape from his mouth and ears. Jonas yelled as the tape took some of his hair with it. The man laughed.

Jonas felt his ears and pulled the cotton plug from each. At last he could hear.

He weighed up the pair who had been guarding him. Both were huge. The heads of both were shaved and one of them had a snake tattooed on his scalp. Even at his best he couldn't have taken on one of them. Two? Out of the question. With no weapons and after several agonisingly painful hours crammed in the box under the van floor he wouldn't have a chance.

'Where am I? Who are you?' His tongue and lips wouldn't work properly after all that time with tape over his mouth and the words came out slurred, as if they were being spoken by a drunk.

'Shut your arse,' snake-head said.

Jonas did a lightning calculation. The options were silence and compliance, or truculence and defiance. He was beginning to feel angry. Who were these people who were doing this to him? He decided to stand up for himself.

'Shut your own,' he said. 'Do you know who you've got here? Do you know who I am? Do you know who my dad is? Man, this is the worst day's business you goons have ever done. Let me loose now and I might just be able to stop my dad having you killed.' By the end of the rant Jonas was shouting.

One of the men looked uncertain but snake-head didn't. He regarded Jonas for a moment and then casually reached forward, took his hand, and abruptly broke one of his fingers. Jonas heard it snap. He screamed and bent double. He fell to his knees as a tsunami of pain shot up his arm. He blinked back tears. The two men stood watching him with amusement. A red wash blurred his vision. The pain was excruciating. Jonas felt sick and almost keeled over.

'Stand up,' said snake-head.

Jonas struggled unsteadily to his feet.

'Piss,' said the other man, pointing to a hole in the wall opposite the bed.

'What?' Jonas had to speak with his teeth clenched. It was the only way he could stop himself howling.

'Piss. In there.'

Jonas didn't move. Snake-head leant towards him. 'Either you piss into that hole in the wall,' he said in a menacing whisper, 'or I move along all your other fingers and break them one at a time.'

'It's all right, pretty boy,' said the other man. 'We won't look.' The two of them sniggered.

Jonas had no idea what was going on. What did these thugs want of him? Was he being ransomed? Was it enemies of his father out to settle some score?

'I don't have any money,' he said.

'We don't want your money, just your slash'

'Today would be nice, pretty boy. If it's not too much trouble.'

Jonas was motionless. He knew he had to comply, in fact he hadn't peed since he'd left the club and he needed to, but he felt completely disorientated and pain made movement impossible.

'It's no good,' said snake-head, 'I'm gonna have to take another finger.'

Jonas stepped forward to dodge the hand that was reaching towards his wrist. The hole in the wall was a recess at groin height, clad in stainless steel and with a drain hole in the bottom. He fumbled with his good hand to unzip himself and he urinated. Now he was doing it he was surprised how much he had wanted to go. When he'd finished he stood back and a shiny metal panel slid down to cover the space.

'There, that wasn't too bad, was it?' said the second man. 'Now eat.' He indicated the plate of sandwiches on the table. The two men left. The door closed with a heavy thud that made it obvious that it was locked.

Jonas flopped onto the chair and cradled his injured hand. It throbbed and he couldn't control the tears that streamed down his cheeks. The idea of the sandwiches made him feel sick.

How long did he sit there, nursing the damage? An hour? How long had all this been going on? It was around one when he'd come out of the club. He felt as though he'd been in the van for a long time. He'd been blindfold when they'd pulled him out, and the room he was in now had no window, so he couldn't tell if it was dark. But it was January, so it probably would be by now. The long time in the van meant he must be far from home. And somebody had mentioned the border. Scotland? The woman who'd come up to him outside the club had a Scottish accent.

The sandwiches didn't look too bad. The nausea which he'd been feeling had passed and he supposed he ought to eat something. He might need all his strength. He fumbled with the film with his good hand and took a sandwich. It was tasty, cheese and some sort of chutney. He finished it and moved onto the second. Once he'd started he realised how hungry he was. Gradually he worked his way through all the sandwiches.

He examined his finger. Although it was feeling a bit better it still hurt. It was swollen and impossible to move. Why had snake-head done that? There had been no need. If he'd done it to scare him he'd sure as shit succeeded. Perhaps it was just that he got it on by hurting people. He'd met arseholes like that before. His dad knew some, and even made use of them sometimes.

The strips of tape that had been torn off his mouth and ears were on the floor. He picked them up, straightened them out as best he could, and set about binding the broken finger to the one next to it. It hurt like hell and the hair they'd pulled away with the tape stopped it sticking properly, but he managed to arrive at some sort of splinting arrangement.

What now? Where was he? The room and the building had a clinical feel. The bed was like a hospital bed, there all that stainless steel, and there was a panel on the wall that seemed to be the sort of thing that patient support services could be hooked up to - drips, monitors, oxygen. Why was he in a hospital? Maybe they thought he was ill. Maybe there'd be someone here who could treat his broken finger.

Would snake-head and the other one be back? Was there anyone else in this godforsaken dump? He could hear no sound. He was tempted to shout, to yell in order to see if he got a response from anyone else who might be here, but he was wary of bringing his tormentors back. He lay down on the bed.

If they meant to kill him they would have done so already he reasoned, so they must be holding him for ransom. His father would know by now that he was missing. How long would it take to find him? How would they know where to look? He needed to do all he could to discover the exact location of this place, so that when he was freed he could lead his father to it and they could burn it to the ground, and he would personally break all eight of snake-head's fingers. And his thumbs.

He was thinking about these things when the door opened and a woman came in. She looked like a nurse - light blue overall, watch pinned to her breast - but she had no hat and her hair was uncovered. She was serious but she had a kind face.

She closed the door behind her. 'Don't even think about it,' she said. She had an accent. Polish?

'What?' Jonas levered himself up on his elbows. 'Think about what?'

'Making for the door. The two guys who brought you in here are just outside, and Genghis is dying for an excuse to rough you up some more.'

Jonas swung his legs off the bed and sat up. 'Genghis, is that the one with the snake...'

'...tattooed on his scalp, yes.'

'I suppose his mate's called Atilla.'

'Well actually, yes, he is.' She smiled. 'I don't expect they're their real names, but that's what they like to be called.'

'He broke my finger.'

'I know. He's a beast. He lives for hurting people. Here, let me look.'

She took his hand, gently removed the tape, and assessed the damage.

'It seems to be a clean break,' she said. 'Not compound, or dislocated.'

She took from her pocket a plastic tube and an aerosol with a small spout. She eased the tube gently over his finger, directed the spout into the end of it and pressed the button on the aerosol. There was a hiss and the tube filled with a clear jelly. It felt very cold but the pressure was comforting. She held his hand.

'Give that a few minutes to set. It will hold your finger in position while the bone knits. You'll need to keep it on for a couple of weeks, more if you can.'

While she did this Jonas studied her. She looked capable, competent. She was probably around thirty.

Long fingers, gentle hands. Nice legs, what he could see of them. Attractive.

'What's your name?'

'Ingrida,' she said, without hesitation.

'Nice name.'

'Thank you.'

'I'm Jonas.'

'I know.'

'Where am I?'

'I can't tell you that, I'm afraid.'

'Why am I here.'

'Sorry, I can't tell you that, either.' She actually did look sorry, Jonas thought, and she nodded her head slightly in the direction of the door, towards where she had told him Genghis and Atilla waited. He had the impression that she would have told him if she could.

Ingrida reached into her other pocket and brought out what looked like a retractable ballpoint.

'What's that?'

'It's just something to stop your finger hurting. Here.' She took his arm, held the pen over a vein and clicked the top. Jonas felt a sharp prick and almost at once the room began to swirl. He felt Ingrida raise his feet, move his hand so that he wasn't lying on it, lift his head and place it on the pillow. Then he was out.

Ingrida left, pulling the door closed behind her. Genghis and Atilla were waiting in the corridor.

'I've put him out,' she said to them. 'Dr Salamar will be along soon to do the tests. You stay away from him. Leave him alone, do you hear? You know the clinic's policy: no unnecessary violence. If you hurt him again I'll report you to Director Folken.'

She walked briskly away. Genghis watched her go, a mocking smile on his face. As far as he was concerned there was no such thing as violence that was unnecessary. No point going into the room now, though, if the guy was knocked out, but he might be able to have some more fun with him between the tests and the op.

8

It was a little later than usual when Director Folken's driver parked his electric Bentley in front of the detached granite mansion he called 'the workhouse'. He owned three other dwellings besides this one. As well as the house in St John's Gardens, which he'd left that morning, he had an apartment in Paris and a long, low villa on an island with stunning views of the Caribbean. Folken liked the workhouse. It was impressive; Victorian, with large rooms and high ceilings. He loved the airiness and the silence, and the sense of security that the thick stone walls brought.

He was alone. Janice, his cook-cum-housekeeper, only worked during the day, and Anita, his wife, was still in Brussels. She was busy on an important case at the European Court. He'd seen her only intermittently in the last few months, a state between them that was usual now. When he was feeling crotchety he told himself that it was no wonder they had no children because they were never together long enough to have sex. But that wasn't the reason. The reason was that Anita wasn't interested in motherhood.

Janice had left his supper on a tray in his study. Cold meat, crusty bread, fruit, a bottle of Chablis in a chiller. He picked a peach from the fruit bowl and bit into it. Juice trickled down his chin and he dabbed where it had dripped onto his shirt. He would eat the other things later. For now there was something else he wanted to do.

He settled in an armchair, took his minipad from his jacket pocket and stabbed the button which called his wife's number. It rang for a long time. He thought she wasn't going to pick up and he was about to close the call when her face appeared. She was in her hotel room. The light was behind her and threw her face into shadows but even so he could see that she looked tired.

'Oh. Hi,' she said.

'Hello, darling. How are things?'

She pulled a face. 'So so. I suppose we're making some progress. We have enough to fix the bastard but his legal team are up to all the tricks in the book and we have to work hard on the presentation. The court has become extremely fussy of late and I've been slogging through paperwork all day.' His wife was a lawyer, and the case she was talking about concerned a former Georgian politician's trial for embezzlement. 'How about you?' she said. 'Good day?'

'A long one, but yes. The kidney donor for the Russian girl has been admitted and the team are running tests straight away. I've spoken to the Russian and he and his daughter will be arriving in the next few hours.'

'Oh.' There was a pause. 'Do these people have names?'

'What do you mean?'

'You call them "the Russian" and "the girl". Don't you think you should pay them the courtesy of using their names, considering how thoroughly you're fleecing them?'

Folken winced inwardly. He also felt a flutter of irritation. His wife always treated making money as beneath her, but that didn't stop her enthusiastic spending. He hoped that this call was not going the same way as several of the others they'd had recently and end in bickering and bad feeling. He gritted his teeth.

'Yes, of course you're right,' he said. 'I didn't want to bore you with details. The young woman's name is Alexandra Christina Ivanovitch and her father is Mikael Dimitri Ivanovitch.'

'That's better,' said Anita icily. 'It didn't hurt a bit, did it? And details are what I do.'

It did look as though they were going to row. His wife was clearly weary and in a bad mood; he'd make allowances. He had information which he was keen to share. In her present frame of mind she might not be receptive, but he had to tell her – partly because she had a right to know, partly because if he kept it to himself and she later found out she could be angry, but mainly because there was no one else he could tell and he had to share it with someone.

'Yes, anyway,' he said, 'I have some news.'

She looked vaguely interested. He noticed she had a glass of wine beside her and she took a sip. He wished he'd poured himself some of the Chablis before starting the call. He thought about taking the minipad to the kitchen so he could get some but he didn't want to cause a distraction. He wanted Anita to concentrate.

'Molly went for her scan today.'

'Molly?'

His wife looked genuinely puzzled but surely she must know who he meant. 'Molly. Our surrogate. Your surrogate.'

'Oh. Yes.'

'The baby is a boy. We're going to have a son.'

'It's not a baby. As yet it's a foetus.'

Folken was becoming exasperated. 'Yes. All right. Whatever it is, it's male.' There was a long pause. 'Aren't you interested?'

Anita's mouth turned down. 'Not really. You know I'm not. This was your idea. I don't want children, I never have wanted children. I find the idea of forty weeks waddling around with some parasite growing inside me revolting. And being pregnant would take me away from important and worthwhile work. You knew that when you married me and my mind hasn't changed since. You, though, tell me you have to have offspring to carry on the Folken dynasty, so I agreed to use a surrogate.'

'And I appreciate that, I do.' Folken had hoped that once the procedure had been carried out and the surrogacy had begun Anita would become more involved, but that hadn't so far happened. 'I thought you'd be interested. After all, it's your egg.'

'I release them every month. This one is no more important to me than any of the others.'

Folken was taken aback. 'How can you say that? This is our child.'

'It's your child, Hans. I've been clear from the start that I take no responsibility for it. I hope it will be healthy and that it will live a full life, but I hope that for everyone. I don't want to hold it, I don't want to hug it, feed it, wind it, change its nappy, or be woken up in the night by it. I don't want to dress it, take it to school, meet its friends. I want nothing to do with it. Nothing. You found a surrogate to host the foetus. You'll have to find a surrogate to bring it up. Or do it yourself.'

There was a dig in the last remark. Folken knew that Anita didn't think he was capable of that. He lacked the skills and most of all he lacked the time. Besides, day-to-day care was not the aspect of parenthood that interested him.

'Jeannie will do it.' He had no idea whether Jeannie would. It had only just occurred to him that she might be a candidate.

'Jeannie?'

'One of the security team at the clinic. Part of McIntyre's crew.'

'Black girl, striking looking, I've met her.'

'Yes. She's very capable, too good for the stuff McIntyre gives her to do. I'm sure I can work something out with her.'

'Well that should be just fine for you. And Hans?'

'Yes.'

'This is the last shot. I won't do this again. I know I said that when we did IVF and a surrogacy before, but then it all went wrong and you were devastated. I felt sorry for you and you went on about it so much that I agreed to try one more time. But that's it. It's all right for you. All you have to do is jerk yourself off into a jar but I have to go through an unpleasant course of treatment and an invasive procedure. If this surrogate miscarries like the other one did, that's it. Game over.'

There was a long silence. A dozen thoughts went through Folken's head. This wasn't the first time Anita had told him her position, but she'd not before expressed it so forcefully. He respected her work. She was an extremely able lawyer and barrister and she used her formidable talents to pursue evil people and bring them to account. She thought that the National Human Genome Database was a noble project, and that the information it provided contributed to the common good. She approved of Aurora. Or, rather, she approved of what she knew about it. If she ever discovered the astonishingly lucrative sideline that Folken had developed, the business that provided the houses and the cars and the exotic holidays and the clothes and the luxury hotels, the business that paid for the endless pro bono work she did, she would be horrified. She had never visited the Aberdeen facility and Folken would see to it that she never did.

Anita must have relented a little because she said in a softer tone, 'I'm pleased for you that the foetus is developing well, I really am. What about the host? Is she staying healthy? I was concerned about her age.'

Folken was soothed by this expression of interest, but he knew Anita well enough not to mistake the gesture. It was politeness rather than genuine concern.

'The medical reports say she's in first class health,' he said. 'Anyway, she's not that old. She's 41, that's all. Nowadays there are plenty of women who aren't having their first child until then, and Molly's had many. She's very experienced. This is her thirteenth surrogacy. I'm sure if there were to be any problems she'd be aware of them at once.'

'I hope so. For your sake.'

There was not much left to say. Anita told him a little more about the case she was working on but he didn't really listen and his expressions of interest were phatic. While she talked he thought about the child, growing several hundred miles away in another woman's womb. He would like his wife to refer to it as a baby, not a foetus, but he was well aware she wouldn't. She would see doing so as a move towards attachment, ownership. She was more enthusiastic about a visit to her hairdresser than she was about seeing their genes merge in a new human being. Whereas he spent time every day dreaming about the child, his son, and the things they would do together.

He went back to the kitchen, poured himself the glass of Chablis he'd been looking forward to, and began on his supper.

Would Jeannie take on the job of caring for his baby? It would be rather more than the usual childcare. He would be asking her to in effect be the mother of his and Anita's child. It never occurred to him to wonder if she was interested in children or had the skills that would be needed. She was a woman, and as far as Folken was concerned it came as second nature to them; with the exception of Anita, of course.

If Jeannie would do what he asked it would be a contract, like the one with the surrogate. Looking after his son would be a full-time job and he would pay her well for it. In fact money was no object. He had enough to pay her what she asked and he would have much more. He would be wealthy. He had solved the problem of organ donation.

The NHGD had had an enormous effect. It meant that medical problems of many sorts could be foreseen, early treatment given and problems forestalled. Lives had been saved. Linking people to particular individuals, places and events had made a huge impact on the detection of murders, assaults, rapes, thefts, and as a result crime had plummeted. The ability to identify potential organ donors had been a bonus, but not at first a particularly obvious one.

Opinion surveys about organ donation were muddled. Many approved of it and said they would be happy for their organs to be used by someone else after their death, but in practice only a tiny proportion of them signed up for that. Aurora had done a lot of work encouraging the donation of organs through living wills. The problem was that although the wills provided a list of usable body parts no one knew when they might be obtainable. What's more, people were living longer and it was increasingly the case that by the time organs were available they were worn out and no longer of use. Another factor was that the Genome Database provided no information at all about the lifestyles of individual donors. They could be smokers. Or they might be drug users, or drink too much alcohol. Living wills weren't enough; more was needed.

One evening he was talking to Salamar about a child who desperately needed a heart transplant. There were potential donors on the Database but they were all very much alive. Salamar looked at the list and clicked her tongue in frustration.

'Why must we wait until they're dead?' she said.

She hadn't meant it – or had she? However, it set Folken thinking. He was awake all night going over the implications of what Salamar had said, and devising how they might be made to work. The concept was so obvious it was astonishing that no one had thought of it before. By the morning he had created a new and different company, with access to all the Aurora resources and data but operating discretely, at more than arms length. He called it Aurora Wellbeing.

That was the business which was making Hans Folken wealthy.

9

'How old are you?'

'I'm five.'

'No you're not, you're four.'

Well I'm nearly five. I'm five next week.'

'So am I.'

That was Cameron and Beth's first conversation. Cameron and Molly had just moved into the area, and this was his introduction to the school that Beth attended. The question was put by a classroom assistant, the exaggerated answer came from Cameron, the correction from Molly, the grudging admission from Cameron, and the information that she too was on the verge of being five came from Beth. It wasn't until their actual birthdays that they realised that they were not only in the same week, but they were on the very same day.

Beth's Gran prepared a lavish celebration for her. When she heard that the new boy's birthday coincided with her granddaughter's, of course he was invited. It was an old fashioned party of the sort that Gran had enjoyed when a child, that she had provided for her own daughter and was now doing for Beth. There were balloons, and hats, and sandwiches with the crusts cut off, and proper Coca-Cola, and jelly, and ice cream, and a cake in the shape of the figure 5.

Despite Gran's efforts the party was a disappointment. The children peeled apart the sandwiches, some taking out the fillings. Some of them had expected what they got at other parties – pizzas, sausages on sticks, MacDonalds – and made known their disappointment. The boys and the girls were interested in different games. The mother of another complained that the vegan options hadn't been clearly explained and her daughter had eaten a cracker with dairy butter on it. Gran's cat scratched one of the boys who was teasing it, and another ate too much too quickly and was sick. But despite these mishaps, it was an important day for both Beth and Cameron, and the start of something more.

Being in the same class meant that they were together every day and a bond grew between them. As they grew older they shared more. They already had a lot of the same interests and they encouraged each other to try out new ones. Beth wanted Cameron to come to the dance club with her, and he said he would if she'd play football. So they both did, and Beth became the only girl on the school soccer team and Cameron the only boy in the dance group.

The main thing that brought them together, though, was the feeling they both had that because of their joint birthdays they were different from the others in their class. Their teacher tried to bring them down to earth by telling them that she'd had half a dozen groups where there'd been children whose birthdays were on the same day. It had no effect. They were convinced that there was something special about them.

Beth's Gran was intrigued by the similarities between the two children. She said it could all be explained by their horoscopes.

'You were both born under the sign of Cancer,' she said, reading from her almanack. 'That means you're determined, highly imaginative, loyal, and emotional. But you can be moody, suspicious, and insecure. The Sun was in Cancer for you, and that makes you sympathetic and attached to people you keep close. You're able to feel other people's moods and emotions.'

'It's not other people, it's just Cameron,' said Beth.

She didn't believe in astrology, but it was true that she and Cameron were loyal to their families and to each other. They also felt close to them. As for imagination, Beth regularly received star ratings from her teacher for the stories she wrote, and Cameron was often told that his drawing ability was exceptional. There might be something in what Gran said.

Cameron asked Archy, who was good at Maths, what the chances were of two people being born on the same day.

'Easy,' said Archy. 'How many days in a year?'

'Three hundred and sixty-five,' said Cameron. 'Except for leap years.'

'Yes, well forget them for now. So if you had three hundred and sixty-five people all together in one room, they could all have been born on different days. Possible?'

'Yes, I suppose so,' said Cameron, 'but it's not likely, is it?'

'No,' said Archy, 'but it is possible, yeah? Now if you had three hundred and sixty-six people together, two of them would have to have been born on the same day. It's a must. Agree?'

'Yes. Obviously.'

'So that's it. The chances of two people sharing the same birthday are one in three hundred and sixty-five.'

'It can't be,' said Cameron. 'I've asked a few of the teachers at school whether they've ever had kids with the same birthday in their classes and they all said they had, and some of them quite a few times. So it can't be that rare.'

'Okay,' said Archy, feeling defensive. 'Ask my dad. He can get you an answer to a millionth decimal place on one of his computers.'

The puzzle didn't need a computer, or not at first.

'This isn't a new problem,' Zak said. 'It's one that's often given to Maths students. It even has a name: The Birthday Paradox.'

'So what's the answer?' said Archy.

'Let's work it out,' said Zak. 'Assume we've got a room full of people, all chosen at random. We walk in and grab one and put them on one side. We then choose another person. Now, the first person we chose was born on one particular day, so there are three hundred and sixty-four days in the year that they were *not* born on. That means that the probability that person two has a different birthday from person one is 364 over 365.'

'There, told you,' said Archy.

'Not so fast,' said Zak. 'I've not finished yet. Let's go do another one. Let's bring in person three. They were born on a different day from both person one and person two, so that means there are three hundred and sixty-three days left that person three's birthday could be on. Expressed mathematically, the probability of person three sharing a birthday with person one or person two is 363 over 365. We keep on bringing in new people and with each of them the probability reduces – 362 over 365, 361 over 365, 360 over 365, and so on. When we've got right down to one we can multiply together all the probabilities.'

'Aw, my head hurts,' said Cameron.

'Easy, really,' said Zak. 'Let's run it. Archy, over to you.'

Archy took Zak's keyboard and began to enter the numbers. Cameron and Zak watched. After a few minutes Archy sat back and hit return.'

'Okay,' said Zak. 'There are easier ways to do that. I'll show you later, but for now, what's the answer?

'49.27,' said Archy.

'See?' said Zak.

'No,' said Cameron, 'I don't see. What does it mean?'

'It means that in any group the probability that no two people share the same birthday is 49.27. What does that tell you?'

'Search me,' said Cameron. He didn't get it.

Zak looked at him with an expression of patience mixed with pity. 'It tells you that if there's a 49.27% probability that no two people in the group we've chosen have the same birthday, there's a 50.73% probability that two of them will.'

'Oh,' said Cameron. He still didn't understand what it all meant. 'And in English?'

Zak pulled a face. 'You see it, don't you Archy? Tell him.'

Beth didn't believe it.

'It's 23,' said Cameron.

'It can't be,' she said. 'It must be more than that.'

'No it's not. If you get 23 people together in a room, the chances are that at least two of them will share a birthday.'

'And who told you that?'

'Zak came up with the formula and Archy worked it out on his computer.'

'Number nerds,' said Beth. Her tone was contemptuous, but in fact she was herself good at Maths.

'It seems right, though,' said Cameron. 'I mean, all the teachers we've asked have said it's quite usual for them to have two people with the same birthday in a class of 25 to 30. So it kind of makes sense.'

After Cameron had gone Beth went online to check what she'd been told. It was all there; The Birthday Paradox, something called The Pigeon Hole Principle, and queries and chats from all kinds of people who shared birthdays. Their situation, hers and Cameron's, wasn't particularly unusual and she couldn't help feeling disappointed about that because she'd thought that might account for the way they were able to share each other's moods and feelings.

Then, just as she was settling into bed, she had a thought. *Twins!* If sharing a birthday was after all the reason why she and Cameron were so often thinking about the same things, then there should be examples of it in twins. She sat up, opened her tablet, and searched the web. Three hours later she fell back on the pillows exhausted. There was just so much. She couldn't wait to tell Cameron.

The next day was Sunday, and after she'd helped her gran with the weekly chores that they always saved for a Sunday morning she got on a bus to Zak's.

Cameron, Archy and Zak were all at home. She'd phoned Cameron to tell him some of what she'd found online and she'd hoped they could talk about it together, but he'd already passed it on to the other two and they were keen to join in the discussion. Beth was irritated, but she hadn't told Cameron to keep it to himself so she couldn't blame him. Although if he really could read her mind, she thought, he would have known that was what she wanted.

Zak was familiar with most of what she'd read about in the night.

'There are plenty of stories about uncanny connections between twins,' he said. 'Some of the most interesting ones feature twins who have lived apart for a long time and then when they come together find they have a lot of things in common. Like marrying people with the same name, having the same pets, choosing the same make and model of car, giving their children the same names. There's one account of twins who hadn't seen each other for years finally meeting and discovering that they were dressed almost identically.'

'But that's just genetics,' said Archy. 'Having identical genomes must be the reason why that happens.'

'Yes,' said Zak, 'the shared genome is an important factor, but there's no way it could account for all of it. For one thing, the human genome isn't complex enough. The Human Genome Project predicted that we'd have more than 100,000 genes. It turns out that we actually have only around 35,000. That's nowhere near enough to cover what we're talking about. That potted plant over there has 25,000.'

'So it's nearly as smart as we are,' said Cameron.

'It's smarter than you,' said Archy.

'Oh, very funny,' said Cameron.

'There's a well known case from 1977 that can't possibly be explained by genetics, or by environment and upbringing. One day a woman was going about her normal day when she felt a terrible pain across her chest and stomach. She said it was as if she had been cut in two. Hours later she discovered that her twin sister had died in a plane crash halfway across the world.'

'She could have made that up after she'd heard the news,' said Archy.

'Her co-workers saw it and they said she was in agony. They thought she was having a heart attack and they called an ambulance. That was before news of the crash came out. They call this sort of thing "crisis telepathy". The problem is, there have only been a few scientific studies to investigate it, and the ones that have been done either haven't been peer reviewed or they've been discredited.'

'So that means it's rubbish?' said Cameron.

'Not at all,' said Zak. 'Peer reviewing something like this is almost impossible. You can review the data, but the actual observations are unrepeatable. You couldn't justify putting one twin in danger just to see if the other could feel it, could you?'

'No, I suppose not.'

'The other thing is that scientific advance requires venturing into the unknown, but mainstream science is so theory-driven that it's only interested in developing existing notions. Telepathy has been dismissed or ignored because the current model of the brain and consciousness says that our brains only get their input from their own eyes and ears. There's no room for anything else, it just doesn't fit, therefore it's discounted.'

'So you believe it,' said Beth.

'I think you and Cameron have a connection of some sort, yes.'

'But you're not saying they're twins,' said Archy. 'Are you?'

'Of course not,' said Zak. 'How could they be? Anyway, just look at them.'

'Do I have to?' said Archy.

Beth sighed. Archy obviously thought remarks like this were funny but to her they were tedious.

'You're not twins, but it would be interesting to know when you were born. I don't mean July 14th, that's just the day. I mean the actual time. I don't know when Cameron was but Molly will.' He turned to Cameron. 'Next time you're with your mother ask her if she has any idea what the time was when you popped out.' And to Beth, 'Do you think your gran would know the time you were born?'

'I've never asked her. She might.'

'They ought to put it on birth certificates,' said Archy.

'They do for twins, and for triplets, but not for the rest of us,' said Zak.

'So do you think that might explain the connection between Cameron and me?' said Beth. 'That we were born not only on the same day but at the same time.'

'Who knows?' said Zak. 'But it would be interesting to find out if you were.'

'Can't be,' said Archy. 'I read somewhere that over the whole world there are up to ten births every second. Do you mean that those ten people can share emotions and feelings like Beth and Cameron say they do?'

'Maybe, maybe not,' said Zak. 'Perhaps they do and don't realise it. If you never meet the person you are sharing with, how would you know? I do know Cameron very well and I know Beth quite well. I think there's something going on there. As they say, watch this space.'

'You mean the space between Cameron's ears?' said Archy.

Beth sighed again. It was a stage that Archy was going through and she would be glad when he grew out of it.

10

'YOU DID WHAT?' Jeannie sat up and looked in horror at Ingrida on the pillow beside her. 'You must be out of your mind.'

'I couldn't do what Salamar wanted. I just couldn't.'

'So let me get this straight.' Jeannie rolled onto one elbow so she could look into Ingrida's face. 'Dr Salamar told you to inject the kidney boy with Tri-thingy...'

'Trimesorphene, yes. It's a nerve agent.'

'Whatever. Salamar told you to inject this guy with it.'

'Yes.'

'And you didn't.'

'No.'

'Jeez.' Jeannie flopped back on to her pillow. 'If Salamar finds this out you're fucked, babe.'

Ingrida thought she probably was. Would she mind

being fired? It would resolve the go or stay issue that was now constantly on her mind.

'Well I did give him some,' she said, 'a bit. I was told to make up a dose of fifty millilitres. That's a lot, so I halved it.'

'What's it supposed to do?'

'Trimesorphene slows the heartbeat and makes it hard to breath. It also lowers the blood pressure and temperature, and affects the central nervous system. It sort of switches you off.'

'Is fifty enough to do that?'

'Not usually, but it depends on what drugs he'd already been given. When I was at home in Lithuania I did a course on dealing with Russian nerve agents. I know that some of them can give the appearance of death without the person actually dying. I hoped that might happen to this boy, that it would shut him down enough to make people think he was gone, at least until he was out of the clinic.'

'So you don't know whether you killed him or not.'

'No.'

Jeannie sighed. 'You're a right eejit, aren't you? Why did you cut down the dose? Why the fuck didn't you do what Salamar said?'

Ingrida shook her head. She was close to tears. 'He was such a nice boy. Young. On his own. I felt sorry for him. I thought he deserved a chance. Besides, in my country when a nurse qualifies they take an oath that they'll do all they can to save lives. I took that oath. I couldn't deliberately do something that would kill him.'

'But you didn't have to give the stuff to him yourself. All you had to do was prepare the syringe. It would have been up to the Undertaker to administer it.'

'It makes no difference,' said Ingrida.

'Didn't the Undertaker check to see that he was dead?'

'She said he was. But she was in a hurry and I don't think she did a thorough job. She left me to turn off the instruments and tell Dr Salamar.'

'So there's a chance he might have been alive when he was taken away.'

'I hope he was.'

Jeannie sighed and laid back on the bed. Ingrida reached for a tissue to wipe her eyes.

'Right,' said Jeannie, 'there are two possibilities. No, three. One is that the Tri-thingy juice finished him off. Quick, painless, just like that. Possibility two: the dose knocked him out and made it look at though he was dead, the disposal crew dumped him in a ditch, and by now he's frozen to death. And number three, they dumped him but he didn't die, he woke up. If it's number three he'll be able to tell people what's happened to him. People like the police. And he'll be able to say roughly where he's been. You'd better hope it's possibility one and that he's dead.'

There was a long pause. Ingrida was conscious that Jeannie was looking at her very closely, her face only centimetres away.

'No, I don't,' said Ingrida. 'I hope he's alive.'

'You're a bit of a softy really, aren't you?' said

Jeannie. 'Anyway, what was wrong with the boy's liver that you couldn't use it.'

'The tests showed he had hepatitis B.'

'Is that bad?'

'It might be, but most people who have it don't know.'

'Then why is it a problem?'

'The virus attacks the liver and it can cause trouble. Cirrhosis and cancer possibly. It means that none of his other organs would be any use for transplant either.'

'Right,' Jeannie said thoughtfully. 'That explains why Folken couldn't use this boy for any of his posh customers. Why didn't this hepatitis show up in his genome screening?'

'I expect he got it after the DNA sample was taken. The NHGD is updated all the time but it can never be a hundred percent accurate.'

'I know that. How do you think he might have caught it?'

'The most likely way is unprotected sex with somebody who already had it.'

'Randy bugger.'

Ingrida laughed, but because that's what her partner expected, not because she thought it was funny. The boy was gone and she was concerned for him. Could she find out where he'd been taken and alert somebody to help him? It was doubtful. Who could she contact? How could she find out where he was? Jeannie might know.

'Where would the crew have taken him?' she asked.

'I don't know,' said Jeannie. 'McIntyre would have told a couple of the security team to do it. It depends who was on call?'

'Could you find out?'

Jeannie frowned. 'Maybe. It would look dodgy, though. People would want to know why I wanted to know.' There was a long silence. Then she continued, 'Anyway, I expect I'll be sent to get a reserve. Folken will have somebody else lined up, somebody to take his place. I just hope you don't fall for this one.' She raised herself on one elbow. 'What I don't understand is why you took this job if you don't like what goes on here.'

It was something Ingrida had been asking herself over the past days.

'I don't know,' she said. 'I answered an online ad that asked for a senior nurse to work in a facility that specialised in organ transplants. I'd never heard of Aurora but I looked it up and it came across as really good, a place where dedicated surgeons used the latest techniques to save frail and ill people by giving them new organs. And that's how it was at first. I saw patients who came in at death's door and then, over a matter of days, turned the corner and began looking forward to a new life.'

'So what changed?'

'It was Salamar. I'd not met her before. I was working at the Aurora clinic in Basingstoke and she turned up one day and asked me to have lunch with her. She said everyone was impressed with my work, and she wanted me to transfer to a different Aurora facility, up here in Scotland.'

'And you accepted.'

'Of course. She said it would be doing the same thing, organ transplants, only more sensitive ones. She said it would be a lot more money, and when I looked at pictures of Scotland it reminded me of my home. It was only after I'd been here a few weeks that I realised something different was going on. When I started I was with the patients who were receiving the organs. They all seemed very rich. They came and went in expensive cars and they had their own staff, and some even flew in by private jet. Most of them were foreign. I was forbidden to speak with them except on medical matters, but from what I overheard I learnt that they were paying for the organs they received.'

'And that was a problem?'

No. I know someone has to pay, it can't be free. But it wasn't what I came into nursing for. Then I found out about the donors. It puzzled me that the donors and receivers were kept completely separate. I thought that they'd meet, that at the very least the receivers would want to thank the donors for the sacrifices they were making. But they never saw each other. They were in different parts of the building with locked doors between. I didn't go into the donor side until Salamar moved me there, and then I saw how it was. The receivers' rooms are like suites in a luxury hotel. Their meals are prepared by a proper chef. They've got flowers, fantastic entertainment systems, visitors whenever they like, everything they want. The donors' wards are different. Things there are very basic. But you know all this.'

'Yes,' said Jeannie, 'I do. But that's how the world is.'

'Perhaps, but should it be? Is it fair?'

Jeannie didn't answer that question. Instead she said, 'Is that why you took pity on the kidney boy, Jonas.'

'Is that his name? I didn't know. Salamar said we mustn't ask their names, they just have numbers.'

'Jonas Eze, yes.'

'It was partly that,' said Ingrida. 'There were other things too. The receivers are handled with kid gloves. Nothing is too much trouble or too good for them. The donors are treated badly, sometimes brutally. One of the guards broke the Jonas boy's finger. Deliberately, just to scare him and cause him pain.'

'That sounds like Snake-head. He's a complete nutcase.'

'He is so. But the worst thing is that I was told that the donors are volunteers. Well, a few of them may be, but most of them are not. They're kidnapped. They're taken away from their lives so that their bodies can be used.'

Jeannie rolled over on to her stomach. She was tempted to tell Ingrida that she had been in charge of the group that had taken Jonas from outside his father's club, but she held back.

'And some of them don't survive,' said Ingrida. 'You

can live without a kidney, or a lung, or an eye. But some donors have been brought in for their hearts. What Folken and Salamar are doing is organising murders, and they're getting paid for it.'

'It's not like that,' said Jeannie. 'You should have been briefed about all this right at the start. Yes, Folken makes money out of the transplants, but it's not just that. That's not the only reason why he works night and day on running this place. He's not a bad man.'

'Well if it's not money, what else it is?' Ingrida was challenging.

'Folken did a lot of work in London and at the Max Plank Institute in Berlin before he started Aurora. And it's all been about improving the human race.'

'And how does taking people's organs against their will do that?'

'Hear me out. The folks who come here in need of help may be rich, but they are all people who have given a lot to society: artists, writers, thinkers, scientists, doctors, musicians, engineers, financiers, you name it. Some of them are benefactors who have given huge sums to charities. Many of them are young and have much more to offer the world. They are people who have faulty organs that are limiting what they can do. With replacements they can function again, carry on with their works and avoid the premature deaths that would be such a loss.'

'Everybody's death is a loss.'

'Of course it is, but some are more of a loss than others. Here at Aurora we assess their need, and then use the NHGD to find matching donors. But we don't just go for the first one. The database might throw up twenty or more names, and each one is carefully screened against some important criteria. They have to be young. They must have no dependents, either children or other family members depending on them. They can't be married. They must not be the only children of elderly parents. They must not have embarked on promising careers. They mustn't be engaged in any work that contributes in any way to the public good.'

'So he's looking for layabouts. Drones.'

'He's looking for people who haven't done much for anyone else, and he gives them a chance to do it.'

'But they don't have a choice. You make it sound like Folken's doing them a favour, but he's making decisions about who lives and who dies.'

'Isn't that what doctors do? And nurses too, sometimes.'

'It's not our decision to make.'

'Whose is it, then?'

Back in her girlhood in the Orthodox Church Ingrida would have replied God. Now she wasn't sure. What Jeannie said about Folken had a sort of logic, but it was twisted. It was Machievellian, reason without feeling. Could she accept it?

The two women lay for a long time in silence, only just touching. It had grown dark. The curtains weren't drawn, and the street light spilling through the bedroom window lit Jeannie's profile, her hair, the curve of her throat. She was beautiful. Ingrida couldn't believe she was really as heartless as she'd sounded.

She traced the line of her shoulder. 'Your skin is so smooth,' she said. 'It's like chocolate.'

Jeannie turned towards her and smiled. She ran a purple nail between Ingrida's breasts. 'And yours is like yoghurt.' Then she giggled. 'The old stuff, what gets left in the bottom of the pot, past its sell-by date.'

Ingrida let out a shriek of protest, and pushed her. The pair rolled and wrestled.

'Okay okay okay,' said Jeannie, gasping to get her breath. 'I didn't mean it.'

They fell apart and lay side by side, both looking at the ceiling.

'You're lovely,' said Jeannie. 'I looked up your name. Ingrida. It means the beautiful one. It's right.'

'Thank you,' Ingrida said quietly. She could feel herself blushing. Neither spoke for a while. Then Ingrida said, 'I'm not really gay, you know.'

Jeannie turned and shot her a look. 'What? Well, you could have fooled me!'

'No, I'm not. I have a boyfriend back in my country. We've been together for three years.'

'What's his name?'

'Stavros.'

'That doesn't sound like a Latvian name.'

'We're not from Latvia. It's Lithuania,'

'Same thing.'

Ingrida let out a shriek of protest, giggled, and punched Jeannie on her arm. 'Anyway, he's Greek.'

'What does he do?'

'He drives a truck. He travels all over.'

'Does he come to Scotland?'

'No. He goes to southern Europe mostly. Sometimes into Russia, or Belarus. He's away a lot but the money's good. And what I'm paid here is much more than a nurse in Lithuania gets. We're saving up, and when we have enough money we'll go to Greece and open a small restaurant, a taverna. Stavros will be the chef, he's a great cook, and I will be the waitress. Then, after a few years, we shall have babies.'

'You've got it all planned out then.'

'Yes, I thought I had.'

Jeannie waited a moment, then she said, 'Well I have news for you too. I'm a first for you, and you're a first for me. You're the only woman I've had sex with. There was a bit when I was a girl but that was just experimental, finding out where everything was and what it did. I broke up with my last boyfriend six months ago. Since then, nothing. Until you came along.'

There was another long silence. During it Ingrida thought about what she'd learnt during her time at Aurora, and what Jeannie had said about Folken and why he did what he did. She couldn't accept it, but what was the answer? Walking out and going back home would solve nothing. The organ factory, with its conveyor belt of unwilling donors on one side and rich predators on the other, would carry on. Could she stop it by staying? She probably couldn't stop it completely, but at least she could do her best to see that some of those the business intended to use and spit out had the chance to survive.

That's what she would do. She would stay, and do her best to right the balance. In the meantime she hoped that the young man, Jonas, lived.

11

THE STORM BEGAN JUST as the van was leaving, torrential rain married to a savage wind. The rain was spiced with hail that rattled on the roof, pelted the windscreen and bounced like mini golf balls on the road ahead. Even the night vision screen was fuzzy.

For the first few minutes the driver and his passenger said nothing. Then the passenger spoke. 'Where are we going?'

'Leyburn,' said the driver, pointing at the destination name on the navigation screen.

'Where the hell's that?'

'I dunno. That's where McIntyre said to dump him. It's in North Yorkshire somewhere, I think.'

'North Yorkshire. Jesus. How long's that going to take?'

'The satnav says six and a half hours, doesn't it?' The driver was irritated by the questions. He'd rather not be doing this tonight, in the rain, in the hail, in the dark, and the passenger could see the data on the screen as well as he.

'Shit. Why there?'

'How the fuck should I know?' The driver peered through the windscreen. 'Big Mac just gave me a map reference. Put that in the satnav, he said, drive there and throw him out.'

'Throw him out where?'

'Behind a wall, at the side of the road, where do you think? We'll find somewhere. For fuck's sake, use your brains.'

There was a pause. The rain battered and the wipers beat hypnotically.

'Who is he, anyway?' The passenger nodded towards the back of the van where a body lay under a blanket. He was a biggish lad and it had been a struggle to get him in. There'd been sod all help from the others, too.

'I have no idea.'

'Why don't they want him?'

'For Christ's sake, I haven't a clue. Now stop with the questions, will you? I don't know any more than you do. Take him to the map ref, find a field, dump him. Those are the orders, that's all I was told.'

'All right, all right.' The passenger adjusted his seat, gave it a bit more recline, and settled down for the six hour drive.

It took them an hour and three quarters to reach the edge of Glasgow and another half hour to get around the sleeping city. Once on the M74, however, they made better speed. The weather had improved but only a little and the conditions were still not easy. Trucks threw up curtains of spray that cut visibility to a few metres. They reached the Scotland-England border, where one guard sheltering in a control box waved them through without looking at them.

Even with night vision, lane-stray alert and auto-stop, driving was stressful and needed concentration. The van was hot and the driver felt himself getting drowsy. He turned the stereo up and the heating down. His passenger stirred.

'Christ, it's cold. Where are we?'

'Nearly at Carlisle.'

'Is that all?'

The driver took his hands off the steering wheel. 'Have a go, if you think you can do better.'

'No, it's not that,' the passenger said quickly. 'I just thought we might have been further on, that's all.'

'Yeah. Well, we're not. And if you'd been awake instead of sawing logs you'd know what it's been like. Like driving through a frigging monsoon. Why couldn't they give us an auto-drive, cheap bastards? Then we could both snore.'

The passenger was silent. He looked at the profile of the driver, eerily lit by the glow from the instruments. Minutes passed. Then he decided there was no way he could wait another three hours. 'I need to drain the lizard,' he said.

He'd expected the driver to grumble but he didn't.

Instead he said, 'All right. I could do with a break myself.'

It was about fifteen minutes to the next service area. Even though the car park was almost empty the driver took the vehicle to a far corner, away from the buildings. They came to a standstill beside a clump of trees and the driver removed the control fob. The wipers died.

The passenger stretched, looked out of the window and sighed. It was still raining. He looked towards the inviting neon signs far away across the rain-washed tarmac. 'You could get a bit closer.'

The driver frowned. 'Best not. Keep our distance, I think, bearing in mind what we've got in the back. Don't want to get ourselves on TV, do we.'

The passenger was getting desperate. 'I need to go first. I'm bursting. I'll be quick, then I'll keep watch while you go.'

'Don't be daft,' said the driver. 'We can both go. He doesn't need watching,' nodding towards the back. 'He's not going anywhere, is he?'

'I suppose he isn't. All right then, come on.'

The two men jumped out of the van. The doors locked with an electronic chirrup and they ran through the downpour to the dry haven of the Highway Café.

There were not many people inside – two truck drivers at separate tables, a couple talking earnestly over empty plates, a man hidden behind a magazine. They all looked as weary and fed up as the few staff on duty at this hour. The driver and the passenger used the lavatory, washed their hands, splashed their faces. Like all the motorway services the driver had visited over the past year, there was no hot water. They had to shake their hands in the air to dry them because the electric blowers had been vandalised and a soothing notice told customers that in order to save the planet paper towels were no longer provided.

Back in the restaurant the driver bought a black coffee and an old prawn sandwich. The coffee was bitter and the sandwich inedible. The bread tasted stale and the prawns were off, and he pushed it aside. He thought about complaining but it wasn't worth it, there was nobody to complain to, so he tipped the sandwich off the plate onto the floor.

The passenger did better; he had a cola and a jam doughnut. He wiped his sugary fingers on his trousers and went over to a fruit machine. He tried to win five hundred pounds but only succeeded in losing twenty.

'Mug's game,' said the driver, with a pitiful shake of the head.

The passenger shrugged. 'Someone's got to win. If you're not in it you can't win it. That's what they say.' It was the same optimism that sustained his twice weekly investment in lottery tickets, ten pounds a time, always the same numbers.

The driver looked at his watch and in unspoken agreement they rose to leave. They'd been forty minutes.

'That yours?' It was one of the staff, an old woman, and she was pointing to the sandwich mess on the floor.

'It was,' said the driver. 'You can have it.'

'Pig,' said the old woman, kneeling to gather up the mess.

'Takes one to know one,' said the driver.

They paused in the foyer by the electric doors to adjust their jackets against the weather. The passenger peered through the steamy glass at the van on the far side of the car park. It looked a long way away.

'You could get the van and drive it over here to pick me up. No point in both of us getting wet.'

The driver gave him a look. 'Fuck off.'

They stepped out into the night. The rain had eased but the wind was still blowing hard and it was very cold. It made the passenger's ears hurt. They hurried across the broad apron of hard-top to the parked van. As they approached the vehicle it obligingly unlocked its doors and switched on its lights. The driver opened his door and heard a metallic clank from the rear. Wind whipped through the cab, sucking out the copy of The Scottish Sun the passenger had left on his seat and distributing the pages across the car park.

'Shit! The back door's open!'

'It can't be!'

Both men rushed to the rear of the van. One rear door was flapping wide. On the load area there was a box of tools, a shovel and a rope. Apart from them the space was empty. The dead man and the blanket had gone.

Long before Jonas regained consciousness something buried deep in his brain warned him to keep still. Keep still, keep still, keep still, keep still, it said in a self-preservation mantra. He gradually became aware of some of the elements of his situation and they were not the same as in the hospital. Again he was in a van. There was transmission and road noise, a rocking. He lay on hard plastic which struck cold through him. Keep still, keep still, keep still.

Not that he had the capacity to move. Jonas was worse than he had ever felt in his life. His head pounded as though someone was beating it repeatedly with an axe, splitting it in two. His feet, his calves and his hands were tormented by cramps. He guessed that these were effects of the drugs he'd been given, the drugs which he knew had been intended to kill him. They had nearly succeeded, too. His muscles tightened and knotted and he was scarcely able to breath for the pain, but he repeated to himself: keep still, keep still, keep still.

He wasn't tied. They must have thought he was dead, and why bind a dead man? He was perished. Somebody had thrown a blanket over 'the body', but there was nothing underneath him, nothing to stop the freezing cold of the van floor striking through his thin clothing.

His captors wouldn't have noticed even if he had moved. There was a panel of tight steel mesh between the back of the vehicle and the cab area. Fighting the agony behind his eyes, Jonas forced them open and, still without moving, looked through it. There were two figures, black shapes silhouetted against the flare from the headlights and the dull, orange glow of the instruments. It wasn't a self-drive; the driver was having to work hard, hunched forward to peer through the steamy windscreen, squinting past the rhythmical swish-flop of the wipers. The passenger was sitting back in his seat, his feet on the dashboard.

Jonas closed his eyes in an attempt to pacify his throbbing brain. The din of the rain on the van roof and the beat of the engine were conspiring to destroy him. He rested his head on his arm to mollify the jolting but his broken finger hurt. He relapsed into unconsciousness.

He woke suddenly. The van was going round a sharp bend and he felt himself rolling against the icy, steel side. He held himself rigid. He'd learnt somewhere that rigor mortis set in three to four hours after death. He didn't know how long he'd been out, but if the drugs had done their work and he was dead his body would probably be rigid by now. When the van crew checked on him they would expect his limbs to be locked.

He had no doubt that if his captors found him alive they'd kill him. Where were they taking him? To a mortuary? A graveyard? A landfill? Would there be the chance to get away before they reached it? What was best? He couldn't fight; all he could do was play dead, hope they wouldn't notice him breathing, and allow himself to be dumped? That might work. But what if they chucked him down a ravine or threw him off a cliff? Or slung him in a reservoir? He wouldn't last more than a couple of minutes in water at this time of the year. Might he land a couple of quick punches and get away? Surprise would be on his side. But there were two of them, and he felt that he could barely stand, let alone fight.

The van came to a standstill. He heard a few mumbled words, then a door opened and the cab filled with light that spilt through the mesh. Would they look through to check on him? The other door opened, and both slammed. Thud. Thud. There was an electronic burble and the doors locked. They were leaving him, assuming he was gone. He strained his ears to hear which way the footsteps were going but the rain and the wind made that impossible. He waited. Nothing happened. He didn't know where they were or why they'd stopped. He didn't know how long they would be. Perhaps it was just a lay-by and the two men had only got out to take a leak. But the steady noise had made him think they'd been travelling on a motorway. No lay-by there. They must be at an oasis, a services area. He propped himself up so he could look through the windscreen but all he could see was a distant glow. It must be a café. So they'd probably get a drink, and maybe a bite to eat. They could be a while. This was his chance, and he was certain it was the only one he would get.

He could bang on the side of the van in the hope that somebody would hear him, but they might not. And the driver and his passenger might. Then they'd know he wasn't dead. They hadn't checked on his 'corpse' before they'd left so they probably wouldn't when they came back. If he could find a way to open the rear doors he might be able to slip out of the back of the van before the pair returned and hide somewhere. Get a grip, he told himself. No use lying there going over things; he had to move.

Cautiously he levered himself onto his knees. His limbs were so stiff he might as well have been dead, he thought. Sharp pains shot through his head with every movement. Slowly, achingly, he turned until he was facing the back of the van. He could see nothing, but he reckoned there must be an internal light somewhere. He reached up and ran one hand over the van roof till he found a smooth disc, and next to it a switch. He was unsure about turning it on but there was no choice. He had to find a way to open the doors and for that he needed light.

The bulb was like a lance striking into his pupils. He squinted between his fingers and his heart leapt. There was an internal handle to the right of the door, and immediately above it a red button. He screwed his eyes to make out the legend beside it: Emergency Lock Override. He switched off the light, groped till he found the button, and depressed it. There was a click. Surely it couldn't be that simple. He turned the handle and the door gave. He gently pushed it, bracing himself for the vehicle alarm to go off but there was no sound. He swung his legs over the edge of the load area, felt for the ground, and stood up.

He was overcome by a wave of nausea and he almost fell over, but he clung onto the van, holding tight until he regained his composure. It was still raining and there was a bone freezing wind. He was dressed in his jeans, a t-shirt and hoodie. They were the clothes he'd been wearing when he was snatched. Thank God they hadn't left him in a hospital gown. Thank God they'd put his trainers on him. There was no time to hang about; he had to get away before the van driver and his mate came back. He snatched the blanket that had been over him and pushed the doors closed.

Everywhere was sodden, great pools of water so his shoes were immediately soaked. Far away across the car park a neon sign read Highway Café. That's where the men would be. There was a familiar shape in his jeans pocket. His phone! He pulled it out. It had a tiny charge left but there was no signal and his hopes were dashed as quickly as they'd been raised. His head still hurt and his limbs were weak. Spells of dizziness blurred his vision. He knew he couldn't go far and that he desperately needed help.

Near the van was a copse that ran back beside the motorway. The trees would offer somewhere to hide, and might provide a bit of shelter from the wind. That would be his best bet. His hope was that the men wouldn't notice straight away that he'd escaped and would drive off. If he could keep out of sight until the van had gone he could come back to the service area and get help. He could at least then find out where he was. But if they did clock he was missing they'd surely look for him. As he stepped off the tarmac his trainers squelched in the mud and he felt them fill with cold water.

It could be worse, he thought; I could be dead.

12

'GONE? Gone? What do you mean, gone?' Director Folken banged the file that he was holding on his desk, so hard it sent a small dish of paperclips spinning to the floor. The clips scattered and the dish landed face up, its winged Aurora logo grounded.

'It seems he's disappeared, sir.' McIntyre, the Head of Security was standing before the Director's desk, and at that moment he was wishing he was somewhere else. He got some relief from imagining what he would say and do to the two dolts who, half an hour before, had phoned him with the news that the body they'd been instructed to dispose of had vanished. 'The crew left here, sir, as per your instructions. I personally gave them the map reference of the location for the dump.'

'And where was that?'

'I chose Leyburn, sir. It's a village in the Yorkshire Dales.'

'I know where Leyburn is,' the Director snapped

irritably. 'Why there? Why not just take him out to sea and tip him overboard?'

'Yes, sir.' Rathbone wished now that he'd done just that, but there had been a reason for choosing Leyburn. 'I did consider that but I thought it would be best if the body was found.'

'Why?'

McIntyre shuffled uncomfortably. This was going to be difficult. 'I have information that the father of the missing boy, a businessman called Solomon Eze, could be troublesome.'

'Troublesome? How?' Folken dealt daily with wealthy and important people, and he prided himself on his skill in handling them. He doubted that this individual of whom he had never heard could present any kind of a problem.

'He has a lot of connections. He owns several northern clubs: Revolution Easy in Leeds, Easy Beat in Manchester, Steel Easy in Sheffield. He also has a chain of home stores called Easy Living, and there's Easy Roller, a casino. And he owns a couple of care homes on the east coast called Rest Easy.'

'He seems to like the sound of his own name,' said Folken dismissively. 'I've always found that to be a characteristic of small fry.' He was already developing a profound contempt for Solomon Eze.

'I don't think he is small fry, sir. It seems that he's already started extensive searches. The boy is, was, his only child, and from what I hear Eze is the sort of man who's unlikely to give up. So I thought it would be a bad idea if his son just disappeared, because in that case he'd carry on looking for him. The best thing would be for his body to turn up somewhere near his home. Leyburn isn't far from where we snatched him. If he was found in a field there, apparently dead from the cold, I reasoned that his father would look for some explanation locally. We left him his phone but we removed his lifecard and his cash, so it would look like a robbery. Dr Salamar told me that the drug he was given breaks down and can easily be mistaken for alcohol, so the obvious conclusion is he went out somewhere, got drunk, was mugged, and died of exposure.'

McIntyre turned to Salamar for back-up.

'A quick look would probably conclude that he was drunk,' she said, 'but it wouldn't get past a detailed forensic examination.' She was sitting to the side of Folken. The arrangement was an indication of her rank, a point not lost on McIntyre.

'I thought that what I had planned was preferable to an unexplained disappearance, or worse, his body being washed up somewhere,' said McIntyre. He was pleased with the case he'd made and hoped his boss would see its merit.

Folken had to admit that McIntyre's plan had logic, but there were problems. 'Finding the body in the way you describe would risk a police enquiry,' he said.

'With respect, sir, I doubt it,' said McIntyre. 'There are no signs of violence on him.'

'He has a broken finger,' said Salamar sharply.

'Yes, but that's in a proper hospital dressing. It can't be linked to the notion of a mugging.'

Folken considered what he'd been told. 'So there would be nothing to connect him with us, nothing to indicate he'd been anywhere near Scotland, let alone Aberdeen.'

Salamar and McIntyre agreed.

The Director sniffed. He grudgingly had to admit that the plan made sense; or it would have done, if it had worked. 'So what went wrong?' he said.

'My men were scheduled to reach Leyburn during the night,' McIntyre explained. 'They stopped for a comfort break at a motorway services south of Carlisle. When they got back to the van the rear doors were open and the body had vanished.'

There was a long, long silence. Dr Salamar sighed. It was meant both to express criticism of McIntyre and to distance herself from him. Folken could be irascible and unpredictable, and he would be perfectly capable of including her as a target for his wrath should she get in the firing line.

'And they both left the van together?' said Folken. 'They left it unattended? With a body in it?'

'The body was a corpse, sir. They saw no need to guard it.'

The Director seemed more weary than angry. He put his head in his hands and rubbed his eyes. 'I don't believe it.' He muttered. 'I do not believe it. Will someone kindly explain to me how a dead man can vanish from a locked van? He was dead, wasn't he? We are sure of that?'

McIntyre looked to Salamar, pleased that the focus had now shifted to her.

'Oh yes,' she said. 'He received 50 millilitres of Trimesorphene. That's well above a lethal dose.'

'Did you administer it yourself?'

Salamar bristled. 'Certainly not. I am a doctor, I do not take life. The dose was administered as usual, by our Undertaker. She examined the patient and there were no vital signs. She pronounced him dead at,' she glanced at her datapad, 'twenty-zero-three. I told the Undertaker to log this and to give instructions to security to dispose of the body. '

'And the van really was locked?' The Director looked sharply at McIntyre.

'Oh yes, sir. The crew are certain that the van was locked.'

'So what do we believe happened?' There was no answer. Salamar stared out of the window. McIntyre shuffled and looked at the floor. 'Come on, people,' said the Director through clenched teeth. 'I want to know what you think.'

Salamar could see that Folken believed that she shared some responsible for the affair and she saw an opportunity to divert the blame.

'It could be that the van crew are lying,' she said.

McIntyre started to protest but the Director shushed him. 'Go on,' he said to Salamar.

'Well, we only have their word for what happened.'

'There's the tracking data,' McIntyre protested. 'It shows that the van stopped where they said it did, and that it didn't go anywhere else.'

'And how long did it stop for?'

'About forty minutes.'

'Precisely my point,' said Salamar. 'We know when and where they stopped but there's no way of knowing what happened while they were there.'

'The service area must have cctv,' said Folken. 'Have we got copies of the recordings?'

'I have asked for them, sir,' said McIntyre. 'It was one of the first things I did, but I'm afraid the manager of the services is not being very helpful.'

The Director scowled. 'What do you mean, not helpful?'

'He's requiring authorisation from his superiors before he'll release the recordings to us.'

Folken was angry. 'Authorisation? Authorisation?' he fumed. 'God help us, doesn't he know who we are?' He had turned puce and Salamar wondered if this would be the occasion on which he would have the heart attack she had long predicted for him.

By contrast McIntyre was the essence of calm. 'I told him we are an agency appointed by the Government of England and I messaged him a copy of our warrant but he still insists he has to get clearance. It probably won't make much difference, though. The crew say that because of the van's contents they left it well away from the main building in what they judged to be a camera blind spot.'

'So all we can expect to see is your men going into the building,' said Folken. 'We won't see how the body disappeared.'

'I think there's only one reasonable assumption,' said Salamar.

'Which is?'

'That the body was stolen.'

Folken snorted. 'Why would anyone do that?'

'Absurd,' said McIntyre. 'Who would do it, and how would they know where the van would be?'

'There are several possibilities,' said Salamar. 'The van could have been followed, or the crew might have tipped somebody off about what they were carrying.'

'That's rubbish,' said McIntyre. It was his turn to be angry now. 'These men have been with us for a long time. I use them regularly for sensitive and confidential work. They're one hundred percent loyal and I trust them. Anyway, I didn't give them the assignment or the destination until just before they left.'

'They could have called somebody on the way,' said Salamar. 'Told them where they were going.'

'No chance,' said McIntyre. 'The van doesn't have two-way radio but it does have a tracker that monitors everything that goes on in the vehicle. It would show if a phone had been used.'

'Has it occurred to you,' Salamar said, her voice heavy with sarcasm, 'that one of the crew might have got out of the van? The tracker wouldn't know about that, would it. It wouldn't know if he'd used a phone then.'

McIntyre was beginning to suspect that the reason Salamar seemed to be intent on putting the blame on his van crew, and therefore on him, was that something had gone wrong at the hospital end.

'The tracker shows that the van didn't stop before it got to the motorway services,' he said. 'So in order to use a phone one of the crew would have had to leave it while it was moving, make the call, catch up with it again and get back on board. My men are able, but I don't think even they could accomplish that.' If Salamar could be patronising and sarcastic, so could he.

Folken was tired of the bickering between two people who in his view were both at fault. 'This is nonsense,' he said. 'Who would want to steal this young man's dead body? It's perfectly clear what happened. While the van was left unattended the "corpse" woke up and got out.'

'But I've explained,' Salamar protested. 'He was given fifty...'

'...milliliters of Trimesorphene. I know. And I accept that he may have shown every sign of being dead when the Undertaker examined him, but we both know there are cases of resistance to Trimesorphene, and of it not killing but inducing a severely catatonic state that can be mistaken for death. It's rare but it can happen.'

McIntyre was pleased to note Salamar's discomfort. 'Well he can't have got far,' he said. 'It's freezing tonight and he's not wrapped up. Unless he's found shelter he'll be in trouble.'

'Not as much trouble as he'll be in if he's still alive when we find him,' said Folken. 'I want the van crew and half a dozen of our best people at that service area. I want them fully equipped - thermal imaging, ultra sound, the lot. I want a helicopter survey. Scour the whole area. I want this man found.'

McIntyre's expression was smug. 'I have it in hand, sir. The search squad have already left, I sent them off as soon as I heard the news. I've organised the helicopter to go up at first light. I've given them all the same instruction: find the boy. If he's dead, leave him. If he's alive, kill him.'

'Good,' said Folken. He looked at his watch. In only a few hours Ivanovitch and his daughter would land at Aberdeen airport. 'What about the back-up?'

'We've located a suitable subject,' said Salamar. 'Caucasian, just eighteen years old.'

'Female.'

'Male. We haven't managed to locate a suitable female within range.'

Folken grunted. Same sex transplants were the least likely to be rejected. Male to female were a higher risk but they'd have to take it. It wasn't perfect but it would have to do. At least this one was white. Ivanovitch hadn't asked about the donor's ethnicity but the fact that he'd cleared players of colour out of the football club he'd bought suggested that he would not have been happy if he'd known the colour of the first donor's skin.

'When can we pick him up?'

'It's already in hand,' said McIntyre. 'I briefed Jeannie to go with a snatch squad as soon as I heard that the Eze boy was unsuitable. Oddly the reserve donor lives in the same city, so the arrangements have been easy, if you'll forgive the pun.' McIntyre thought that was quite good but Salamar and the Director didn't smile. Neither was minded to lighten the tone yet. 'I'm expecting to hear from the snatchers tomorrow before the end of the day,' McIntyre added.

'Good,' said Folken. 'Tell me when you do. Make sure I'm kept informed. Fully informed.' McIntyre and Salamar were dismissed.

As soon as they were clear of Folken's office McIntyre challenged his colleague. 'It sounded in there as if you were trying to lay the blame for this mess on my people.'

'Well who else's fault could it be?'

'You heard the boss. He said the drug you gave Eze didn't work...'

'Impossible. That is so rare...'

'...and anyway your lot didn't properly examine his genome and missed that his liver was useless.'

Rows between the clinic's medical staff and security were commonplace. This one was settling into the familiar pattern of carping and accusation.

'There was nothing wrong with our screening,' Salamar snapped. 'Nothing wrong at all.'

'So hepatitis B is nothing,' McIntyre retorted. 'If he'd been a healthy donor we wouldn't have had to get rid of him and we wouldn't be in this mess. You missed it.'

'We didn't miss it. He must have contracted the condition after we carried out the genome check.'

'Of course he must,' said McIntyre, meaning anything but. 'I hope the screening of this new one has been better.'

Salamar offered no answer and McIntyre walked away. I won that one, he thought to himself.

Back in his office Director Folken had a call to make. It would be a difficult one. He glanced at the file on his desk and dialled the private number for Mikael Dimitri Ivanovitch.

13

CAMERON VISITED his mother at least every week, almost always on a Friday. Often he took Beth with him because Molly liked her and they got on. He preferred it when Beth went with him because they could talk while they were walking and on the bus, and when they got there Beth and Molly would chatter on together and leave him free to amuse himself on his phone. This time, however, it was different; Molly had asked him to be sure to come on his own. He'd been puzzled by the request, and curious to find out the reason for it. What Molly told him was nothing he could have predicted, and it turned his life upside down.

The visit began normally. Molly sat him down, opened a half bottle of Prosecco and poured him a glass, 'To celebrate your birthday,' she said. 'Your eighteenth. That's special.'

'I'm all for another glass,' said Cameron, 'or even

two, but Beth's and my birthdays were last week. We did celebrate then.' Cameron took a sip of the fizzy wine. It was ice cold, and even though Prosecco wasn't his favourite this one tasted good. 'You're not having one?' His mother hadn't been drinking last week either, but he'd thought that was because she was driving.

Molly shook her head.

Cameron raised his eyebrows. 'Again?'

Molly nodded.

'When?' said Cameron.

'Five months,' said Molly.

It didn't show, but his mother was in any case well built and she usually wore loose-fitting garments, so it was hard to tell.

'Mm,' he said. 'Boy or girl?'

'Boy.'

'Whose is it this time?'

'You know I can't tell you that. I can't tell anybody, not even you.' Molly gave a weary smile. It was a question he asked her every time, one that people always put to surrogates and one that they were pledged never to answer. Confidentiality was essential for what they did. 'There is something I do want to tell you, though.'

'Oh yeah?' She's going to give up surrogacy, Cameron thought, and about time too. She wasn't young any more. He was so sure it would be that, it made what she actually said a complete bombshell.

'It's about your father.'

Cameron sat up. His father was a shadowy figure.

The little he knew about him had come in dribs and drabs throughout his childhood. He'd been something of a hero, a test pilot in the RAF who'd been killed when Cameron was a baby. He'd been trying out a new strike fighter. It had been a top secret mission, and that was why there was no reference to him anywhere, not in MOD records, not online, not anywhere. Distance and mystery generated romance. Was his mother going to give him some memento of his father to mark his eighteenth? His medals perhaps? Some sort of commemoration of his service? He got up and went to the sideboard, and picked up the photograph of a good looking young man in pilot's uniform.

'No,' said Molly.

Cameron turned. 'No what?'

'No, that's not your father.'

Cameron was confused. 'What do you mean, not my father?' He looked at the fresh face staring out from the frame. He'd always thought the young man in the picture resembled him. Beth said so too.

'What I say. That young man is not your father.'

'Who is my father then? Zak?'

Cameron was five when Zak married his mother. He could remember the ceremony very well. He'd been a page boy, Beth a bridesmaid. He could remember all the fuss and the hugging. He'd always thought that Zak had come into Molly's life well after he was born, but maybe that wasn't so. Maybe they'd been together for a long time before that.

'No. Not Zak.'

'Who, then?'

'I don't know.'

Cameron felt as though the room was spinning. Nothing was making any sense. 'What do you mean you don't know? You don't know who my dad is? That picture's been on your sideboard as long as I can remember. You've told me loads of times it's my dad. You've told me stories about some of the things you did together, some of the places you went. You said he was your first love, somebody really special.'

'No.'

'Don't keep saying that. You know you did.'

Molly sighed. 'Yes, I know what I told you, but it wasn't true. That isn't your father.'

'Then who is it?'

'I don't know. It's a photo I found in a second hand shop. I liked the frame, and that picture was in it. I thought he would do.'

Cameron sat down, hard. He couldn't take in any of this. 'Well if he isn't my dad, and Zak isn't, who is?'

'I can't tell you.'

Molly looked down and seemed to be tearful, but despite this Cameron was angry. 'You can't tell me, or you won't?'

'I can't.'

'You can't tell me who my own father is? Really? Are you serious?' Possibilities raced through his head. Was he the outcome of a one-night stand? The result of a rape? What?

Molly dabbed her eyes with a tissue. She said

nothing for a few seconds, then she patted the space beside her on the sofa. Cameron hesitated a moment, then he moved over to sit beside her.

'I know this is a shock,' she said, 'but hear me out, please. I want to explain.'

Cameron was starting to get a feeling of dread. Surely he wasn't... surely he couldn't be...? 'You don't mean I'm a... that I'm like all your others?'

Molly took his hand. He resisted at first, then he gave in.

'Yes, and no,' she said. He made to get up but she clung on to his hand. 'Please listen. I want to tell you the truth. Now you're eighteen you have to know.'

Cameron said nothing, but he left his hand in hers and she took this as a willingness for her to go on.

'You need to understand something about me, how I got to do what I do, why I do it, and what it means for both of us.'

Cameron felt lost. As long as he could remember his mother had been bearing children for other people. At first he'd not even been curious, he'd just accepted it; it was what his mother did. For a time after marrying Zak she'd stopped, but then they separated and she'd started again. Cameron had never questioned it, even though he'd been teased about it at school – your ma's a gussie, gussie boy, gussie pussy, etc. Later, in his early teens, he had begun to resent it and he and his mother had rows. Then as he grew up he came to accept it again. What had kept him going, through the doubts and the teasing and the embarrassment of the gossip, was his father. Zak was his step-father. Nobody could have been more caring than Zak and Cameron loved him dearly, but he wasn't his true father; his true father had been a hero.

'I know that what I do has sometimes been difficult for you and you've often called me out for it, but you've never asked why I do it.'

Cameron nodded. That was true. The why of it had never been important to him.

'Right. Well, this is how it was. I had my first surrogate baby when I was only nineteen. I didn't do it for the money, not then. At that time it was illegal for surrogates to charge. No, it was for some people I knew. They were a lovely couple, neighbours, and they'd been trying to have a baby for ages. They'd tried everything – fertility drugs, IVF, IUI, managed sex, hormone treatments for both of them, injections, special diets, you name it. Whatever they did, Susie, that was her name, didn't get pregnant and then, when at last she did, she miscarried.

'She was heartbroken. Steve, her bloke, was away at the time and I went round to her house. She was really down. She said she thought there was something wrong with her, and maybe it was a judgement on her for being too free and easy with sex when she was younger. She said she was thinking of ending it all. She really meant it, she was going to kill herself. We talked all night, and we drank a lot of wine. I told her not to be daft, that it wasn't her fault. Then, I don't know what possessed me, I just came out with it. I said I'd carry a baby for her. I didn't know how it was done or what was involved, I just said it because it seemed to be something I could do to help her. It may have been the wine talking and anyway she turned it down. But the next day she called me and said did I mean it. She and Steve had talked about it and it was what they wanted. I had to say yes. Well I did, didn't I, because I couldn't let them down, not after everything they'd been through. Besides, I was worried that if I did go back on the offer Susie really would do something bad to herself.

'It turned out to be easy. I thought it would be awful but it wasn't. I was examined and passed as super fit.' She laughed. 'Hard to believe, I know, but I was in those days. And so we did it. She went through the IVF again and the fertilised egg was implanted in me. That bit wasn't too nice, I admit, but then it was plain sailing. For nine and a bit months I carried her baby, and at the end I gave birth to a bouncing, healthy boy. Eight pounds seven ounces. Not bad for a first attempt, the midwife said. His name's Sam.

'Susie and Steve keep in touch. They send me a card at Christmas and on my birthday. They wanted to pay me but it wasn't allowed. Then, soon after, the law changed. There were a lot more people wanting surrogates than there were women prepared to do it, so something had to be done. At first it was improving the expenses. They used to just cover basics like transport, special diets, medication, that sort of thing, but they got to include accommodation, and what you would have earned if you'd been working. Finally they brought in fees. It was only fair. From getting pregnant to giving birth to recovering afterwards is a year of your life, sometimes more, so it's right you get a year's pay for it.

'So after Sam was born I thought there must be other people in the same boat as Susie and Steve. Maybe I could help them too. I'd been bugger all use at school and I'd left without any qualifications, so the only job I could get was in a packing warehouse where the hours and the pay were terrible and the supervisor was a total dick. Up till then I'd been no good at anything, but this was something I did seem to be good at. I contacted an agency and they took me on, and this time I did get money for it. It seemed a fortune in those days. I remember the day the bank transfer for the first payment came through. I took Suzie and Steve out for a slap-up meal. No alcohol for me, though. The agency were keen as mustard about that. They'd do random tests; somebody would just turn up and take a blood sample and if there was any trace of alcohol they'd cut your fee.'

'So what has this got to do with me?' Cameron had a nasty suspicion and his voice was cold. 'Are you saying that I'm one of those?'

Molly didn't answer his question directly. 'I did three surrogacies,' she said. 'During the last one I started to develop a yearning for a baby of my own, one I could keep. It was unbearable. When you're a surrogate you hardly get to see the baby. Maybe you'll give it a couple of feeds, but they don't want you to bond with it so they don't leave it with you. It's taken away. That hurts. It still hurts, every time. There's this tiny thing that's grown inside you for all those months, that you've looked after, kept yourself healthy for. It's kicked you and you've talked to it, and then suddenly it's gone. You're emptied out. And the mums and dads are so made up. They're over the moon. So I thought, I want a baby of my own. One I can love, and provide for, and watch growing up.

'The problem was, I didn't have a fella. You're not exactly top of the list of hot dates when you're pregnant pretty much all the time, and anyway some of the dating sites ban gussies. Besides, there was no one I fancied. AID? I didn't want to go in for all that, thumbing through the cvs of donors, like choosing a puppy at the pet shop. So I thought, the next surrogacy I do, if it all goes well I'll just keep it. Of course, you sign a form to say you're not going to do that, but I thought "What the hell?"

'I went through the usual rigmarole, had the injections, the implant, and it took. At 12 weeks I had an ultrasound scan, and it was a boy. I didn't care, I would have been just as happy with either. This baby felt different. It felt special. I don't think it was just that I'd decided to keep it, it was something more. It had a personality; it kicked like a striker but if I put music on it would go quiet. It didn't wake me in the night and I felt great. From the get go it was mine.

'I took a holiday. I told the agency I'd been sleeping badly and I was going abroad for a couple of weeks to get some sunshine and a change of scene. They didn't like it but at that time there was nothing in the contract to stop me. I'd contacted a doctor in Romania online who I thought would do what I wanted, and he did. At the end of my first week away I messaged the agency and told them that I'd miscarried. I said I'd had food poisoning and severe stomach cramps, and the next day the foetus was stillborn. The Romanian doctor gave me a letter backing it all up.'

Molly stopped talking and put her arm around Cameron's shoulder.

'And that was me?'

'Yes, that was you.'

'I was born in Romania?'

'No. I stayed there until just before you were due. Then I came home and you were born here.'

'And nobody twigged anything?'

'No. The agency was pissed, of course, because they'd been forced to return the money they'd got from the parents, and they might have suspected something but I kept low. I rented a little cottage on the east coast, and you and me holed up there. We spent the winter together. It was amazing, one of the very best times of my life. Just the two of us, and the sea and the gulls. I could have stayed there for ever but I was running out of money, so I came back and started again.'

'More surrogacy.'

'It was the only thing I knew, and it meant I could be home to look after you. Then you went to nursery, and I met Zak, and, well, you know the rest.'

'So who is my dad?'

'I don't know. I meant it when I said I can't tell you. I really can't. The agency I was working for then kept the details of the parents confidential. The one I'm with now is different, but most of them still ban any communication between the biological parents and the surrogate. They say it avoids complications later.'

'So when you and Zak split up, why did you leave me there?'

'That's what you chose. I wanted you with me but Archy was your best friend and I thought that being with him would give you a more normal childhood.'

Cameron thought about that. Life with Zak was not what most people would consider normal, but he let it pass. Then something else struck him, and he wondered why it hadn't before. He let go of Molly's hand.

'So not only do I not know who my real dad is, you're not my mother either.'

'Not technically. No.'

Suddenly it all boiled over and he got up. Everything he'd believed about his life was unravelling. He'd been lied to for years. Somewhere were two people who were his biological parents, whose genes he had, whose blood he shared, and he had no idea who they were. Or where they were. Or even if they were still alive. Did he have brothers? Sisters? Aunts and uncles? A whole family? And this woman looking at him, concern all over her face, was no relation to him. 'Not technically,' he repeated. 'Jesus!'

Molly reached out her hand to him but Cameron kept his distance.

'I'm not your biological mother,' she said, gloomily. 'But for nine months you lived and grew inside me. Where I went, you went. My body fed yours, my body built yours. You knew my movements and I knew when you moved. And then when you were born you drank my milk. When you were teething I was there. I helped you learn to walk, and to talk. When you fell over and hurt yourself I picked you up and comforted you. When you woke in the night it was me that went to you. So no, I'm not your true mother, but I think I have a pretty good claim to the title.'

Cameron flopped into an armchair and leant forward, his head in his hands. This was turning out to be probably the worst day in his life.

'All these years, all this time, you've lied to me. You and Zak.'

'Grown ups lie to children all the time,' Molly said, and now she sounded weary rather than sad. 'The Tooth Fairy. Santa Claus. "Cheer up, you'll soon feel better." "Daddy and I weren't really arguing." "We'll go there tomorrow." Yes, all lies. We sometimes tell children things that aren't true because we think that's best for them. We tell them what we think will make them happy. I wanted you to have as happy a life as possible, and I wanted you to think of me as your mother.'

'So why tell me different now?'

'Because last week you were eighteen, and on that

day your genome went onto the NHGD. That's a public record. All sorts of people have access to it for all sorts of reasons. Anybody could see from it that you and I aren't related.' Cameron made to interrupt but Molly held up her hand. 'It's unlikely anybody would, I know, but I couldn't risk it. I didn't want you to hear the truth from anyone but me. It also means that if you want you should be able to find out who your biological parents are. If you want.'

Questions clamoured in Cameron's head. What were his true parents like? Was his father a handsome hero, like the guy in the photo on the sideboard? Or would he be a disappointment? Who was his mother?

'Will they come looking for me now I'm on the NHGD?'

Molly shook her head. 'No. They don't think you survived. For them it was just a failed business transaction.'

'You simply sold them your body for a spell.' It was like being a prostitute, he thought, and that made the words come out more bitterly than he'd intended.

'That's what a gussie does,' Molly said, and there was defiance in her tone.

'Who else knows about this?' he said.

'No one else. Just you, Zak and me.'

'Archy?'

'No.'

'Beth?'

'No. Like I said, just you, Zak and me.'

'Does Zak know you're telling me this today?'

'Yes.'

So what next? Cameron thought. Go on as before? Could he, knowing what he did now? What would Beth think of it all? Would he even tell her? But could he hide it from her? She often knew his moods and feelings. She'd be bound to realise something was different about him and she'd want the details. And what about Archy, who was his best mate? And Zak? Would things with them ever again be the same? There was so much to think about. He was drowning. He needed time.

He left then. Molly wanted him to stay until he felt calmer but he had to be alone. They hugged, and Molly kissed him on the cheek like she always had, but now it was different and Cameron held himself rigid in her embrace.

He always called on Beth on the way home after visiting Molly and she would be expecting him, but he needed to be on his own while he tried to process what he'd been told. He left Molly's and instead of going to the bus stop he turned into the park.

It was because he had so much on his mind that he didn't notice the couple following him; or the car loitering by the railings on the outside.

14

Solomon Eze was musing on how quickly a person's priorities can change. A few days ago the main thing on his mind had been the completion of his new house, and trying to restrain Marcella's more extravagant schemes for its decor. Now all that meant nothing. As far as he cared Marcella could paint the whole place purple if she wanted. She could have all the gold taps she could find. The fancy Italian tiles she'd chosen for the swimming pool? No problem. All he could think about now was his son, Jonas, sleeping on the bed at his side, and about what had happened to him. The boy was looking better and his breathing was less ragged, but he was still ill. Solomon's number one concern now was to find the bastards who had done this.

It had been a harrowing time. When he'd walked back to the club after his afternoon appointment he'd been pleased to see that Jonas's car had still been there because it meant that uncharacteristically he wasn't skiving off for the afternoon. But he wasn't in the building and no one had seen him. He assumed that the boy had gone out on foot somewhere and would be back soon. But he wasn't. After a couple of hours he'd tried Jonas's mobile; there was no answer. By the end of the afternoon he was starting to get annoyed. He knew very well what had happened. Jonas had gone to a pub to get some lunch, met some mates, and spent the afternoon getting drunk. He'd be at somebody's pad somewhere sleeping it off. He was already planning what he'd say and do to the boy when he finally came home. Marcella hadn't seemed bothered, convinced that he'd turn up at any minute. He didn't. Solomon had gone to bed still angry, and fallen into a troubled sleep.

He got up at six, as he usually did, and immediately went to Jonas's room. He didn't care if the boy had a hangover. Serve him right if he had, it was time he pulled himself together. He flung the door open and his anger deflated like a split tyre. The bed was empty and it was obvious that it hadn't been slept in. He went downstairs. There was no sign of Jonas. He called his mobile yet again. Still no reply. That was when he started to worry.

Solomon and Marcella spent a day phoning all Jonas's friends they could think of. They put out calls on social media. They contacted everywhere they thought he might have gone. Nobody had seen him, nobody had any idea where he might be. A knot of misery was forming in Solomon's heart. He'd been picky with Jonas all morning. There'd been a number of irritations and he'd taken out his displeasure on his son. He hadn't even said goodbye to him when he'd left the club.

Then, in the small hours of the morning, Solomon's mobile rang. He snatched it and switched on the bedside light. It was Jonas's number.

'Jo, my boy, what's happening? Where are you?'

There had been a pause. Then a sound like choking. Then, 'Dad? Dad? It's me.'

'Jonas? Jonas? Jesus Christ almighty, boy, what's going on? Are you all right?'

'Yeah. I mean, no. Oh, dad, I'm bad. Come and get me, dad. Please.'

He sounded about nine, sounded like he'd done when he used to wake up in the middle of the night from a bad dream. He hit the Where's My Caller? app. A map and coordinates unrolled on the screen. 'You stay right there, my son. Don't you move. I'm coming.'

Jeans, a sweatshirt, shoes. Dressing was difficult because his hands were trembling, something unusual for Solomon. Jonas hadn't sounded good. What had happened to him? Why was his boy in a field beside the M6, in the middle of the night?

Marcella, who had at last been persuaded to take a sleeping pill, propped herself up on her elbows, looking dazed.

'It's Jonas. He called. I've got to go get him.'

'Oh my God. Where? Where is he?'

'Near Carlisle.'

'What's he doing there? Is he all right?'

'I don't know. He don't sound good.'

Solomon did up his belt, pocketed his phone and wallet, and turned to see his wife swinging her legs off the bed.

'Hey, what're you doin'?'

'Carlisle,' she mumbled. 'It's a long way. I'll come too.' She tried to stand up but couldn't make it and sat down hard.

'No, sweet cheeks,' he said. 'You stay right here. I've sent Draven and Gunner the coordinates. They'll meet me. You get some rest so you can look after our boy when I bring him home. Besides, we might need you here.'

He kissed his wife on the forehead. She nodded sleepily and sank back onto the bed.

Solomon rushed down the stairs, into the laundry room and grabbed an armful of blankets. Then out to the car.

The roads were deserted and it took Solomon less than an hour to get to the spot where his phone said Jonas was. It was very dark, very windy, and very cold. It had been raining and there were standing pools of water, so Solomon's feet were immediately wet through. He called Jonas's name, straining against the wind for a reply. The gale roared in his ears and stung his face. He pulled his coat around him and walked beside the wall that bounded the road. The lights from his parked car threw his shadow ahead of him.

Solomon scoured the road, the ditch beside it, the other side of the dry stone wall. He found Jonas a hundred yards along, beside a gate. He was unconscious, appallingly cold, wringing wet, and when Solomon roused him he couldn't speak. Solomon wrapped the blankets around him and tried to rub some life into his frozen limbs.

'What this? What have you done to your hand?' Solomon said as he encountered the dressing.

Jonas just shook his head. His face was wet, rain or tears. The priority for Solomon was to get him out of the cold and warm him up.

'Come on,' he said. 'Let's get you to the car.'

He got his hands under Jonas's arms and pulled him to his feet. It wasn't easy. Although Solomon was strong Jonas was heavy, he was weak, and the ground was soggy and infirm. Eventually he got the boy upright but he couldn't stand on his own. He began to tremble violently. The problem was to get him to the car hundred or so metres away. He'd just got his son into the road when another car drew up behind his: Draven and Gunner.

Between them they got Jonas into Solomon's car, cranked up the heater, removed his wet, cold, stained clothes, and wrapped him in blankets. As the young man warmed he came to. Draven had brought a flask of hot tea laced with whisky. Jonas took a sip and was seized by a fit of coughing.

They took him straight home, put him in bed and sent for medical support. The doctor came within the hour, examined him, took his pulse and blood pressure, listened to his heart, drew off some blood samples, put him on a drip.

'One of his fingers has been broken, but apart from that there's no obvious physical damage. But he has been heavily sedated. Christ knows what he's taken. It will take me a couple of hours to get the blood analysed, then we'll know what it is and I can start to rebalance his system. For now, keep him quiet and give him plenty of liquids, but no alcohol. Make sure he gets lots of rest but don't let him sleep for too long, wake him up every hour or so.'

'Is he all right?'

The doctor considered his answer. 'It's too soon to say. There's no obvious immediate threat to his life. He doesn't seem to have suffered anything permanent from the cold. He's a strong boy, but we won't know for sure about the longer term until we've found out what drugs are in his system. I don't like to say this, but might he have picked something up at the club?'

Solomon didn't know. They had a strict no drugs policy but it was almost impossible to enforce in dimly lit spaces crammed with young bodies. It was possible that Jonas had found something stashed when he'd been cleaning up, but surely he wouldn't have taken it without knowing what it was. And what was he doing in Carlisle? How did he get there without his car?

The doctor had been examining Jonas again. He looked at Solomon thoughtfully. 'I don't think what he's taken is any of the recreational drugs that the kids are using at the moment. It looks heavier than that. I doubt he took it himself. There are marks on his arms from needles.'

'What are you saying?'

'I'm saying that what's been done to your lad is deliberate. Whatever it is, somebody made him take it. What concerns me is that it could be some sort of nerve agent. We need to watch out for damage to his liver or kidneys'

'Nerve agent? What the fuck? Who would have given him that? Why?'

'Your guess is as good as mine, but you've got a bad enemy out there somewhere. Whoever did this, junked up your boy and dumped him in a field on a freezing night, whoever did that meant him serious harm.'

After the doctor had gone, after Marcella had fussed over Jonas and cried over him and hugged him and managed to get him to take a sweet drink, the boy had been able to tell them what he remembered of what had happened: leaving the club, his car boxed in by a van, talking to a young woman, a man arriving, then waking in the van and being unloaded at a hospital. He told them about a friendly nurse, Polish he thought, who was the only one who was nice to him. He told them about an older woman – a doctor, severe and unpleasant – who'd taken samples for tests. Then another woman had come in and the Polish nurse had given her a syringe. She'd asked was it enough and the nurse had said plenty. This new woman jabbed him, and after that he remembered nothing until he'd woken in the van.

'I think they thought I was dead. I wasn't tied up or nothing, just chucked in the back of this van on an old blanket. There were two dudes in the front. After a bit the van stopped and they got out. I looked out the window and saw it was a services. I thought I was shut in but I tried the door and it wasn't locked or nothing. My head felt like shit and I kept trying to throw up. I got out of the van and hid behind some skips. They'd taken my card with my credits and a bit of cash I had but they left me my phone, it was in my pocket and it still had some charge. I went through the trees until I could get a signal and I could call you. Then I hid in the field. It was fucking freezing.'

'Who were they, these guys in the van? What did they look like?

Jonas couldn't say. He hadn't got a proper look at them.

He fell asleep again, and Solomon let him. There was time to seek out the van crew, time to discover the why's and wherefores of it all later. What mattered now was that his son was safe and they had to get him healthy. But it was only a temporary rest; soon the time would come to make somebody pay. He called Draven.

'Hey,' he said, 'Jonas has been filling me in on what happened to him. He says he was grabbed by some people right outside the club. Check the security cameras, especially the one on the front. See if it's picked up anything.'

Twenty minutes later Draven came back. He'd found some security footage and was messaging it to Solomon. And there it was: Jonas's car, the van, the girl, and another man who seemed to watch them from the other side of the street before coming over. It wasn't possible to see exactly what happened because the man and the woman were standing too close to Jonas, but the camera had a clear view of him collapsing and being bundled into the van, and of the registration plate as it drove away.

He keyed a speed dial number on his phone.

'Zak?'

'Sol, hi. What gives at this splendid hour of the morning?'

'I've got a little job for you. I'm messaging you a video clip of a white van. Do me a favour and see if you can find out who it belongs to, huh?'

'It's as good as done,' said Zak.

Solomon checked his watch. Jonas had been sleeping for well over an hour. In an armchair on the other side of the bed Marcella too was asleep. Shame to wake either of them, sleeping there clean and quiet like little babies. But the doctor had insisted that Jonas must be woken regularly, so Solomon took the boy's shoulder and gave it a gentle shake.

'Hey Jonas, my boy. How're you doin? Time to rouse.' He patted his son's cheek.

Suddenly Jonas jumped with a force that almost took him off the bed. His eyes snapped open and there was a look of wild panic on his face. Solomon was startled and stepped back. The boy's teeth were clenched, his neck muscles stood out, and his eyes darted around the room. He was rigid for a moment, then he gave a huge sigh and shuddered. The tension eased.

'Jesus, dad. I thought I was back there, in the hospital.'

'Well you're not. You're home now, in your own bed.'

Jonas sighed again, and managed a weak smile. He sank back. Marcella had woken too, and she moved to fluff up his pillows.

'This hospital,' said Solomon. 'Feel like talking about it?'

Jonas nodded. He bit on his bottom lip, gathering his thoughts.

'Can you remember anything about it?' Solomon prompted. 'What was it like?'

'I didn't see much of it. Two morons took me in there. One of them, a gruesome dude with a snake tattooed on his scalp, did this.' He held up his finger. 'The Polish nurse put this tube thing on it. She was nice but the others never said anything. Except the doctor woman who was in charge. She was nasty. The place seemed weird, really weird. It was a hospital all right, all clean and white and with beds and equipment and stuff, but it was like a prison.'

'Did you see anybody else there, talk to anybody?'

'No, just the nice nurse. And the doctor woman. She gave me injections. I don't know what it was but it made stuff seem all vague, hard to see properly or think straight.' He started to shiver. 'Dad, they were gonna operate on me, take my kidney!'

Solomon froze. 'How do you know this?'

'One of the guards told me, the same one who bust my hand. The others didn't say nothin', ignored me, but this was a creepy dude. He seemed to think it was all a big joke. Said they were goin' to take my kidney and give it to some Russian babe. He said I was lucky to be getting inside a Russian doll. Said after they'd got my kidney they'd take a whole load of other stuff, chuck away what was left.'

Solomon was trying to appear calm, he didn't want to excite his son, but inside he was raging. He'd done some rough things in his time, sometimes you had to to enforce your will, but this was different.

'So why didn't it happen, what this guy said?'

Jonas shook his head. 'I dunno. After all the tests they left me, and then this doctor woman came in. She seemed angry. She told the nice nurse to jab me, try me on something I think she said. I was strapped down and I couldn't do anything, but after the doctor woman had gone the nice nurse whispered to me that it was okay. Then another woman came in and she gave me the jab and the next thing I knew I was bumping around in the van with my head pounding like a beat-hammer.'

There was a long silence. Marcella was still, sitting on the bed and she leant forward and stroked her son's forehead.

Solomon stood up. When he spoke his voice was

quiet, cool, determined. 'I'm going to find this hospital. When I do I'm going to torch it. Burn it down, with that guard and the doctor and as many of the others as I can round up inside it. I'm going to find it.'

'Oh, I know where it is,' said Jonas. 'Well, roughly, anyway. It's in Scotland.'

'How do you know that?'

'The woman who spoke to me outside the club had a Scottish accent. The dudes who took me put me in a kind of box thing under the back seat because they said they wanted to be sure I was out of sight when they crossed the border. That must have been the England-Scotland border. And the services where I got out were near Carlisle, that's almost in Scotland. And there's another thing,' Jonas went on. 'The nurses had this logo on their uniforms. A big letter A with wings. I think that must be something to do with the hospital.'

There was a long pause while Solomon digested this information. He knew about the winged A, knew what the logo meant. He was surprised his son didn't.

'Dad,' said Jonas, and he sounded like a little boy. 'They were gonna kill me.'

15

'DID YOU WIN?'

Beth dropped the bag containing her kit on the floor and closed the door behind her. 'Yes, two nil.'

'Oh good,' said Gran. She wasn't the least bit interested in football but she liked Beth to do well whatever she did. 'Did you score?'

'No. I made one though. I beat three of their defenders. And I got a couple of really good shots at goal but their goalie stopped them.'

'Oh, that's a shame.' Gran tried to sound as though she knew what Beth was talking about but as Cameron said, she didn't know one end of a football from the other.

'Yeah, it was, but this girl's a giant. She's about seven feet tall! I know her a bit. I've seen her at Revolution.'

'Revolution?'

'Revolution Easy. The club near the shopping centre. You know it.'

'Oh yes. Used to be Dobbs department store in my day. Really nice shop that was. Anyway, I'm glad you're back, it's nearly time for the show.'

'Cameron not here?' It was obvious he wasn't, but he always came to hers after he seen Molly and so he should have arrived by now.

'No, he's not been here, love.'

'Funny, I can't get him to answer his mobile either.' Beth settled on the couch and examined her ankle. Well into the second half of the game she'd been tripped, and a livid bruise was developing. When she and Cameron had parted things had been a bit strained, but it was a minor disagreement, that was all. He wouldn't ignore her calls. He never did that.

'I expect his mobile's dead,' said Gran.

Beth grunted. It probably was. He was always forgetting to charge it. She adjusted the cushions. The room was tiny and the only armchair was occupied by her gran. The couch was old and sagging – a bit like me, Gran often said.

'He'll be here directly,' said Gran. 'Turn the TV on will you, love? It's my show and we don't want to miss the start.'

'Oh Gran,' said Beth, sighing. 'You know how to do that yourself.'

'Yes, but I don't like talking to that thing. It's not natural.'

Beth groaned. Gran seemed convinced that the

innocent looking virtual assistant sitting in the corner of the room was an intruder plotting to take over her life. 'Gina, TV channel ten,' she called.

There was a pause, then the TV screen came to life.

'Just in time,' said Gran.

'Ladies and gentlemen,' boomed a disembodied voice from the set. 'It's Saturday, it's live, it's Aurora New Dawn.' The image on the screen erupted in star bursts. There was a blast of music, and whooping and cheering from the studio audience.

'And here,' the voice rose to a new pitch of intensity, 'are your very own New Dawn hosts, Mika Brown and Candice Bell.'

The music swelled and the camera pulled back. A huge, scarlet letter A with golden wings descended from above to the accompaniment of a fanfare of electronic chords. Two people were seated on the structure, one on each wing. The man was bronzed and wore a skin-tight catsuit, cleft to the waist. The woman was a vision in a shimmering silver dress. She had a silver tiara in her long, silver hair. Silver sparkles twinkled on her perfect cheekbones and her creamy shoulders; an argent angel descending to the Earth

'Who does she think she is?' Beth said with a snort. 'Some stupid fairy?'

'Lovely though, isn't she,' said Gran.

Beth glanced at her phone again. She'd messaged Cameron half a dozen times. He should surely have replied by now.

The giant letter A came to a stop a metre above the stage and the voice of the unseen compere bellowed: 'Ladies and gentlemen, welcome to the Aurora New Dawn Show!'

Candice and Mika waved and smiled. Mika leapt down from his wing. Candice – she liked to be called Candy – slid gracefully from hers and took Mika's outstretched hand. The audience, warmed up for more than an hour by a well-known stand-up and now at fever pitch, went berserk. Candy pirouetted into Mika's arms and they began to waltz. The winged A floated away.

The dance slowed, the music changed and the lighting dimmed. Threatening figures appeared from all sides. Some were semi-human, some were beasts, some were insects, some were indescribably alien. All were in black. They crawled and writhed across the floor, moving menacingly towards the silver pair. The incessant pounding of a human heartbeat swelled over the music until it drowned it out. The invaders reached Mika and Candy, who recoiled in horror. Candy swooned and Mika supported her but was himself faint. They both staggered as the crawling creatures jabbed, stabbed and clawed towards them, threatening but never quite touching. The lights pulsed in time to the heartbeat, now thunderously loud.

Abruptly the noise and the flashing stopped. The dark figures froze. There was silence as the whole audience held its breath. Then ethereal tones, clear as a mountain stream, began. They were so very quiet that at first it was hard to be sure they were really there. Two figures, a boy and a girl clad in scarlet, moved smoothly and slowly across the stage. Each held a winged letter A, smaller versions of the one that had descended earlier. The boy presented his to Candy and the girl gave hers to Mika. The effect was magical. As soon as they touched the letters Candy and Mika recovered, shedding their torpor and swaying into their waltz once more, first tentatively and then with growing vigour. The black creatures cringed from them as if scalded, and scampered away, hissing and beaten.

In the centre of the stage the silver couple embraced. The music was now triumphant and the two stars acknowledged the wild applause.

'Aw,' said Gran, clearly moved.

'It's boring,' said Beth. 'It's always the same. They always do something naff like that.'

'It's the Dance of Life. It shows how the folk at Aurora save people from horrible diseases.'

Beth knew what the scene was meant to convey. Some version of it started every Aurora show. She sighed. 'Gina, show a movie,' she said. The channel abruptly switched to a an old musical.

Her grandmother was disappointed. 'I was watching that.'

Beth didn't do anything. She knew they would change back because Gran loved the show so much, but she was making a point. In her view the Aurora New Dawn extravaganza was crap.

'Put it back on, love. Please. You know how I look forward to this show. It's my favourite.'

Beth sighed again. 'Gina, find Aurora New Dawn.' The picture reverted to the original channel.

Mika was speaking. 'And what a show we have for you tonight. We have the magic of Annette and Anton (a cheer from the audience), comedy from Dicky Quip (a louder cheer), and music from Bagatelle (even louder still). But is that all?' Mika put his hand to his ear and leant towards the audience. There were obliging shouts of 'No!'

'No, no, no,' Mika went on. 'We have more. Candy, tell them what else we've got.'

The picture cut to Candice. Her silver gown caught multicoloured lights so that as she twirled subtle rainbow hues rippled over the fabric. 'Yes, Mika. Tonight we look at some of those people who have been helped by Aurora. People who, because of the generosity of our New Dawn donors, can begin to live again.'

'Aw,' sighed Gran. 'Isn't that lovely?'

Beth snorted. As far as she was concerned the show was creepy; Mika was a plastic man and Candice was a Botoxed Barbie doll, Dicky Quip was a sexist scumbag, and the saccharine pop of Bagatelle made her want to throw up. She could have gone to her bedroom to watch something on her tablet except it was bust, so for screen entertainment she was stuck with the system in the sitting room. Might as well make the best of it, she thought. She tucked her legs underneath her, put in her earbuds, found her current favourite playlist on her cloud player and picked up a magazine.

She rammed the earbuds in as tight as she could but she could still hear the irritating voices. Candice was talking about what would be the show's climax. In a voice dripping with breathy sincerity she murmured, 'And finally we'll enter the Gallery of Heroes and meet those brave souls who have voluntarily donated their own organs to help others. We'll meet Dale, who's giving one of his kidneys to his son (cheering and applause) and Pansy, who's offering one of hers to some lucky receiver she doesn't even know. Later we'll watch live as the New Dawn computer searches the records to see who that might be.'

Mika took over. 'And we'll catch up with this month's Aurora Angels, those huge hearted citizens who have sadly died this month but before they did so pledged their organs to help others. We'll learn about their lives and we'll hear from their families. If you want to be an Angel yourself and leave your organs to save the life of another after you've gone, you can do so at www.newdawn.org. And don't forget that every hundredth pledger wins a star prize.' Images of a sports car, a jet (cautiously labelled in small letters 'flight only'), an older couple enjoying a rooftop drink in Istanbul, a glitzy wrist watch, a smiling and sunny picture-book family rising in a balloon.

The audience was drenched in feel-good. Music played and people shrieked, cried, stamped, clapped. The show droned on and on, and Beth continued trying to ignore it until suddenly something jumped out from the screen and hit her like a bus.

She'd seen out of the corner of her eye the Gallery of Heroes caption, followed by a parade of faces, some young, some not so. Each image was held for no more than a couple of seconds before merging into the next. They could be anybody, nice, clean, friendly looking people, and no one could deny the selflessness of what they'd committed themselves to do.

She was turning back to her magazine when one image grabbed her. The photo was fuzzy and appeared only briefly, but it was enough to make her freeze. Among the organ donors was a face she knew almost as well as her own. She sat bolt upright in her chair.

'Did you see that?' she gasped.

'See what, love?'

'That picture. In the Gallery. It was Cameron!'

'No,' said Gran. 'He hasn't done anything like that. It couldn't be.'

'It was, I tell you. Gina, rewind. Stop. Play.' The procession of images began again and there it was: longish slightly mussed hair, dark brows, square jaw, straight mouth that might be about to smile, or might not. Beth was sure of it. 'It is, it's Cameron.'

'Well yes,' said Gran, 'I must say it does look a bit like him.'

'It is him.' Beth was so bewildered she could hardly speak.

'But why would he be on TV? Did he say anything to you about that?'

'No.' Cameron was the most generous and kind-hearted person she knew, and he would give his own life to save a friend, but like her he found the New Dawn Show a cloying charade. He'd said so loads of times. He wouldn't have changed his mind, not just like that, without telling her. And if he had, if he'd agreed to go through this pantomime, she would have known anyway. She would have felt the change in him.

She picked up her phone and hit number one on her speed-dial list. The call seemed to take an age to connect, then she heard it sound. After a dozen or so rings there was a familiar message.

'Hi, this is Cameron. I can't talk right now, but you know what to do and you know when to do it.' There was a pause and a beep.

'Hi,' she said, 'it's me. Where are you? I thought you were coming round after you'd seen your mum. I've being trying to call you but you don't pick up. Is something wrong? Call me.'

She was about to put her phone aside but changed her mind. She called Molly's number. She didn't bother with any preliminary courtesies. 'Hi, it's Beth. Is Cameron with you?'

'No dear. He left. I thought he was coming to see you.'

'I thought so too but he's not here yet. What time did he leave?'

'Ooh, hours ago.'

'Did he seem all right?'

Molly hesitated just long enough for it to be

noticeable. 'Yes, he was okay. Maybe he's stopped off at Zak's.'

'Maybe. I'll give him a call.'

Beth didn't call Zak, she phoned Archy. He hadn't seen Cameron either; neither when Archy asked him had Zak. Beth put down her phone. She'd been feeling uneasy for the past couple of hours. It was a bit like stage fright; it was distant and it was indistinct, but it was there. Something was wrong, and it concerned Cameron.

Gran was watching her. 'He'll be here soon, love, I'm sure he will. He's probably met a friend.'

'I expect so,' said Beth, although she didn't believe it. One of the things she loved about Cameron was that he always did what he said he would. He'd said he would come straight from Molly's to her. If something had happened to change that he would have called her; if he could. The fact that he hadn't meant he couldn't, and that worried her.

She told Gina to resume the show and Gran's attention was drawn back to the screen, where Dickie Quip was doing his best to embarrass an overweight woman in the studio audience.

She kept telling herself that it was probably nothing, but she didn't believe that. She took a deep breath and tried to empty her mind of everything, to shut out the banal rubbish on the TV. She reached out, and out, and out. It was a void. All she felt was a hollow sensation, like waiting to take an exam or to see the dentist. Was that because they'd recently had a row? It hadn't been a row, not really. She and Cameron didn't row. They sometimes disagreed and occasionally those disagreements might become heated, but they weren't the sort of altercations some of her mates had with their boyfriends or girlfriends, where they threw things or stamped out and didn't speak for days.

It had been about something so trivial that it seemed ridiculous now. Her tablet had developed a fault. It was dead. It wouldn't charge up, wouldn't switch on, nothing. She asked Cameron – told him, she had to admit when she thought about it – to take it to Archy and get him to put a new battery in it. Cameron didn't want to. He said it was a cheap machine and it had never been any good. He said it wasn't worth the cost of a new battery or Archy's time. That was a bad start, because Gran had bought it for her and even though Beth was well aware it wasn't top of the range she also knew that Gran couldn't afford any better.

'It's fine,' she'd said. 'It just needs a new battery.'

'Hark at you, Miss Teccy,' Cameron had said.

That got to her and she'd called him a chauvinist dick.

'All right,' he'd said. 'I'll get you a new one.'

'Don't be daft. You can't.'

'Yes I can. Of course I can. Zak gave me some money for my birthday but I don't need it at the moment because I get enough from my Saturday job. I'll buy you a new tablet and you can pay me back later.'

Cameron was naturally generous and he meant the

offer, but it had seemed patronising; two women, Beth and her gran, couldn't handle something technical like this and it needed a man to jump in and sort them out. The sub-text certainly wasn't there, Cameron wasn't like that, but that was how it had seemed to her at the time. She refused his offer, and when she thought about it she'd done it rather coldly.

Cameron had acted like he'd been slapped across the face and gone very quiet, which was always a sign he was upset. Shortly after that he left to see Molly. When he'd gone she felt awful and she tried to reach out to him, to touch his mind, but each time she ran into the scarlet globe of his anger; until the last time, when there'd been nothing.

16

BETH LIVED with Gran in a small terrace of six red brick houses in a street behind the library. Archy rang the bell and shivered on the step while Beth checked through the spyhole and unfastened the door chains. He had a car – an eighteenth birthday present from Zak – but he'd not passed his test so he'd had to come on his pushbike. He'd put on a thick quilted jacket and biker's gloves but he was still perished.

Beth was wearing ripped jeans and a tattered jumper. Her hair was dishevelled and her eyes were puffy and red. She stood aside to let him in and as he passed her she flung her arms around him. Archy was surprised and had the fleeting thought that it was worth riding across town in the freezing dark just for that.

'Thanks for coming,' Beth said

'No problem. Any news?'

'No, nothing.' Beth dabbed her eyes with her sleeve.

Archy followed her inside. She took his wet coat and gloves and hung them beside the heater.

'Is your gran up?'

'No. She said there's nothing we can do till morning and she's gone to bed. She doesn't think there's anything wrong anyway, just that Cameron is holed up with his mates somewhere.'

'But you do.'

'Yes. It's not like him to ignore his phone and texts. He goes on at me something chronic if I don't answer him. Then there was the Aurora show. Did you see it?'

'No,' said Archy. 'I can't stand it.'

'Nor me, but Gran likes it, otherwise we might not have seen. Watch this.'

The room they went into was small and clean, but meagrely furnished. There was a settee and a single armchair. The armchair was Gran's and the old woman had filled the sagging frame with cushions to construct a sort of nest. There was a small table made of some orange wood. The only things on the walls were a couple of Beth's photos and the huge screen over the top of a home entertainment system that looked the business but which, Archy knew, was bottom end of the market. The room was mostly beige but the drawn curtains had a cheerful pattern.

Archy sat on the chair, Beth on the settee.

Beth fiddled with the remote and the screen came to life, picking up the show just as Candy was gushingly introducing "those wonderful, wonderful people who will this week be making donations that will give others a new dawn". The faces flashed through quickly, barely a breath for each, until it got to one and Beth clicked pause.

'There,' she said. 'What do you think?'

The picture was fuzzy and the image grainy. 'I suppose it does look a bit like Cameron.'

'It is him,' said Beth. 'It's the photo ID from his life card. I know it is because he had a pimple on his chin when it was taken. Can you see it?' She zoomed in on the face; the pimple was clearly there. 'He's gone missing and his face is on the New Dawn Show as a volunteer donor.' She shook her head and looked at Archy with bewildered helplessness. 'What does it mean? How can that be? What's happened?'

Archy was as puzzled as she was. 'I don't know. Some sort of mistake? An error in their system?' Archy didn't believe that, and neither did Beth.

'What's worse is that I can't reach out to him. When I try to connect there's nothing. I can *feel* there's something wrong.'

'What do you think it might be?' Archy said.

Beth shook her head. 'I don't know. It's not clear. It's a sort of ache.' Her voice caught as she said this, as if choking back a sob. 'It's like he's scared of something.'

'But you can't tell where he is.'

'No. But I know he's a long way off.'

Okay,' said Archy, 'your gran's right, there is nothing we can do right now, but we can plan what we'll do as soon as it gets light. There's no point going to the police yet. They won't listen until someone's been gone for more than twenty-four hours. I think the first thing we should do is to phone the TV company and see if we can get from them why Cameron's face appeared on their show. They might know where he is.'

Beth nodded. She was looking better now that there was the prospect of some action. 'Shouldn't we look for him?'

'Yes, we can search around here. He might have been mugged, or he could be holed up somewhere. But you said you think he's further away.'

Beth got up. 'Yes. No. I don't know.' The idea of Cameron lying somewhere injured was awful. 'We should go now.'

Archy shook his head. 'There's no point. I'm really sorry, but there isn't. Where would we start? And it's pitch dark.' Archy thought for a moment. He believed Beth, but they had to cover all bases. 'There's another thing,' he said. 'You won't like this, but we should check the records of hospital admissions.'

'Yes,' said Beth, and there was a chill in her tone. 'I thought of that too. But if he'd had an accident or something the hospital would have called us.'

'Not if he'd lost his ID. They'd have to take a DNA swab to match against the database to find out who he was. That would take time. And lying in hospital might account for you not being able to reach him.'

Suddenly she sat down. With an awful realisation it dawned on her what Archy was getting at: Cameron might have been taken into hospital after some potentially fatal accident, and been just conscious enough to agree to the organ donation before passing away.

'It's a possibility,' said Archy. 'We have to think of it.' He moved over to the settee and put his arms around her. She leant on his shoulder and her hair tickled his face. 'I still think there's a chance he's met some friends and gone off with them, and that he's left his phone somewhere. I know that's not what you think, but you've said before that when you connect with each other you can sometimes be mistaken about what the other's feeling. He's probably sleeping on someone's floor right now and waiting for the morning to call you.'

Archy didn't really think that, he was just trying to make Beth feel better.

'And the TV thing?' she said.

'A coincidence. Either someone who looks like Cameron, or just some crazy cock-up.'

Beth didn't reply. Archy was being kind but he was wrong. Cameron was in trouble. A dull gnawing was growing in the pit of her stomach.

Archy stood up. 'As soon as it's daylight we'll start the search.'

He got his jacket. It was still very wet.

'Will you stay over?' said Beth. 'I know we don't have a spare room but we've got an airbed. I could pump that up for you. Or I can make you comfortable on the settee.'

Archy looked at the settee. It didn't appear to be in any better shape than Gran's chair but he wanted to stay, and he had an inkling of the reason why Beth wanted him to. A knock on the door in the small hours, two police officers standing there with grave faces and bad news; she wouldn't want to deal with that on her own, and he wouldn't want her to.

'Yeah, course,' he said. 'The settee will be fine.'

Beth smiled for the first time since he'd got there.

17

'It's Mr Ivanovitch, Dr Folken. He's here!' The PA sounded flustered.

'What, here now?'

'Yes. He just barged in and he's on the way up. He's angry.'

Folken felt his heart sink by a couple of feet.

There was no knock. Alexander Dimitri Ivanovitch flung open the door and marched into Folken's office without waiting for an invitation. Two men were with him. They were the same ones who had accompanied him to Folken's London house, except this time they didn't wait outside.

Folken was nervous but he tried not to show it. 'Mr Ivanovitch, this is a surprise. Did I miss a notification? I wasn't expecting a meeting.'

'Well you should have expected it,' the Russian growled. 'My little girl is sick. She is getting sicker. You jokers are supposed to be making her better. A procedure is fixed, and then it's cancelled. What is going on?'

The two minders moved round behind Folken's desk. One of them stood at the window, the other at the Director's shoulder.

'I am really very sorry,' said Folken, trying keep his voice steady. 'We're doing all we can.'

'You have two minutes to explain the problem to me. After that, if I'm not satisfied my two friends here will start to break things.' Ivanovitch sat down, taking the chair immediately in front of Folken's desk.

The man at the window picked up an ornament from the sill, a delicate fan of gingko leaves rendered in gilded porcelain. Folken had bought it from a London gallery and it had cost a lot of money. The man weighed the object in his hands, then looked at the floor as if considering the possibility of dropping it. Folken rested his hands on his knees under the desk, partly to still them but mainly to hide that they were shaking. He also wanted them to be within reach of the panic button.

Things had been going so well. He'd spoken with the woman who was hosting his and Anita's embryo and she'd reported that she and the baby were in excellent health and that the pregnancy was on track. He'd called Anita, and without any prompting she'd asked him about their child. He'd been elated, taking this as an indication that she was starting to become interested in it. It was what he had hoped for. There had been news about his investments, which were growing impressively. Finally he'd had a meeting with McIntyre, who told him that although his team had not yet managed to locate the body of the Eze boy there had been no reports of him turning up alive. The longer there was no news the more likely it was that he was lying dead somewhere. By now the Trimesorphene in his system would almost completely broken down, so when he was found no one would suspect he'd been poisoned.

Yes, it had been an excellent day; until this!

'Speak,' said Ivanovitch, glaring at him. He cracked his knuckles. 'Explain this cock-up.'

Folken felt his heart speed up and for a moment he was stuck for words. He could sense violence in the air and he was not a violent man. He bullied his staff, but his default approach for people who were more powerful than he was sweet reason. That was what he tried now.

'Please calm yourself,' he said. 'Everything is in hand. What happened is a minor setback, that's all. I can assure you that your daughter is very comfortable and is receiving the best possible care.'

'She had better be.'

Folken decided that the best way to calm his angry visitor was to turn a negative into a positive. 'It was a pity that the donor we had chosen turned out to be unsuitable. Fortunately we don't just rely on the information we get from the National Human Genome Database, we also screen them very carefully ourselves. When we ran our tests on this one we found hepatitis

B. It was as well that my staff spotted it, because their vigilance prevented your daughter from receiving an infected organ.'

The effect wasn't what Folken wanted. Ivanovitch leapt up and leant across the desk. He was a big man and he towered over Folken, who shrank back in his chair. 'If that had happened you would be dead. Pidaras!'

Folken didn't speak Russian but there was no doubt what the word meant.

'Please, Mr Ivanovitch, sit down. Please.'

Ivanovitch took a deep breath and looked as if he was going to explode, but to Folken's relief he did sit. His eyes were the coldest blue the Director had ever seen.

'We could not have known anything was wrong,' Folken said, trying to keep his voice steady. 'Hepatitis B can be serious but usually it's not, and it's possible for someone to have it and not know. They feel nothing, so they carry on as normal. There are several ways to get it but two main ones. The first is by sharing a needle. We know that the donor was not a drug user, so it was most likely the second way, which is by having unprotected sex with someone infected. We have no way of knowing if that had happened, we don't watch potential donors that closely.'

'Well you should.' Ivanovitch was still angry but Folken was relieved to see he was becoming calmer, if only a little. 'God damn it, can I believe you people? You guaranteed me a top class service and this is what I get. And after what you've charged me, too. In my own country I could have bought a whole hospital for what I've paid you!'

Folken at last began to relax. He had manoeuvred the Russian into exactly the response he wanted.

'I realise that this is a huge disappointment for you,' he said, 'and for your daughter. And I understand that the money is an issue too.'

The remark threw Ivanovich into retreat, as Folken intended. 'The money's nothing,' he spluttered. 'I don't give a monkey's fuck for the money. That's not the point at all. It's the bloody incompetence your people have shown.'

'On the contrary,' said Folken, 'what has been demonstrated is the opposite of that. If our systems had not been so stringent and my staff so careful this problem would not have been spotted. Anywhere else in the world that would certainly have been the outcome.'

It was not true. Any routine blood test would show if someone had hepatitis B. Folken was banking on Ivanovitch not knowing that, and thankful that he seemed to accept it.

'All right, what are you going to do now?' the Russian grunted.

'What we do now,' said the Director, 'is move to our back-up position. We already have another donor selected, just as good a match as the first one, possibly even better. That person will arrive here within the next few hours and as soon as they do we'll carry out the tests. We don't expect any problems with this one. We're satisfied there's no drug use, and as they have a long term steady partner casual sex is unlikely. We will begin preparing your daughter at the same time as we're carrying out the tests. The delay will be minimal, the transplant will be carried out only marginally behind the original schedule.'

'Let's hope you're right,' said the Russian, 'and that this stupid bimbo has had the sense to keep her knickers on.' He stood up again. There was a fountain pen on Folken's desk, a Montegrappa 1930 in turtle brown. It had cost Folken more than a thousand pounds and he was very fond of it.

He watched anxiously as Ivanovitch held the pen to the light. 'I rarely allow a second chance,' he said, 'and never ever a third one. If there are any more mistakes I'll hold you personally responsible. You will be the one who pays.'

Ivanovitch carefully put the Montegrappa in his jacket pocket and walked to the door. He treated Folken to one last glare, then left. His two thugs followed.

It had been all Folken could do to keep himself together. Had he shown how afraid he was? He desperately hoped not, but now that the immediate danger had passed he started to tremble uncontrollably. The spasm continued for several minutes.

The problem with wealthy clients, Folken thought as he calmed down, is that they don't know how to wait. They have no experience of it. The endless pauses, halts, hiccups, delays that plague ordinary people every day are foreign to them. They all expect to be able to go straight to the head of the queue. Rational men and women, intelligent, entrepreneurial people, magnates used to directing the lives of countless others as well as shady racketeers like Ivanovitch, none of them seem able to understand one simple fact: that it is impossible for everyone to be first. The Russian certainly couldn't accept it. As far as that was concerned he was in a league of his own: a top notch, world-class, gold medal, egomaniac.

Folken was feeling better. He smiled, and gave himself a pat on the back for being alert enough to ensure that the Russian persisted in his misapprehension of the donor's gender. At least this one was white.

18

It seemed an interminable night. The settee was back-breakingly awful. It wasn't long enough for Archy to stretch out and the sagging cushions were lumpy. In the end he gave up and got up. He went to the kitchen and splashed his face with cold water. He filled a kettle, trying to make as little noise as possible, and set it to boil while he found a tea bag. Then he took his mug back to the living room and switched on the home entertainment system. He turned the volume right down and picked up the keyboard.

He'd only been working for a few minutes when he heard the stairs creak and Beth came in. She was wearing one of Cameron's shirts and black panties. Archy tried not to stare.

'Can't you sleep either?' she said. Her eyes were bleary. She rubbed them and pushed a lock of hair behind her ear.

'I was just looking on the hospital websites,' said Archy. 'I thought I'd see if Cameron's been checked in.'

She nodded and sat beside him. She smelt sweet, like a marshmallow with a trace of perspiration. They searched the accident and emergency lists on the websites of all three hospitals in the area, scrolling down the names of the patients who had been admitted in the past twenty-four hours and checking their photos. Cameron wasn't amongst them.

'I knew he wouldn't be,' said Beth. 'And I'm relieved. His photo being on the show last night, I thought maybe...' Her voice trailed away, unable to express the horror of what she'd been considering.

Archy pursed his lips. He was still not sure the photo on the show was of Cameron. It did look a bit like him but it was blurred, and he thought the face was older.

'If we're going to ask around we need a recent pic,' said Archy. 'A good one.'

'I've got this,' Beth said, holding out her phone. The wallpaper was a selfie of her and Cameron, cheek to cheek. It was a great photo of two smiling, happy young people on top of the world.

'Airdrop it to me. As soon as it's light we'll start our search. We'll show people this and ask if they remember seeing somebody like that yesterday, early evening.'

They couldn't wait until it was light. Beth was unable to settle, pacing like a caged animal. In the end Archy suggested they start. While Beth put on some clothes he went to the bathroom and cleaned his teeth using toothpaste and his forefinger. Downstairs he felt his jacket. It was almost dry. Almost, but not quite, and he winced as he put it on and the damp collar wrapped around his neck. Beth came down in a sweater and jeans, and grabbed from the hooks a parka which Archy recognised as Cameron's.

Outside they shivered in the chilly dawn.

'Let's split up,' said Beth. 'We can take a street each and cover more ground than if we're together.'

'I'm not sure,' said Archy. 'You know what they say about four eyes being better than two. Best to be thorough, even if it does take a bit longer.'

They started with the area immediately around Beth's block. They looked in yards, behind lock-ups and sheds, along hedges and walls.

'If he'd been tanked up he might have just baled out somewhere,' Archy said. 'Or if somebody'd tried to jump him these might be places he'd hide.'

They combed alleys, the scrub behind the houses where a small factory had been demolished, the yards of derelict properties. And all the time the cameras on the street corners and on the tops of lamp posts followed them, watching with detached yet persistent interest.

There was a row of garages in the next street, beaten down and smothered in graffiti. Some were unlocked and others had had their doors kicked in. They explored them all in case Cameron had blundered in there, or had been dumped. The little concrete boxes stank of urine and excrement. There was rubbish, debris, evidence of rats, but there was no Cameron.

'Does he always come on the bus when he's been to his mum's?' Archie asked.

'Not always. Sometimes he walks.'

They followed the path Cameron would have taken from his mother's house, covering the whole route. They got to Molly's no wiser and Beth knocked on her door. She answered it in her dressing gown. Her face was heavy and she looked tired.

'Come in,' she said. 'You look like a pair of lost souls.'

They went through to her living room. She made them tea and gave them biscuits, then sat down herself. She seemed to Archy much older than she had the last time he'd seen her. Her face looked flabby and her ankles were swollen.

'Can you tell us what happened yesterday?' said Archy. 'When Cameron came round here.'

Molly confirmed what she'd already told Beth about the previous day. Cameron had sat with her for a while and they'd chatted. Then, after an hour or so, he had left.

'Did he say where he was going?' said Archy.

'Yes, straight to Beth's.'

'Did he say how he was going to get there?'

'Walk, I think. He had some things on his mind and he said he needed time to chill.'

'What things?' said Beth.

Molly hesitated. 'I had some information for him, about his dad. I knew it would come as a shock but I thought that at eighteen he should know. I'd share it with you but I think it ought to come from him.'

Molly wanted to join them in the search, but they all three knew that wasn't an option. As they were leaving and while Beth went to the bathroom Molly drew Archy aside.

'I didn't want to say anything in front of Beth 'cos I don't want to worry her, but I'm not happy about this. I saw on the Nextdoor app that someone else around here went missing only a couple of days ago. A young lad not much older than Cameron, in broad daylight. Just gone. The police don't want to know about stuff like that, and these bloody cameras they've got everywhere see nothing. Useless.' She gripped Archy's hand and looked earnestly into his face. 'Find him, won't you.'

Archy nodded. 'I hope so. I'll certainly try.'

He and Beth left. Molly stood on her doorstep and watched them until they turned the corner.

'What now?' said Archy.

'We go on looking,' said Beth.

They tried three possible routes between Molly's home and Beth's. They must have shown Cameron's picture to more than fifty people but only a few had been in the area at the right time and none of them remembered seeing him. Archy bought a street map and a pack of coloured felt-tip pens and marked the routes. Beth added every camera she could see, using an elaborate code.

'Those things must have picked up something,' she said.

'Zak says most of them don't function, they're just for show to keep people quiet,' Archy said. 'And the cops say they don't have the manpower to check the ones that do work.

The pair were weary and dejected by the time they got back to Beth's home. Before going into the house they stood and looked blankly at each other. What should they do? They'd scoured the area. They'd tried the hospital websites. They'd asked other people. They'd knocked on the doors of neighbours. In every case the response had been the same, a blank look. Not only did no one seem to know anything, no one appeared interested.

Gran made them a cup of tea. Archy accepted the offer of a sandwich, Beth said she felt sick and couldn't eat anything. They gave Gran an update, which was basically nothing to report, and took their drinks into the living room. Beth flopped down on the sofa. Archy had noticed her becoming increasingly edgy as the day wore on and now she looked more dejected than he had ever seen her.

'Something is wrong,' Beth said.

Archy didn't know what to say in response to that. Of course there was.

'Really really wrong. Cameron's in trouble,' she went on. 'At first I couldn't connect with him but now I can. I can feel it. I can sense it in my stomach. It's hollow, as if something's been ripped out of it. I think he's in pain.' She spoke very quietly. 'It was Cameron we saw on the New Dawn show. I know it was.'

'Yes,' said Archy. 'I don't know what it means, though. I don't know how it could have been him. And I don't know what to do about it.'

'No,' she said, 'neither do I. We said we'd contact the TV people, see if they can tell us anything. We said we'd do that first.' There was an accusation in her tone, as if she was blaming Archy for ignoring what had only been a suggestion.

'We could try,' he said. 'We might not get anything. Maybe best to wait for Zak. He could probably hack into their servers and see if there's anything there.'

Beth nodded.

'We need help,' said Archy. 'I need to tell Zak what's going on. I don't want to talk about it on my mobile. I'll go home and tell him, and then I'll come back.'

'All right,' said Beth. She liked Zak. He could work things. He had a lot of contacts and he could get stuff done. If anyone knew what to do it would be Zak.

'I'll be right back,' Archy said. 'Why don't you check the hospital websites again for admissions? Something might have come in since we looked.' He was sure it was pointless, but it would be a distraction from searching the streets on her own, which he thought she might be tempted to do if he wasn't there.

'OK,' she said. 'But don't be long, will you.'

She gave him a kiss on his cheek. She'd never done that before. There was the brush of her hair on his face and a whiff of her closeness.

Archy felt a mixture of emotions. Cameron was his brother. He desperately wanted to find him and end Beth's misery. At the same time he was fearful of him turning up the victim of an attack or an accident; injured, or perhaps even dead. So in a way it was almost a relief that they hadn't found him. When Beth had called the night before he had thought that there must be a simple explanation and it would be easy to find where Cameron had gone. He'd met a friend, or he'd remembered there was someone he had to see. Or he'd lost his phone. Now, though, time had passed and there had been no word, no contact, and their searching had been fruitless. On top of that there was Beth's feeling of doom.

Even so, he found it hard to believe that it could be anything really bad. This was Cameron. Cameron, who got on well with everybody. Cameron, who was never serious. Cameron, who would drive him mad because he mucked about when they should have been getting on with something important. Cameron, who was liked by everyone and was everyone's friend. It just didn't seem possible.

19

CAMERON'S MIND *is as tight as a drumskin and close to splitting. Jagged shards of memory spin and flicker, the milestones of his life, as vivid and disjointed as a movie trailer.*

• *The man is smiling. 'That's your daddy,' says Molly. 'He flew aeroplanes.' 'Where is he now?' Cameron asks. She hugs him. 'He's gone. He was a very brave man.'*

• *Cameron looks up from playing. A tall man is standing with his mother in the doorway. He has long, dark hair and a black beard. He has tattoos, and his ears are pierced. Things that the five-year-old thinks look interesting.*

• *Molly sits him down. 'We're going to go live with Zak,' she says. 'Me and Zak are going to get married. Zak will be your new daddy and Archy your new brother.'*

• *There's a boy. He's about Cameron's age. He has*

ginger hair and glasses. 'Do you want to play?' he says. 'My name's Archy. What's yours?'

• 'Ah, the new boy,' the tall woman says. She's so tall that Cameron can barely see her face. So tall her head almost touches the ceiling. 'This is Cameron, everyone. Here, Cameron, sit next to Beth. It's her birthday next week too. Isn't that lovely, both of you having your birthday on the same day.'

• 'I know what you're thinking,' says Beth. He's known her for a month. It's the first time she's said that. She's said it many times since. It's true.

• Archy says he'll meet Cameron and Beth in the pub later. It's no secret that Archy is keen on Beth. Oddly, Cameron doesn't mind. He and Beth go back a long way. Nothing could separate them.

• Beth strips off her top and turns her back to him. Between her shoulder blades is a new tattoo. 'It's a dream catcher,' she says. 'What do you think?' To Cameron it looks like a tennis racket but he doesn't say so. Instead, 'It looks cool,' he says.

• He's in an uncomfortable chair in A&E. His arm is in a sling. Beth comes through the door. 'How did you know I was here?' he says. 'I just did,' she says.

• He's at his mother's, at Molly's. He's on the sofa, reeling at the news she's just given him. Nothing that he thought was true is true. He is not the person he thought he was.

• He's supposed to be going to Beth's house but he needs time on his own. He turns left to walk across the park. He can hear children playing in the distance. He is making for the gate on the far side of the park, where a couple have just entered. The woman is holding a phone. They seem to be arguing.

• She is looking at a map. The man comes towards him. He asks for directions to Begonia Avenue. He's never heard of it.

• 'I don't know,' he tells the man. 'Is it on your map?' Too late he hears a sound behind him and he feels a sharp sting in his neck.

• There are voices, distant and hollow, as if resonating down long tube. He can see nothing. He reaches for Beth. He feels her question: where are you? He tries to answer but he can't.

• There's somebody with him. It's Beth. She's come for him. His heart speeds. Then he sees it's not. It's a nurse. She has a kind face. She lifts his head and gives him water. He tries to raise his hand to help but it's strapped to the bed.

• 'Better than the last one?' says a man. 'Yes,' says a white-coated woman. 'Everything's clear.' 'Very well,' the man says. 'Get him ready.'

• The nurse strokes his forehead. He thinks she's crying. He has tubes coming out of him. He can move his hands far enough to feel strapping around his middle.

Where is he? Does Beth know? Beth, where are you? Beth, I'm in trouble. Beth, please find me.

• Beth can't sleep. She's tried to link with Callum but she can't, and that gnaws at her. Where he should have been is blank, a void. Even when he was asleep she had sometimes been able to hover like a moth on the fringes of his dreams. Now there is nothing. It's if he's vanished from the face of the earth.

• She sits up. She is exhausted. Where is he? The street light in the road has found a gap in her bedroom curtains and shines on to her pillow. She goes to the window and stands at the window looking for Cameron. Cameron, rounding the corner and coming towards her house. Cameron, with his long, determined strides, his hunched shoulders, loping along lost in the music on his earbuds. But there is no one there. The pavements are dark and empty.

• She turns back to the room. It's full of reminders: his guitar that he often leaves with her; his second best trainers stuffed under her bed; the empty bottles from two nights ago when they'd shared beers; a faint trace of his cologne on her pillow. There are books too – art books, sport, superheroes. His portfolio is jammed between her bed and the wall. Sometimes she thought there was more of his stuff in her home than in his own. It's almost as if he is with her.

• But he's not, and Beth knows he won't be. She feels it with a force that shakes her to the core. She can't put it into words, although if she is to do something to save him she'll have to do exactly that. How can she explain what she feels?

• She doesn't know she's crying. It's not a sudden

disintegration into helpless sobbing, it comes on more slowly and more intensely. The pain is a knife, entering her flesh and twisting to part it. She stands at the window with tears running silently down her cheeks and falling from her chin. She knows Cameron is in trouble.

20

Archy hadn't planned to call at the police station but it wasn't far out of his way. He knew that there was no point in reporting Cameron's disappearance yet because the police wouldn't do anything so soon, but he wanted to do something to ease Beth's pain, and he wanted to find the mate who he thought of as his brother. If he could persuade the police to start searching sooner they might be able to locate him before something bad happened.

He wasn't optimistic; the police have a poor reputation for finding missing people, but there must be a chance somebody had seen something. The problem was locating that somebody, and the police were the only ones who might be able to do that. Some of the dozens of cameras that seemed to be everywhere must work. Some of them must have a record. If he could persuade the police to take a look at the ones from along the route that Cameron would have taken they might explain what had happened to him, and from that they might learn where he was.

The police station was huge, blank faced and anonymous. The only indication of its purpose was a garage door that from time to time opened to discharge or admit a police vehicle. Archy had passed it many times but never been in. He got off his bike and wheeled it around the corner. It seemed best to hide it. He had no lights, and although no one bothered about that any more it was still technically an offence and he didn't want it to be a distraction. So he padlocked it to the railings and went to the public entrance at the front of the building.

The door was hefty, metal, and firmly shut, with a notice warning that wasting police time would not be tolerated. There was a card slot beside the door with the instruction to insert his life card. Once he'd done that a screen headed 'Purpose of visit' offered a list of options with check boxes. None of them seemed to fit reporting someone missing, so he checked 'Report a felony or misdemeanour', reasoning that he could give a proper explanation once he was inside.

The door clicked open and he found himself in a shabby lobby with bars dividing it into two and a metal detector in the centre. A recorded voice told him to put all his possessions in a slot and pass through the detector. He unloaded his bike key, his phone, his cards, his watch, wrist band, neck chain, even his glasses. A steel panel closed off the slot and they were gone. He was aware of the cyclopean eye of a camera studying him from the top corner of the room.

He had to go through now, no choice. Nervously he shuffled past the detector, worried that he'd forgotten something and there would be an electronic shriek. There was none, and another door clicked open. He was in a vestibule with several rows of cheap plastic chairs. It was dingy and smelt of puke. The walls were covered in graffiti, most of it telling the police to carry out a variety of imaginative and obscene activities. There were three other people in there; all eyed him suspiciously. They looked like tramps and were dressed in random items of not very clean clothing.

He sat down, leaving a decent gap between himself and the others. He'd expected that after all the entry rigmarole he'd be able to go ahead, but nothing happened. He waited for more than an hour. His chair was broken, the seat coming away from its metal frame. The tramps were summoned one at a time to the innards of the building. They seemed to be regulars because the officer who called them through addressed them by their names. Two more people came in, a man on his own who looked shifty and uncertain, then a woman with a swollen eye and a face streaked with blood and mascara. Archy wanted to find out if she was okay, whether he could help her, but a large notice said that conversation was prohibited and talkers would be ejected. He didn't want to get kicked out at this stage.

At last it was his turn and he was directed into a small room. It was only marginally less dismal than the first. A weary looking middle aged man was seated at a desk. He was almost hidden by a large screen, and a computer that was so battered and stained it looked as though it had seen service in a cowshed. He didn't speak, just pointed with a plastic ballpoint at the chair opposite. It was against the wall, two metres away. The physical space between him and the desk mirrored the chasm that Archy felt was between himself and the authorities. The whole experience was debilitating, as if his life force was being drained out of him. He wondered if everyone felt this way in a police station, the police as well as the public.

Archy could see that the man had his ID card. It must have been somehow retrieved from the tray into which he'd consigned his possessions. What had happened to the rest of them? The man swiped the card and tapped his keyboard. Archy knew about IT systems and could guess what he was doing. He was checking his ID against the police database to see if he was known and had any convictions. Cameron's record was clean but Archy himself had once been convicted of shoplifting. He'd pinched a memory cube from the Compusmart store when he was thirteen, but Zak had shown him how to hack into the criminal record system and he'd removed any reference to that a long time ago. There would be nothing about him for the man to see.

'Says here you want to report a felony or misdemeanour,' said the man.

'Not really,' said Archy. The man frowned and his hand made a reflex move towards a red button set into his desk. Wasting police time, perverting the course of justice, false reporting, unauthorised entry to a police facility. Archy felt a wave of panic as he anticipated the book being thrown at him. 'No, it's something else,' he said hurriedly. 'I want to report a missing person.'

'Missing person,' said the man, peering at the screen. 'All right then. Name?'

'Mine or the missing person's?' said Archy.

The man looked exasperated and flicked the ID card with his fingernail. 'The missing person's, of course. I know who you are.'

Archy felt stupid. 'Sorry. It's Cameron Bradley.'

'Age?'

'Eighteen.'

'Address?'

Archy gave it.

The man did some more data entry, some more short-sighted peering at the screen. 'When did this Cameron Bradley go missing?'

'Yesterday. Late afternoon.'

The man looked doubtful. 'Mm. That's barely twenty-four hours. With a lad of his age we don't take any action until they've been gone for forty eight. Mostly it turns out they've just gone off somewhere without telling you and they turn up, meanwhile we've wasted a lot of time. What's your relationship to him?'

'Sort of step brother.'

The man thought for a moment, then said, 'All right. It's early but as you're here I'll log it. Do you have Cameron Bradley's life card?'

It was such a stupid question that Archy wondered if it was some sort of trick, but the man seemed completely serious. 'No,' he said. 'He would have had it with him.'

'Right. What were his last known whereabouts?' said the man.

Archy gave the details of Cameron's visit to Molly and his failure to return. The man entered the information at a pace that would have embarrassed a sloth. Didn't the people given these jobs have any keyboard training?

'Got a picture?' Archy held up his mobile with the photo of Cameron and Beth. He started to get up but the man waved him to go back to his seat. 'Beam it over,' he said, and gave a code.

Archy couldn't see, but the image must have appeared on the man's screen because he leant forward to study it.

'Who's the girl?'

'That's Beth, Cameron's girlfriend.'

'And you're sure he's not with her?'

'No, he's not.'

'Because that's where I'd be.'

The thought of this tired, glum clerk and Beth together was so ludicrous it almost made Archy laugh. But he was old enough to be her grandfather so it was also a bit creepy too, and that killed the humour.

The man typed again, stubby fingers poking at the keys. He took a printed slip from a machine under his desk and waved it at Archy. 'We'll contact you if we need to,' he said. 'Don't leave the district.'

'What's this?' said Archy, crossing to collect the paper.

'It's your acknowledgement. Confirmation that you've reported a missing person and the details have been logged on our system.'

'So what happens now?'

'We find him, of course,' the man said sourly. 'It should take about five minutes.'

———

Archy waved his ID card at a scanner, a slot in the wall opened and a metal tray slid out. It contained the personal items he'd had to surrender when he entered.

Outside a thin rain had started. Around the corner there was a space where his bike should have been. The lockchain had been neatly sliced through with a bolt cutter and was dropped by the railings. Archy couldn't believe it; his bike had been nicked from right outside the police station! Just around the corner from the main entrance! Then again, he could believe it. Nothing about that place or anything that went on in it gave him any confidence in law and order. He looked up at the corner of the building. There were two cameras in plain sight. They would surely have seen something. He ought to go in and report it, but he couldn't face another hour inside that dismal hole, with more tedious questions and ponderous form filling. It wasn't an expensive bike; he'd leave it, he'd walk home.

He raised a middle finger at the security camera – you never knew who might be watching, he hoped it would be somebody important – and turned towards the main road. There was no pavement beside the dual carriageway, just a broad grass strip. The surface was uneven and he made poor progress. He needed a lift but he was worried about thumbing. If the police found him trying to hitchhike they could get him for vagrancy, and if they were in a bad mood maybe for begging too. Nevertheless, he stuck out his arm, watching his footing and keeping a look out for the law at the same time. He'd been walking for about fifteen minutes and was passing a patch of scrubby woodland when he glanced over his shoulder and saw a police car.

He ducked into the trees. The car slowed down and a window opened. A policewoman in the front swept the edge of the woodland with an infra-red scanner. They'd obviously spotted him at the side of the road and were interested in where he'd gone. Archy flattened himself behind a tree trunk and stayed still, hoping that it was big enough to hide him from the scanner. There were a couple of quick whoops on the car siren, probably to spook him into making a run for it and revealing himself, but then the officers decided they couldn't be bothered any more and the car moved off.

Archy waited for a few minutes to make sure that

the police had really gone. The car might turn around and cruise back along the dual carriageway to surprise him. Or they might send a drone. Better to stay in the woods, he thought. If he could find a way through he'd cut off a corner and come out only a few streets away from the leafy avenue where his home was.

There was a pile of junk a little way in – a soggy mattress, a rusty washing machine, split and stinking plastic sacks, some tyres. There seemed to be a path going roughly in the direction he wanted around the edge of this heap. It was a bit muddy and he was conscious of the threat to his trainers, but he took it.

Next, two things happened very quickly. The first was that huge hands like pincers seized Archy's upper arms. The second was that another someone hit him in the stomach. Very hard.

The breath was crushed out of him. He doubled up and fell to the ground, where he lay in a foetal position clutching his midriff and trying to breathe. His head was spinning. The pain was excruciating. He was suffocating. He wanted to retch. This was it. He was going to be killed. Was this what had happened to Cameron?

A heavy boot poked him. His eyes were tear flushed and his vision blurred. All he could see were the boots, and two dark figures standing over him. Even though the pain was obliterating his reason he was able to register that the poke was a good sign. If they'd meant to hurt him more they would be kicking him. A few kicks from those boots would burst his spleen, break his spine, crack his skull.

'Who are you?' Poke. The voice was deep, dark and came from a long way away. Archy tried to answer but couldn't.

'I said, who the fuck are you?' Poke again, harder this time.

Archy's throat felt as though he'd swallowed a golf ball. 'Archy,' he croaked.

'Whassat?'

A hand grabbed him by his collar and heaved him roughly into a sitting position. He gasped as the pain lanced him. Another hand frisked his pockets and found his phone and the plastic wallet with his life card.

'Archibald Sparks,' said a different voice, reading the card.

'Archibald Sparks?' This was the first voice again. 'What kind of a name is that? Let's see.'

The second voice handed over the card, and the first voice pulled a portable reader out of his pocket to scan it. Even in his weakened state Archy was surprised that casual muggers had equipment as sophisticated as this.

'Nothin',' the first voice said, with an expression of disgust. 'No fuel credits, no food credits, no fuckin' credits at all. This bunny's broke.' He flung the card away, sending it spinning into the scrub, and spat in Archy 's general direction. 'Anyway, what are you doin' on this plot, Archibald Sparks? Where are you goin'?'

'I'm going home,' Archy managed to say. His interrogator expected more. He squatted down facing Archy. It was hard for him to see the man's face clearly in the dim light. 'I took a short cut to dodge the police,' Archy added. At least while they were talking to him they weren't punching him. The pain in his stomach had eased but it still hurt. He didn't want to feel another of those sledge-hammer blows.

'And why would you be worried about the police, Sparky my man? What is it you've done?'

'I haven't done anything.' Archy saw the man's fist curl up and he flinched, bracing himself for another blow. 'I was trying to thumb a lift and a police car saw me so I dodged out of the road. I just want to go home.'

The second man had been examining Archy's phone. 'Hey boss, look at this.'

He gave the phone to the third man, who had been in the background and hadn't yet spoken. There was an immediate and noticeable reaction. The man who had been squatting before him stood up and exchanged a glance with his partner. The third man took a step forward. He held the phone in front of Archy's face and pointed to a name and number in his call list. It was Zak's.

'You got a name here that I know,' said the man.

Was that good? Was it bad? Archy didn't know.

'Now listen, Sparkyboy. You tell me why you have this man's name on your call list.'

Archy thought fast. Was it to his advantage that his persecutor seemed to know Zak? Was it something he could use or should he play it down? These men weren't to be trifled with. His best bet would be to tell the truth.

'I'm his son.'

One of the men snorted and the other laughed. The third man bent over him and said, 'So why are you going around using the name Sparks?'

'I'm not his actual son. He's my step-dad.'

There was the snorting laugh again, but less certain. 'You're not his actual son!'

The third man spoke. 'Tell me something about this man you've got on your call list who isn't your actual dad.'

'Tell you what? What do you want to know?' Archy was so nervous he could scarcely speak. He was desperate to say the right thing but there were no clues to what these huge men wanted.

'Some things,' said the man. 'You tell me some things you know 'bout this man Zak who's not your actual dad.' The repetition of Archy's words about the relationship was mocking and threatening. 'You lie to me an' I'll twist your balls off,' he added as an afterthought.

Archy's mind raced. Something told him that the men might be meaning to harm Zak. Better to keep his answers general if he could. 'He's thin, got a lot of hair, a beard, ears pierced, tattoo of a guitar on his arm, another of a humming bird on his hand.'

'Sounds like him,' said one of the men to the third one.

'Anybody who saw him in the street could know that,' the man said. 'Tell me some more 'bout him. Somethin' you couldn't see.'

Archy thought. 'He's got a motor bike, a Pangea 1000, gunmetal grey.'

'More.'

'He's got a big, sloppy black dog called Rufus.'

'More.'

He plays the guitar well but wishes he could play it better.'

'More.'

'He makes the worst coffee in the world.'

The man let out a huge guffaw and the other two joined in. 'That's Zak all right. That sure is Zak!'

The man who had punched him, bent down, took Archy's hand and pulled him to his feet. The other one retrieved his life card from the bushes, replaced it in the plastic folder and handed it back to him. The third man gave him his phone.

'I was gonna have you for my supper, Sparky,' said the leader, putting a hand on Archy's shoulder, 'but you go home, and when you see Zak tell him that you met his pal Solomon.'

The three men stood back and one of them made an exaggerated gesture inviting Archy to continue along the path he'd been taking when they ambushed him.

'And you get some credits on that card, Sparkyboy, or you're fucked,' said the man who'd punched him.

Archy felt awful. His stomach hurt and he could

hardly walk. He wasn't sure what had happened. Had the trio really let him go, or was it some charade, some game, and they'd come rushing after him and hit him again? He stumbled through the woods, blundering in the deepening dark and letting out a yelp when his foot got caught on a tree root and in trying to stop himself falling he wrenched his side. Brambles snatched at his jeans and branches whipped his face, but eventually he was through. He crossed the road and looked nervously behind him. He hadn't heard anything, but he wanted to be sure that Solomon and his thugs weren't following him.

Who were they? What did they want? Why did they attack him? What did they have to do with Zak?

21

Mikael Dimitri Ivanovitch was in an armchair beside Alexandra Christina's bed, watching the shallow rise and fall of her chest. There seemed to be tubes everywhere, from her mouth and nose, from her arm and beneath the covers. On the far side of the bed screens in a rack showed multicoloured graphs and numbers. He looked at her hair spread across the pillow, her delicate eyelids, her pale cheeks. Please God this will give her a normal life, he murmured, a life where she will be able to enjoy all the riches he has amassed for her. A life where she can realise the full extent of her talent.

He turned to Folken. 'What's her name?'

Folken was puzzled. 'Who?'

'The new girl, the replacement, the one whose kidney you've put in my daughter.'

'I'm sorry, but the donor has asked for their identity to be kept secret, and it's our policy to respect this request.' Folken smiled wearily. He had told Ivanovitch this before.

The Russian shrugged. 'I know she's getting well paid for it but it would be good to meet her, see what she's like, tell her thank you.'

Folken didn't reply. He didn't say that none of the money Ivanovitch had paid for the kidney was going to the donor. He didn't say that actually the donor wasn't a girl.

The door opened and a dark haired woman came in. Ivanovitch didn't like Dr Salamar but he respected her skill. He had watched through the glass screen while she led the three hour operation, painstakingly inserting the kidney which shortly before had been removed from the donor in an adjacent operating theatre. The kidney had been examined, tested, pronounced healthy, and now it was beginning its work inside his daughter. Pompous Folken – Ivanovitch didn't like him either – had explained that over the previous decade there had been huge advances in understanding the human leukocyte antigen system, and that combined with the NHGD made ensuring compatibility between organ donors and recipients relatively simple. The accuracy and reliability of the matching at Aurora was far better than back home in Russia. China might have been a possibility, but you could never be quite sure with them.

However, Ivanovitch knew that even with the new kidney accepted and functioning properly in his daughter's body, her life would never be completely normal. Folken had told him that a kidney from a young, healthy donor should last more than twenty years, but at some stage in the future it was possible that Alexandra Christina would have to go through all this again. The location of the new kidney in her pelvis meant that she'd be unable to give birth to her own children, but few wealthy women did that nowadays. Give her a few months to get over this, thought Ivanovitch, and he'll talk to Folken about harvesting some eggs. Later, when they've found a suitable father, they'll be fertilised and a surrogate mother lined up to host one of them. He would then have the grandson he longed for.

Dr Salamar examined the screens at Alexandra Christina's bedside. Then she consulted the tablet notes and exchanged a few words with the nurse who had followed her in.

'She's not awake yet,' said Ivanovitch, more gruffly than he'd intended. 'When's she going to wake up?'

Dr Salamar didn't respond right away. She was aware of the man's hostility and it puzzled her. She knew she was one of the best in her profession and she had that morning spent several hours giving his daughter a new life. Didn't that count for something?

'She'll come round soon. She was unconscious for several hours so it will take a while. I'll ask Dr Baldry, the anaesthetist, to look in. You can help by stroking her hand and talking to her. Often patients are aware of external stimuli before they fully regain consciousness.

'Get Baldry.'

Dr Salamar bristled. Really this man's truculence was insufferable. 'I'll see what I can do,' she said.

She left and Folken followed. The room was still again, except for his daughter's shallow breathing and the nurse tidying a trolley.

Ivanovitch took the girl's hand and stroked it gently, above where the tube entered. 'Sdrastvooy, mayo solnyshkuh. Sdrastvooy, kotik. Vsyo boodyt harasho.'

Ingrida was surprised. She had come from the secure wing, where the boy they'd brought in last night was still insensate after having his kidney removed. She hated the Russian, and the girl in the bed, for what had been done to him. But like many Lithuanians she spoke Russian, and she was moved by the tender words she heard. It seemed incongruous that this overbearing and frightening man should be calling someone his kitten, his sunshine, telling them everything would be all right, even if it was his daughter. Jeannie often said that turds can't feel, but it seemed that this one could.

She left without speaking and went to the bathroom. She needed a few minutes alone. She'd been feeling sad for most of the day and was now on the verge of tears. On the way to the Russian girl's room, Salamar had been giving her instructions about getting the kidney donor ready for another procedure; they were going to remove one of his lungs. He could live without a kidney. He could live without a lung. He could even live without both, although it would be a limited sort of life. But there was a strong possibility that taking the two so close together would be fatal. They were going to dispose of this boy, take what they needed from him and throw the rest away, like so much garbage.

She hadn't spoken to him. He'd been out cold when they'd brought him in and had remained so since, but she was sure he'd not signed up for what was happening to him. He was young, nice looking, fit. He was somebody's son, somebody's brother, somebody's friend. She wanted to help him.

22

BETH WAS LOOKING at a spider on Zak's neck. Solomon and two other men were in three large armchairs in a private room upstairs at Revolution Easy. Solomon was dressed in a light grey suit, lilac shirt and a silk tie with a bold black and white pattern. The suit was beautiful and looked expensive. The other two men were also very well dressed. They didn't look a bit like the bomber jacketed thugs who Archy said had attacked him.

The spider was Zak's latest tattoo. It looked very realistic, almost three dimensional as it emerged from his shirt collar under his ear. Body art was a talking point between them. As well as the spider Zak had a two-headed dragon on his back, a guitar and several abstract designs on his legs and forearms, and on his left shoulder the one he prized the most: a girl's face over the name of his dead wife, Hella. Beth's latest was an anchor on her left side, just above her bra line.

She also had a dream catcher in the centre of her back, a rose on one arm, and an elephant on the other. It was a baby elephant, cheerfully waving its trunk while it balanced on a ball. She regretted the elephant. It had looked cute at first but now it embarrassed her so much that most of the time she kept it covered. When she could afford to she would get another design overlaid to mask it. Your arm will be a palimpsest, Cameron had said. He knew words like that.

Solomon was relaxed, sitting sideways in his chair, his legs loosely crossed and one arm draped along the back. When Archy came in he had welcomed him like an old friend.

'Hey, Sparkyboy,' he'd rumbled in his big voice, 'roll in, my man, roll in.' He made an expansive welcoming gesture and stood up. 'Zakarias. Great to see you again. Thanks for coming.'

'You've met my stepson,' Zak said coldly.

'I have. Archibald Sparks. I have.' Solomon pinched his nose between his fingers and thumb and looked for a moment shamefaced. 'That was a misunderstanding. Unfortunate.' He looked to Archy. 'You okay?'

Archy was still angry at what happened and he felt the blood rushing to his cheeks. He also felt a lot braver with Zak at his side.

'My name's not Sparkyboy. It's not Archibald. It's Archy, Archy Sparks.'

The force of his reply surprised even Archy

himself. Zak put a hand on his arm and the two men in the chairs exchanged a glance.

Solomon continued smiling. 'Archy, Archy Sparks. That's how it'll be.' He made a circular hand motion, as if to indicate that his acceptance went for the other two as well.

Archy felt he'd achieved a minor victory. Now he wanted someone to say they were sorry for what they did to him. 'Who was it who hit me?'

One of the men in the chairs grinned sheepishly and raised his forefinger.

'That would be my friend here,' said Solomon, turning to the man. 'Mr Draven.'

'You'd got no reason to hit him,' said Zak. 'All right, you didn't know who he is, but what you did was out of order. It was common assault.'

Solomon's broad smile, which had been in place since they came in, remained but narrowed a little. 'Hey, come down, man. You're gonna fall off that horse.' His deep voice was calming, gentle almost. 'We made a judgement call because he was acting suspiciously.'

'Suspiciously?' said Archy.

'Yeah,' said Draven. 'We'd been watching you. You'd been kinda furtive, dodging away from that police cruiser, looking out for drones. You came into the woods like you was home late and you was scared your momma might hear you.'

Solomon took over. 'A few days back Jonas, my boy, was snatched by some people who took him away.

They were going to hurt him and he was lucky to get away. We've been rooting to find out something about that, looking around places where no-goods hang out, folks who might have seen something, or even been tied up in it. We saw you and thought you was one of them.'

Archy was finding the gangsta talk and the drawl Solomon and his cronies used flakey and irritating.

'Let's not be enemies,' said Solomon. 'It was a misunderstanding, is all. We're on the same side. You got a problem that sounds the same as ours and we want to help you.' He held out a huge hand. 'I'm sorry you got yourself hurt.'

Archy felt a little mollified. You got yourself hurt, not we hurt you, but that was probably the closest to an apology he would get. He took the hand. The grip was firm but not crushing.

'Draven, shake the man's hand.'

Draven's grip was the same.

Solomon beckoned to the third man. 'And this is Gunner.'

Where do they get these names? thought Archy. Gunner came over and went through the handshake ritual.

Solomon beckoned Zak to join them. As soon as he came close he put one arm around him and the other around Draven, who put his arm around Archy. Archy connected with Gunner in the same way because that seemed to be what was expected, so the five of them were in a circle, heads bent. It seemed something

Solomon and his men were used to, but to Archy it was completely bizarre.

Beth waited at the edge of this performance. She looked at her watch. She was feeling irritated. It was fifteen minutes since she, Archy and Zak had come into the room and she was wondering when someone might take notice of her. The show of testosterone-fuelled male bonding was almost the last straw. She was tempted to tell them all to fuck off and walk out, but Zak had told her that Solomon and his crew might be able to help them find Cameron, so she put up with it.

At last Solomon broke the circle. He looked towards Beth and appeared to see her for the first time. 'Introduce me to the lady,' he said to Zak.

Before Zak could speak Beth walked up to Solomon and held out her hand. 'I'm Beth Flowers,' she said.

Solomon smiled. He was half again as tall as she. 'Pretty name, pretty girl.'

Beth winced at the patronising remark. Her name wasn't pretty. To her it sounded like something between a cough and a sneeze. She didn't think she was pretty either. This man was coming across as a slime ball. She hoped that they weren't wasting valuable time, time they could be spending searching. She pulled her hand away.

Solomon gestured to two chairs. 'You sit here, please Miss Beth, next to your boyfriend.'

Archy blushed. He felt he ought to correct the mistake but he didn't want to. Beth darted a look at him. 'I'm not, she's not...' he stammered. Then he saw the twinkle in Solomon's eyes. He knew exactly who Beth was, what her connection was with him and with Zak. Solomon put his hand on Archy's shoulder and pressed him gently but firmly down into his chair. 'Sit with us,' he said. 'All friends now, and we got plans to make.'

The steady pounding of a dance beat came from two floors below. It was early yet and the club had only just opened but things were warming up.

'I sent you a video grab of the van that took Jonas,' Solomon said to Zak. 'You get anything on that?'

Zak shook his head. 'Yes, but it's no help to you. The number plate relates to a vehicle that belongs to a hire firm in Newark.'

'Is that so?' said Solomon.

'It is. And the firm's records say that it was in their own yard on the day you caught it on your camera.'

'How can that be?'

'The plate in the photo you sent me is a clone. It's the oldest trick in the book. You find a vehicle as close as you can to the one you want to hide – same make, same model, same year if possible – and you use its plate. If anyone looks it up it checks out as a genuine vehicle with a registered owner. You do your job and then you chuck the plate away.

'But don't you need documents if you want to get a plate made?' said Archy. 'Registration forms and stuff like that?'

Zak looked at him pityingly. 'These guys are well

able to make their own plates, as many as they want and whenever.' He turned to Beth. 'I explained our problem to Solomon on the phone. Tell him what we know about Cameron.'

Beth did. When she'd finished there was silence. 'Something's happened to him,' she said. 'I can feel it.' They were getting nowhere and she'd had enough. She stood up and started towards the door.

Archy got up too, not sure where she was going or what was happening but knowing he must follow her.

'Hang on,' said Zak. 'Where are you off to?'

'I'm going to find him,' said Beth. 'He's hurt and he needs help and I'm going to find him.'

'Good for you, girl,' said Solomon, 'but give it a minute. There's somebody you should meet first.' He pulled a slim miniphone from his inside pocket and stabbed the screen. 'Jonas, my boy. Get your sorry ass in here.'

23

JONAS TOLD the story of what had happened to him. Beth thought he seemed remarkably calm about it, but an occasional catch in his voice showed that the memories hurt. Zak wanted to go over everything in the minutest detail, asking questions, getting the boy to repeat things. She felt sorry for Jonas but couldn't see how all this was helping them to find out where Cameron was. It took an age, and she was becoming more and more anxious. Cameron was in danger, and with every hour it grew worse. She fidgeted and bit her nails while Zak, Solomon and Archy talked about what they ought to do.

Zak had already done some research before they'd come to the club. He'd started with the possibility that it really was a photo of Cameron that had flashed up on the TV. The show's sponsor was the Aurora Group. There were a number of companies within it and one name was common to all: Hans Folken. Zak looked him up. He'd had a distinguished career in medical research, some prestige appointments and the usual batch of degrees and papers in learned journals. However, even though he looked squeaky clean something didn't feel quite right.

The main company, the one everyone had heard of, was the one that had been set up for the National Human Genome Database. Soon after came Aurora New Dawn. This seemed to be Folken's own baby, and it used information from the NHGD to link volunteer donors with people who needed transplants. There were scores of success stories and enthusiastic testimonials from grateful patients who thought Folken was a saint and his staff angels. This was what the New Dawn TV show was all about.

'Look at this,' said Zak. He opened his laptop and found the edition of the show that Beth had seen. He scrolled through to the Gallery of Heroes. 'Now watch.' The images rolled across the screen. There was no picture of Cameron.

'He was there!' Beth protested. 'Right there, after the woman with the plait and before the guy with glasses. He was. Honestly. Right there.'

'I know he was,' said Zak, 'I've watched the recording you gave to Archy. But there's no sign of him now. Last night I hacked into the production company's system and found all the images that had been on the Gallery of Heroes that night, the woman with the plait, the man in glasses, all of them. But there was no Cameron. 'He's been removed.'

Beth's heart sank. It seemed to be a dead end.

'Jonas, my boy,' said Solomon. 'Tell the good people where you think they took you.'

'I think it was somewhere in Scotland,' said Jonas. He told them why.

'Funny,' said Zak, 'because there's another Aurora company. Look at this.' He tapped the keyboard and turned the laptop around to where everyone could see the screen. It was a simple website, the home page showing a long, low building in designer glass and steel. 'It's called Aurora Wellbeing. It's much lower profile than Aurora New Dawn. It's not clear exactly what it does but there's a message inviting people interested in specialist medical services to contact them.'

'Is that all?' Beth said.

'Yes,' said Zak. 'That's the whole site, just a home page and a click through to a contact form. I guess that anyone coming here already knows what they do. But here's the thing: Aurora Wellbeing is located in Aberdeen.' He paused for a moment. 'Now I'm only guessing here,' he went on, 'but I think that just like its big sister, this branch of Aurora is into transplants, except in a different way. Jonas says the people who grabbed him were going to take his kidney, and they certainly didn't have his okay for that...'

'No they did not,' said Jonas.

'...so I think that's where he was taken.'

'Cameron's there,' Beth said. 'I know he is. He's a long way away. It has to be Aberdeen.'

'Can you hack into their site?' Archy said.

'I expect I could,' said Zak, 'but it might take me some time.'

'We haven't got any more time,' Beth said. 'We have to do something now.'

'The lady is right,' Solomon said. 'I think we go pay this Dr Folken dude a visit.'

Beth could have hugged him, she was so relieved that at last something was happening. She wanted to leave straight away but there were some things to fix first. Naturally they had to work out what they'd do when they got to Aberdeen but the first thing to settle was the journey itself.

'Why would three large men of African origin, their smaller companion, a middle aged Welshman and two teenagers be travelling to Scotland together? You have to ask that,' said Zak.

'Why do we need a reason?' Beth asked. Why can't we just go?'

'Well,' said Zak, 'we could, but the governments both sides of the border would rather people stayed home. Besides, travel nowadays is is for the rich. The cost of fuel credits puts long distance trips out of the reach of most ordinary folks, so the security forces start from the assumption that if you're away from your home without a good reason you're up to no good.'

'So let's give a reason,' said Beth.

'Which takes us back to my question, why would we be going there?'

The plan they eventually settled on was mostly suggested by Archy. The seven of them would split up.

Beth, Archy and Zak would go together. Beth and Archy were to be step-brother and sister.

'But we're not a bit alike,' said Beth.

Zak looked at her dark hair and smooth brows and at Archy's ginger mop and freckles. 'True.'

'And we've got different names.'

'So what are we going to do if they ask us?' Zak said.

'We tell them we don't have the same father,' said Archy. 'Zak's our uncle and we're going with him.'

'Good.'

To Beth it seemed rather doubtful, and given a few minutes checking by the authorities it would unravel very quickly. However, she couldn't think of anything better.

'I could knock up some fake life cards, all showing the same family name,' Archy said.

'Bad idea,' said Zak. 'You know well that possession of fake ID is a criminal offence. If the police catch you they can lock you up until they can verify who you are, and you can bet they'd take their time over that. No, we'll stick with your story, Archy.'

'Okay,' said Beth, 'so you're mine and Archy's uncle. How are we going to get there? Car?'

'I don't think so,' said Zak. 'We'll go by train. I'll book open tickets to Inverness. Returns, of course, the authorities like to know that people are planning to go back to where they came from. The Inverness train goes through Aberdeen and we'll be taking a break there. I'll book a couple of visits or tours or something, so it looks like we've got a good reason to stop off.'

'We need some transport,' said Beth. 'We might need to get away in a hurry.' She couldn't imagine them waiting for a train with Cameron's captors after them. She didn't say that Cameron might not be capable of going on public transport. She didn't say it because she couldn't bear to think about it.

'My dad's got a people carrier,' Jonas said.

'I sure have,' said Solomon. 'It will take all seven of us if need be.'

'And Cameron?' said Beth.

'Room for him too. Me, Jonas, Draven, and Gunner, we'll drive there. We don't know you, we've never heard of you. And the reason we're going to be in Aberdeen is easy. I'm visiting Britain from Nigeria. I have interests in the oil business, which is why I'll be in Aberdeen. I'll get my secretary to book me an appointment with Dr Hans Folken, to discuss "a family medical matter".' His fingers indicated the inverted commas. 'If the man really is doing bad things like we think, that should be enough to get him drooling.'

'Please please please can we go?' Beth pleaded. She was so frustrated at the length of time it was all taking that she was on the point of bursting. But they still weren't ready.

'There's a matter I need to check with Molly before we go,' said Zak. 'It was something she said the other day about her surrogacy. I didn't take much notice at the time and thought it was nothing, but then something clicked and I've a feeling it could be important.' He smiled at Beth and shook his head. 'Don't worry,' he said, 'I'll make it quick.'

Solomon went to a cupboard and took out a cardboard box. It was full of phones, new ones, each wrapped in a plastic sheath. He gave them two each, one black, the other red. 'Call each other a lot on these,' he said, holding up a red one. 'Two times a day, maybe more. Talk about the weather, the wonderful scenery, where you've been, what you've seen, where you're goin'. Say what a great time you're having. Call your granny, Beth. Make stuff up. When you talk about this dude,' he put his huge hand on Zak's shoulder, 'don't forget he's your sacred uncle. You want to call me, or to tell each other something you wouldn't want anyone else to hear, use these.' He picked up the other three phones, the black ones. He held out a handful of SIM cards. 'Take some. Use them only in the black phones, use each once and then trash it. Don't just throw it away, break the sucker up. Burn it if you can, or at least snap it and separate the two parts. New card every time. Don't think that just 'cos maybe you ain't said nothing special you can use it again. No way. New card every single time.'

Beth and Archy nodded seriously and took two of the phones each. Zak smiled and took the remaining pair, slipping one into each back pocket.

24

Beth didn't sleep.

Suppose Cameron wasn't in Aberdeen. Suppose he wasn't in Scotland at all. Suppose they'd be searching totally in the wrong place. Suppose he was one of those who went missing and never came back. Suppose suppose suppose. It was a long, long night.

Morning came eventually and she was up much earlier than she needed to be. She told her gran that Cameron had gone to stay with a friend and that she was going with Archy and Zak to pick him up and give him a lift home. She hated lying to her but she had to because the old woman would have worried herself sick if she'd known Cameron was really missing.

'Well take care, love,' Gran had said. 'When will you be back?'

'Oh soon, but I may stay a night or two at Zak's place. I'll call you.'

She left without breakfast, explaining that Zak and

Archy were picking her up at the station. Another lie; or perhaps not quite.

She was there far too early and had a long wait. More panic and anxiety. Zak and Archy weren't coming. They'd overslept. They'd had an accident on the way to the station. However, they were there in good time, smiling and reassuring. The overnight bag she'd borrowed from Gran looked tatty beside their smart backpacks.

'I thought you'd be here before us,' said Zak, greeting her with a hug. 'Cheer up, soon be in Scotland.'

'How long does it take?'

'About six hours. We'll arrive in Aberdeen early afternoon.'

Beth prayed they would not be too late.

The journey seemed endless and she fidgeted for the whole time. Maybe the Aurora clinic in Aberdeen would turn out to be simply that, a clinic, doing ordinary things to ordinary people. Maybe Cameron wouldn't be there. He could be in a different part of the country – or the world. All she could pick up from him now was that he was in trouble, sometimes in pain, and a long way away. But a long way away could be out of Britain altogether – in France, or Holland, or ... anywhere.

The train seemed painfully slow and there were several stops. Then it came to a standstill on an open stretch of track.

Beth leant forward to peer through the window. 'Oh no, what now?'

'It's the Scottish border,' said Zak.

'But why have we stopped? There's supposed to be free movement. I thought we'd just go straight through.'

'There is. Free movement and free trade, but there've been a lot of problems about drugs and counterfeit goods passing between the two countries.' Zak sighed. 'Don't you young folks keep up with the news? Anyway, the authorities on both sides are clamping down and are doing random checks. I expect this is one.'

It was. A Scottish border patrol worked its way along the train, and it took a long time. They weren't unfriendly but they were thorough. They stopped at the table where Zak, Archy and Beth sat. She worried that here, at the first test, their story would unravel.

'Where are you bound for?' one of patrol said.

'Inverness,' said Zak, and handed over their tickets and ID cards. 'I'm taking my niece and nephew here to see if we can find the Loch Ness monster.'

The man smiled. 'Good luck with that,' he said. He checked his datapad. 'I see you gave advance notification of your journey. I wish everybody would do that. It would make my life a lot easier.' He returned the tickets and IDs to Zak and smiled at Beth. 'Welcome to Scotland.'

Beth had assumed that once they crossed the border they'd soon be there, but it was another three and a half hours before the train pulled into Aberdeen.

Then they had to find their accommodation. Zak had got rooms for them in a budget hotel in the town centre. It was near the station so they walked.

The day was cold with a thick mist off the sea, and it was growing dark. The online guide Beth had seen showed pictures of impressive buildings, parks, a pretty coastline, but all that was hidden by the damp cloud. The buildings she could see were grey and gloomy.

'Is this it? said Archy, dismayed by the threadbare and grimy appearance of the building Zak led them to.

'I'm afraid so,' said Zak. 'We couldn't go anywhere too flash because we want to keep a low profile.'

'What about Solomon and his lot?'

'They're at the Royal Arcadia. It's a five star hotel on the edge of the Trump Golf Resort.'

Archy raised his eyebrows. 'Jammy, or what?'

'Solomon thinks it's the sort of place a rich visitor from overseas would stay.'

'Lucky him.'

'How do we find the Aurora place?' said Beth.

'I know where it is,' said Zak. 'It's only a couple of streets away.' His phone buzzed an alert. 'That's Solomon now. I'll text him to meet us.'

They checked in and found their rooms. Zak and Archy shared one, Beth had her own a couple of doors along the corridor. It was clean but basic, with a narrow bed and a cramped ensuite. The window was grimy and gave onto a scruffy rear yard with wheelie bins and outdoor furniture stacked for the winter. Beyond that she could see nothing apart from the glow of a street lamp through the murk.

She was impatient to get going. She flung her bag on the bed, splashed her face, tidied her hair, and was waiting in the lobby when Zak and Archy came down. They were only there for a few minutes before Solomon's big Merc. pulled up outside the hotel.

'I found the clinic,' said Solomon as the car moved off. 'Jonas thinks it could be the place he was taken but he doesn't know.'

'I'd got a bag over my head when they took me in and I was knocked out when I left so I can't recognise anything. Sorry.'

'How can we find out if Cameron's in there?' said Beth.

'Well, Gunner and Draven are checking the place out now. Maybe they'll come back with something.'

'Can you feel anything?' Archy asked Beth.

She shut her eyes and tried to empty her mind. Did she feel that Cameron was near? She didn't, but then she did. There was an emptiness, but there was also a nearness.

'I don't know,' she said. 'I think he might be but I'm not sure. He could be asleep, that would account for it all being so vague.'

'I think I could recognise the nurse who helped me,' said Jonas. 'If we watch the clinic I could see if she goes in or out.'

'How long would that take?' said Beth. 'And what could we do if you did see her?' Jonas was trying to help, but where would it get them if he managed to identify the nurse? They couldn't just walk up to her and ask if there was a boy called Cameron in the clinic.

'It's a start,' said Zak. 'If Jonas can spot her we might have a way in, but it will be over to you, Beth.'

'How do you mean?'

'Well, someone will have to talk to her. None of us guys can do it, it would look like we were trying to pick her up. But as a woman you might find a way to get into conversation with her. Maybe if you did you could then drop a hint or too. According to Jonas she took pity on him and was kind. She might feel the same if there was another boy his age in a similar situation.'

It had to be worth a try, and no one had any better suggestion, although Solomon seemed quite keen to take Folken on one side and beat the information out of him.

They all got into the car and stopped near the clinic. The mist was lifting and turning to drizzle, and the building Beth could see looked like the one she'd seen on the Aurora Wellbeing website.

'You stay here with Beth,' Solomon said to Jonas. 'The rest of us will go. We don't want to look like no coach party. We'll take a cab to my hotel and wait there. You call us. And don't forget, use the black phones and trash the SIM card each time.'

25

Jonas and Beth were left in the cruiser, parked where they could see both the front entrance to the clinic and a side door which seemed to be used by staff.

At least it was a comfortable vehicle to wait in. It was more than that; it was fantastic. Beth hadn't ever ridden in anything like it. There were nine seats, there was a drinks cabinet, and a stereo that wouldn't have been out of place in a luxury apartment. Lacquered wood glowed and there was the smell of new leather. Beth thought she could live in it. However, she reckoned that it would be best not to stay there for long. The thing was so big and black and shiny that it might attract attention they didn't want.

Beth was pleased they were doing something, but frustrated that they still didn't know whether they were on the right track. She was still unable to connect to Cameron. The car was warm and her missed sleep was catching up. The stereo was playing quietly and she began to doze.

'There,' said Jonas, suddenly sitting up straight. 'That one there. She's the one.'

Beth started. Jonas was indicating a woman who was leaving the clinic. She was about Beth's height and had short, dark hair. She was walking with brisk purpose, almost trotting, one hand steadying her shoulder bag. Her navy blue raincoat was buttoned to the neck against the drizzle. Her head was tilted away, which made it hard to get a good look at her face.

'You're sure?' said Beth, suddenly alert.

'I'm sure all right.'

Jonas had been groggy all the time he had been in the clinic, though not always as much as he'd pretended. He had reasoned that if he made them think he was barely conscious they wouldn't bother giving him more drugs. It had worked. When the doctor, the nasty looking woman in her crisp, white coat came round he tried to relax and slowed his breathing. It had worked. She'd taken a quick look at him, grunted and gone off without ordering for any more poison to be pumped into his system, which meant he'd been able to observe the nurse who had spent so much time in his room. He knew her now.

'We should follow her,' said Beth.

The woman crossed the road to a tram stop and stood under the shelter. Beth and Jonas had been sitting in the back of the cruiser where they'd been hidden by the tinted windows. Now they moved to the front. At the same time a tram crawled around the corner and the woman got on.

'Let it get ahead,' Beth said. 'There's hardly any traffic and it will be easy enough to follow it now the fog's lifted.'

'Fair enough,' said Jonas. 'I expect she won't be getting off for a stop or two.'

They trailed the tram all the way into town until it halted on Market Street, close to the docks. Jonas slowed the car, pretending to be looking for somewhere to park.

'Look,' said Beth. 'Isn't that her? That woman who's just got off.'

'Yes, it is.'

Beth loosened her seatbelt. 'I'm going after her. Let the others know and wait for me. I'll call you.'

Beth slid out of the cruiser and followed the woman, who was walking quickly, looking neither to right nor left. She was glad she'd brought a waterproof with her. The drizzle, fresh off the North Sea, seemed colder and wetter than any rain she'd ever felt before.

At the corner of Trinity Street the woman turned. The road was short, narrow and dark, the buildings grey, fronting directly onto the pavement. She stopped at a door, opened it with a key and went in. Beth hid in the doorway of a house opposite that had been boarded up. It gave some protection from the weather but not much. In the house the woman had entered the upstairs lights came on, and Beth saw her come to a window and draw the curtains.

She took out the black phone Solomon had given her and called Jonas.

'What are you going to do?' he said.

'I don't know. Stay here for a bit and see if she comes out again.'

'It could be a long wait. She might be there for the rest of the night.'

'That's possible, but I'll hang around for a bit. Call Zak and your dad so they know what's happening.'

'Sure will.'

'And if you haven't heard from me in an hour bring me a bag of chips.'

Beth took the SIM card out of the phone as Solomon had instructed, bent it in two and dropped it though a drain grating. Then she put in a new one. She stared at the drawn curtains. Jonas was right. The woman was at home, and she might not come out again until the next day. How could she make contact with her? This watching might go on for some time.

As it turned out she didn't have to wait long.

26

THERE WAS NO WARNING. The upstairs light was still on, but suddenly the street door opened and the woman came out. Beth felt she'd been waiting in the doorway for hours and her legs were numb. She was so drawn in against the cold that she almost missed her. Quickly she turned her back and pretended to be looking for something in her bag but the woman never even glanced in her direction. Instead she walked briskly towards the main street. She was wearing heels now, and the hollow clip-clop rang off the granite walls.

Beth had regretted wearing trainers because her feet were feeling as though they were wrapped in ice, but she was glad now because they made no noise. Her heart was pounding. The woman looked as though she was aiming to meet someone. If she was going to their home that would be hopeless, but if she was heading for somewhere public like a bar or a cinema there might be a way to talk to her. What should she say? How could she find the words that would open up a conversation but not scare her away? Adrenaline flushed through her.

The woman turned right into a broader, busier street. She didn't once look back, but even so Beth tried to appear casual, stopping to look in shop windows while being careful not to allow her target to get too far ahead. Just like in most of the towns in England, a lot of the shops were boarded up, which meant that Beth found herself staring at the windows of those that remained – charity shops, a mobile phone outlet, a betting shop. She thought about calling Jonas, Archy or Zak but she didn't want to risk losing the woman. She could do with a bit of help, though.

Ahead the street broadened at a junction, where there looked to be a sort of castle. Just before she reached it the woman crossed the road and went into a large, majestic building on the corner. It had a curved portico and imposing pillars and looked like a bank, but it was clearly a bar. Beth walked past, sneaking a quick glance into what seemed a dark interior with low lights and plenty of wooden panelling. She turned into what a sign said was King Street and waited a minute or two. She was trembling, and she took some deep breaths to calm herself. She turned back towards the bar and went in.

There weren't many people in there and the woman was easy to spot. For an awful moment Beth thought she'd been joined by a man, but he turned away from the table and with relief Beth saw a cloth over his arm and realised he was one of the staff. She got out her black phone and called Jonas. She told him where she was, to bring the car, park up the street, and be ready to pick her up.

The room was long, with a large mahogany bar at the far end. On the wall half way down was a big TV screen showing a basketball game. Beth went to the bar and ordered a lemon sparkle. While the barman mixed it she watched the woman in the mirror behind him. Her table was in a corner. There was a tumbler in front of her and she was swirling ice cubes with a straw. She must be meeting somebody. Or was she killing time before going on somewhere else?

The barman gave Beth her drink and leant forward as if settling in for a chat. Beth gave him a smile but turned away towards the room. There were plenty of empty tables but she chose the one nearest to the woman. Closer and in better light she could get a proper look at her face. She was a bit older than Beth herself, probably in her early thirties. Her hair was mid-length and cut around her neck in the popular casual style, a bit like Beth's own. Her face was open and friendly. She checked her watch and looked towards the door.

Oh shit, she is expecting somebody, Beth thought. I don't have much time. Oh well, here goes. She opened her bag and took out a leaflet. It was from a whisky distillery, and Zak had given it to her to back up their story that they were tourists. She pretended to study it for a minute, then gave an exaggerated sigh and leant towards the woman's table.

'Sorry to bother you,' she said, 'but are you local?'

The woman smiled at her. She had a nice smile. Beth thought that was a good sign.

'I'm not really local,' she said, 'but I do live here. Perhaps I can help you.'

The woman had a slight accent which sounded eastern European. That was good. Jonas had said he thought that the nurse who'd helped him was Polish. Beth put the leaflet on the woman's table and slid over to the seat opposite her.

The woman frowned. 'I'm expecting a friend,' she said.

Beth was worried she might have blown it but she pressed on. 'It's okay, I'll go as soon as your friend gets here. I'm trying to find this place,' she said, pointing to the map showing the distillery on the edge of the town, 'and I was wondering what's the best way to get there. Do the trams go out that far? Is there a bus?'

The woman gave Beth an odd look. 'I've not been there myself, but it tells you here how to get to it.' She pointed to a square on the corner of the leaflet, which was clearly labelled *How to find us* and contained exactly the information Beth had asked for.

'Oh, yeah,' said Beth. 'Silly me. I should have seen that.' She smiled at the woman, folded the leaflet and put her phone on top of it. 'You're not from around here, are you?' she said, leaning back in her chair. 'Poland?'

'Lithuania. We sound a lot like the Poles.'

'Your English is very good.'

'Thank you. I try hard.'

'So what brings you to Aberdeen?'

'I work here.'

'Oh yes? What do you do?' This was going better than Beth had expected.

'I am a nurse.'

Good, good, Beth thought. Take it easy, don't rush it, don't scare her off. Go slowly, one step at a time. She took a sip of her drink. 'My name's Beth, by the way.'

'Beth. That is a nice name. I am Ingrida.'

'Thank you. That's a nice name too.'

Ingrida smiled. She's got a great smile, Beth thought, the sort that makes you want to join in. She was taking a liking to her. Time to move on.

'Do you work at the hospital?' said Beth, trying to sound casual.

There was a momentary change in Ingrida's expression, a tiny cloud, and a brief pause before she answered. 'Not the hospital, no. There is a clinic here, an important one. I work there.'

Beth waited, wearing what she hoped was an expression of friendly interest and trying to hide her desperation for Ingrida to say more.

'It is a private clinic. For people with much money.'

'It must be wonderful to help people who are sick,' Beth said. Then, more briskly, 'I'd love to be a nurse myself, but I'm not sure I could.'

'Oh? Why not?'

Beth laughed. 'I'm squeamish. I don't like the sight of blood. It's a bit of a disadvantage for a nursing career, really.'

'Oh, yes,' said Ingrida, laughing too. 'You would not like my job. I work in the operating theatres. Much blood there!'

Beth's heart leapt. This surely must be the woman who had helped Jonas. If Cameron was here she would know it. She told herself to keep calm but when she spoke again her voice was unsteady. She tried to cover it by coughing. 'You said theatres. Is it a big clinic? A lot of operations?'

'It isn't huge, but the work is very special and we do do many operations. We have two theatres and they're busy every day, sometimes at night too.'

Beth was surprised. 'I didn't know there were so many rich people in Aberdeen.'

'Oh, the patients are not from Aberdeen. They come from all over the world.'

'Well,' said Beth, 'if that's so I think I might stick with the nursing idea after all.'

Ingrida laughed again. 'But do you know,' she said, leaning closer, 'the blood of the rich is red, just like ours, so you would be no good nursing them, either.'

Beth was thinking that she really liked Ingrida and that they were getting on well when she heard another woman's voice behind her.

'So what's the joke?' This time the accent was Scots.

Beth turned to see the speaker. She was dark,

dressed in black, and she held a glass of red wine in her hand. She slid onto the stool next to Ingrida and kissed her on the cheek. Ingrida put her hand on the newcomer's arm. 'This is Jeannie,' she said. And then with just a trace of defiance, 'Jeannie is my girlfriend. Jeannie, this is my new friend, Beth.'

Jeannie waved a finger and raised her glass. 'Cheers, Beth. Pleased to meet you.'

There were a few minutes while Jeannie settled and she and Ingrida exchanged a few words about their days.

'Anyway,' Jeannie said, looking at Beth. 'What was so funny?'

Ingrida answered. 'We were laughing because Beth said she wants to be a nurse but she does not like the sight of blood. I told her that would be no good for my job in the operating theatres.' She turned to Beth. 'Jeannie works at the clinic, too.'

'Oh? What do you do?' Please let her say doctor, or even a surgeon, thought Beth, but Jeannie said nothing of the kind.

'Security.'

That was bad news. If Cameron was in the clinic and if they were to get him out security would be a problem. Beth hoped that her disappointment didn't show. 'I should think that's very important,' she went on, as lightly as she could. 'Ingrida was saying you get a lot of rich people at the clinic. I expect they need some careful protection.'

Jeannie shot Ingrida a sharp glance, as though she'd

said things she shouldn't. Then she seemed to thaw a little.

'Yes, security's important, although a lot of our patients bring their own.'

'Tell me, why do so many rich people come here?' Beth said. 'I mean, Aberdeen is a nice town, make no mistake, but it's not the obvious place for the well off to come for treatment. It must be special.'

'It is because of what we do,' said Ingrida. 'We specialise in organ transplants.'

Yes, yes, yes, thought Beth and under the table clenched her fists. Jeannie scowled at Ingrida and appeared to nudge her.

'Oh it's all right, Jeannie,' said Ingrida. 'Beth is a friend.'

'Maybe,' said Jeannie, 'but...' She frowned. 'Some of the patients we get are famous,' she explained. 'Celebrities, stars, business people, politicians. They don't want what they're going through to be made public. So the clinic has a strict rule: we do not talk about our work outside.' She gave Ingrida a meaningful look.

'Of course,' said Beth. 'I understand that. I didn't mean to pry.'

More people had come in to the bar now and it was busier, although the tables near them were still unoccupied. Jeannie's phone sounded. She got up and moved away to take the call. This was likely to be Beth's last chance.

'The clinic must be quite a swish place if you get so many influential patients,' she said.

Ingrida looked around, leant forward, and spoke quietly. 'It's swish enough if you're a rich Russian. Not so swish if you're one of the poor donors.'

Beth held her breath. She had almost got what she came for, but not quite. Jeannie was still on her call but kept glancing towards them.

'It is like two separate places,' Ingrida whispered. 'On one side are the rooms for the rich patients. They are 5 star. They have all the best medical equipment, phones, computers, big TVs. Then there are the rooms for the donors. They are no better than 2 star, very basic.'

'But I thought the organs used for transplants came from dead people.'

'Some of them do,' said Ingrida, 'but some people sell them.'

'What, really? Isn't that illegal.'

'Not in Scotland. It is illegal to ask someone to sell you an organ but not illegal for you to offer one for sale. Is it the same in England?'

Beth shook her head. She didn't know. Suddenly her own phone buzzed, the screen lit up and Cameron's face and her own smiled out at her.

'It's my gran,' she explained. 'Until a year ago she wouldn't go near a mobile. Now she's learnt to text and she does it all the time.' She put the phone back on the table.

Jeannie sat down again, her own call over.

'A problem?' said Ingrida.

'No, just Jock McIntyre wanting to change the shifts around. I told him to piss off. Anyway, we'd better go, we don't want to be late.'

'No, of course not,' said Ingrida, gathering her things to get up.

'Good to meet you,' said Jeannie.

'Sure,' said Beth. 'Very nice to meet you too.' Things were slipping away from her. She made a final play. She knew even as she said it that it sounded desperate, but she had to try. 'Your clinic sounds fantastic. I don't suppose, I mean, is there any chance I could have a look round? Being as I'm thinking about becoming a nurse? Are visitors allowed?'

Ingrida smiled and nodded and Jeannie frowned and shook her head, both at the same time.

Beth rushed on, hoping she didn't sound too imploring. 'It would be marvellous if I could. I've been round a big hospital in England, but to see a specialist place like yours, well it might open up a new direction for me.'

Jeannie had linked her arm in Ingrida's and was drawing her away.

'Here's my number,' said Beth, and held out a card she'd written it on. 'Please call me if you think it would be all right. Please. I would be really grateful.'

Ingrida took the card, put it in her pocket, and allowed herself to be led towards the door. Beth held her breath. Would it work? Would Ingrida phone?

27

THEY MET in the hotel room that Zak and Archy were sharing. Zak had wondered if Solomon's big flashy car would stand out too much in the car park, but he needn't have worried. There were several expensive cars there - another big Mercedes, a Porsche, a Lexus 4x4. It suggested to Beth that perhaps the wealthy were sometimes happy to slum it. Maybe that's how they stayed rich, by not splashing out on what they didn't need. Gran would approve of that.

The men were full of admiration for Beth's performance.

'You did good,' said Zak. 'It took guts to do what you took on and you did it well.'

'Five stars for thinking on your feet,' said Jonas.

Gran had taught Beth that it was polite to respond to praise modestly and so was about to demur; then she thought no, he's right, it was a tough job and I gave it my best. So she smiled and did a mock bow.

'How do you rate this Ingrida lady?' Solomon asked.

'I don't know,' said Beth. 'I liked her. She seems kind, just the sort of person who would try to save Jonas. I think she might help us, but I've no idea. I got the idea that Jeannie wasn't keen. She thought Ingrida was telling me too much and she might be a problem.'

'Jeannie?' said Zak.

'Her girlfriend.'

'Are they a couple?'

'They kissed when they met, and they went off arm in arm, so I guess they are.'

'You say this Jeannie works at the clinic too. What does she do?' said Solomon.

'Something in security,' said Beth.

'Mm. Could be a problem,' Solomon said thoughtfully.

'Or she might be useful, you know, somebody on the inside,' said Zak. 'Depends on which of them is the dominant one. What do you think, Beth? What's Jeannie like?'

'Youngish, black, cool looking. She wasn't there for long so I didn't have time to get much of an impression. I don't think she liked my questions about the clinic, though. She didn't want Ingrida to tell me about what they do there.'

'Young, black and cool?' said Jonas.

'Yes.'

'She sounds like the one who got talking to me just before I was taken.'

'Could be the same,' said Solomon.

'The question is, will she be on our side or not?' said Zak.

Beth considered for a moment. 'I don't know. I don't think Ingrida lets herself be pushed around but Jeannie did seem quite bossy. Anyway, what do we do now? There's no reason for me to meet her again, and if I did I don't know how I could find out about Cameron without questioning her directly, and that might sink the whole thing.'

'You asked if you could visit the clinic and you gave her your number. She might call you.' This was Archy.

'Yes, she might, but it was a bit desperate. She was leaving and it was all I could think of so I just pushed at her a card I'd written my number on. I don't think she believed my story that I wanted to look around because I was interested in nursing. Jeannie didn't buy it for a second. Maybe Ingrida just stuck the card in her pocket and forgot about it.'

'So let's decide what we do,' said Solomon.

They tossed it around for a while, but in the end there was no more they could settle on. Draven and Gunner had spent some time casing the clinic and they reported that it was well guarded. Ingrida seemed the best way in but they hadn't yet hooked her.

'Sure is a place,' said Gunner. 'Cameras everywhere. Steel doors at the back that would stop a tank. And two heavy dudes in the foyer at the front.'

'We could take 'em, though,' said Draven.

Archy had no doubt that they could. He was still

tender from where Draven had 'taken' him. However, there was no doubt that the clinic was too well defended for them to just walk in. Besides, they still didn't know for sure that Cameron was inside. Beth was becoming increasingly fretful because if he was they needed to do something quickly, and if he was somewhere else they were wasting their time, and his. What they could all agree on was that wherever Cameron was, every hour added to his danger. It was three days since he'd featured as a donor on the New Dawn show. They might have already harvested from him whatever it was they were saying he'd volunteered to donate. Rescue might already be too late.

'I have a way in,' said Solomon. 'but it might take a bit of time. I have an arrangement to meet this Hans Folken guy, the Director.'

'When?' said Zak.

'Eleven o'clock tomorrow. He thinks I'm looking for a transplant for my wife, and I'll expect to be given a tour of the place. I've never met Cameron but Beth's shown me photos of him. If he's there I should be able to recognise him.'

'If he's trussed up in bed with an oxygen mask over his face you might not be able to pick him out,' said Jonas.

'I bet they won't even take you to the part of the clinic where he is,' said Beth. 'Ingrida told me that the section for the organ receivers may be five star but the bit for the donors is nowhere near as plush. You're a prospective client so there are no prizes for guessing which you'll be taken to see.'

'And of course we still have the problem of what to do even if we know Cameron's there,' said Zak. 'Beth, what do you feel? Are you getting any vibes from him?'

Beth didn't answer right away. The last time she'd tried to reach out to her friend she'd drawn a blank. She tried again, turning inwards to focus on the emptiness he often occupied. Immediately she felt something so strong that she almost drew back. For most of the last three days the space had been empty, but now it was not. It was filled with an intense ache. She'd never had toothache but she could imagine it, and this feeling was like a toothache of the spirit. It was as if something in the very core of her being had been scooped out and the wound left raw.

'He's in there,' she said. 'He's in the clinic.'

'How sure are you?' said Zak. 'Out of ten.'

'I'm very sure. He's close, I can feel it. And he's in trouble. That's where he must be, in the clinic.'

'That's good enough for me,' said Zak.

Beth could have hugged him. Zak was one of the very few adults who took the gift that she and Cameron possessed seriously.

'Right,' said Zak. 'Solomon's appointment is at eleven, so that's when we'll start our rescue operation. The meeting can be both a way in and a distraction. Take Gunner or Draven as your assistant. You'll be expected to have some staff with you.'

'Jonas too,' said Solomon. 'It's important I have Jonas there.'

'But there'll be people in the clinic who know him,' said Beth. 'Somebody will recognise him, for sure.'

'He'll be my PA and he'll stay in the background. Wearing a suit and specs and with a document case, nobody will clock him as a sick guy in a bed. I need him there.'

'Okay,' said Zak. 'That means that the rest of us have to find a way in. The preferred option is that Ingrida comes through and she can at least get Beth in.'

'And what if not?' said Beth.

'Then we make it up as we go along.'

There was no more that they could do and the meeting broke up. Solomon's group went back to their luxury hotel and Beth to her own room.

Despite her tiredness and a welcoming mattress, she found it hard to rest. Her head was teeming with plans, schemes, thoughts, fears which became wilder and wilder as the night wore on. She thought of everything, from turning up at the clinic's reception and saying she was there to donate one of her kidneys, to standing on the front step screaming at passers by that they were holding her boyfriend prisoner. She thought about going to the police but she knew that if the authorities this side of the border were as mired in officialdom and red tape as they were in England she would get nowhere, and she might even be arrested herself.

Eventually in the small hours she sank into a deep

slumber. She felt she'd only been asleep for moments when her phone woke her. Blearily, she blinked at the screen. It was seven o'clock. The number showed as unknown. She didn't usually respond to unknown numbers, especially when she was alone. They were usually either somebody trying to sell you something, or a pervert. Pervy calls could be funny when you were with your friends and everyone could listen in, but not when you were by yourself. This time it was different, though. She knew who it might be, who she hoped it would be, and so she answered.

'Beth?'

She recognised at once the gentle voice, the accent. 'Yes.'

'It's Ingrida.'

Beth was afraid to speak. Her hand was trembling so much that she dropped the phone on the mattress and had to fumble to retrieve it. She didn't expect what came next.

'Beth. I know I know why you're here.'

Beth froze. Her mind was racing. Very quietly she said, 'Do you?'

'Yes. You have come here because you think your friend is in the clinic and you want to see him. It didn't dawn on me right away but then in the night it clicked.'

There was a long pause. 'Oh my God,' said Beth. 'How did you guess?'

'Never mind now. But I think you have come to take him away.'

'Yes.' There was no point in trying to deny it now.

That's it then, it's all over she thought. 'Yes. I want to take him home. Yes.'

The line was silent. It was such a long pause she wondered if Ingrida had dropped the call. Beth held her breath. Then Ingrida spoke.

'All right,' she said. 'I will help you.'

28

'SHE'S LATE,' said Zak. He was right, she was.

After the phone call Beth had lost no time in contacting the others. Ingrida was due to be on duty at noon, so they'd arranged with her to come to Solomon's hotel at nine-thirty. It seemed the right place to choose because there would be plenty of room in his suite and they'd be able to meet without anyone else close to the clinic knowing. It was now almost nine forty-five and Beth was feeling increasingly edgy. Perhaps Ingrida had changed her mind about helping. She'd told Beth that Jeannie was on an early shift and it was best if at least for now she didn't know that they were meeting. Beth wondered if maybe Jeannie had found out and was causing trouble. Finally the tension got to her.

'She's *got* to come,' she exploded. 'We can't leave it any longer. If we don't get Cameron out soon it will be too late.'

Since she'd woken up that morning she'd been

feeling those spasms again, the ones she'd felt before, and they'd got worse. It was a pain that could dig sharply into her and make her helpless. It was telling her that Cameron had been hurt. That he was afraid. She felt herself getting tearful. She wished she didn't cry so easily. Gran said it was a good thing, that it showed she was a big-hearted girl. She saw it as being soft and she hated herself for it. Cameron needed her to be tough. Tough and determined.

The four of them waited, silent people in a circle of armchairs. Jonas wasn't there; he was keeping an eye on the clinic from a cafe opposite and had instructions to phone if he saw anything that looked relevant to their task. Solomon had dispatched Gunner to watch the lobby and posted Draven round the back. 'You never do know,' he had said with the air of a man uttering something wise.

Archy got up and walked to the window. He knew that if the butchers in that clinic really had taken Cameron's kidney he wouldn't be in a state to be moved for some time. He'd read up on the internet what was involved and he knew that removing a kidney wasn't a simple matter. Without top class care there was a strong chance of infection. Would Cameron be getting top class care? From what Beth had told them of her conversation with Ingrida he doubted it. And although he hadn't said as much to Beth, there was also the possibility that they wouldn't stop at one kidney. While they had him there they might take the other one as well - and his liver, and his heart, and his lungs.

If they did there would be nothing left of Cameron to save.

Draven, who had been taking a turn in the round-the-clock surveillance of the clinic that Solomon had ordered, had reported that the evening before, while Beth was watching Ingrida, he had seen a limo with tinted windows arrive at the main entrance. A tall man with a mop of silver-grey hair had got out, and a frail-looking woman. The woman had been helped into a wheelchair and the party had been taken into the clinic. They'd been greeted by someone Draven recognised from the website pictures as the Director, Hans Folken. He and several others had given an effusive welcome to the visitors.

'Main people,' Draven had declared. 'This Director dude, he almost licked their shoes.'

The car had waited. After about an hour the silver haired man had come out on his own and been driven off. The same car had brought him back that morning. This time there had been no welcome from the Director. The man had walked quickly into the clinic while the car was parked in one of the VIP spaces. It was there now, with its driver and another man.

'Mean looking dudes,' was Draven's assessment. 'Packin' too, no doubt 'bout it.'

It was obvious that the woman must be a candidate for a transplant. It was the morning of Cameron's fourth day in the clinic. They wouldn't keep him there indefinitely, it was not a hotel. They must be preparing for some major activity involving the woman in the wheelchair, and it was worrying that it might well involve him.

Beth's impatience was almost out of control. She couldn't sit down but paced about like a tigress, listening at the door, looking out of the window. 'Where is she? Perhaps she's sick. Maybe she's had an accident.' She flopped into a chair and gnawed at a fingernail.

Archy took her hand. A week ago that would have seemed very strange. Today she welcomed it, and what he said. 'No. She'll be here. Hang on. You'll see.' Archy had no idea whether Ingrida would show up or not, but he did know that Beth needed comforting.

It was almost ten o'clock when the hotel room door opened and Draven came in. Beth let out a huge sigh of relief when she saw that Ingrida was with him. Her heart sank, though, when she saw that Jeannie was there too. What did that mean?

'I am sorry we are late,' Ingrida said briskly, loosening her coat and sitting down. 'We had a lot to talk about.'

Ingrida immediately took control. There were the briefest of introductions, then she started to fill them in. She said they were late because she and Jeannie had been discussing the situation since the early hours of the morning, since she told her who Beth was.

'How did you find out?' said Zak. His tone was suspicious, hostile even, but that didn't seem to disturb Ingrida at all.

'Last night in the bar,' she said, 'Beth put her phone

262

on the table. For most of the time it was dead, but then she got a text and it came to life. I saw her screen picture.'

'Me and Cameron,' said Beth. 'It's a selfie I took at the seaside a few months ago.'

'Yes, you and a boy,' said Ingrida. 'I didn't know his name, but I recognised him as someone we have in the clinic. Someone who's donating organs.'

Zak exploded. 'Donating! He's not donating. He's being forced to do it. For Christ's sake, you know this happens? You know and you don't do anything about it?'

Jeannie, who was still standing, took a step forward. Ingrida looked at the carpet, but her voice was steady when she answered.

'I came to the clinic because I was recruited from Lithuania. I knew its business was organ transplants, and I was told that the donors were all either dead, or people who had volunteered to donate an organ they could live without, a kidney or a lung, to keep someone else alive. I thought they were noble people. I thought it was worthy work. It's only very recently that I've come to understand that some of the donors are not volunteers. That is why I have decided to help you.'

'Why should we trust you?' said Zak.

Beth couldn't understand his attitude. They desperately needed this woman's help and his hostility seemed to risk turning her away. However, Ingrida didn't seem bothered.

'A few days ago,' she said, 'we had a young man

taken in to give a kidney. It turned out that the kidney couldn't be used, and I was told to make ready a lethal injection. I didn't. I prepared the injection but I diluted it so that it would not be lethal, so that the young man might live. I hope he did.'

Solomon stood up, walked slowly across the room, and stood before Ingrida. Then he stooped, raised her as if she weighed nothing, and hugged her tightly.

'You blissful angel,' he murmured. 'That young man is my son. And yes, he did live. At this very moment he's on watch but when he comes up here he'll thank you himself.'

They stood together, Ingrida held in the arms of this great bear of a man. Jeannie looked uneasy, not happy about the little tableau but unable to do anything about it. Beth wondered how long they were going to go on like that, time was drawing on.

Eventually Ingrida pulled herself away and stepped back. She was clearly moved and dabbed her eyes.

'You must hurry,' she said. 'There is another operation scheduled for later today. A woman was brought in yesterday, the wife of some Argentinian bigwig, and she needs a lung. Cameron is a perfect match and they plan to take his. There is little time to save him from this.'

'Why have you decided to help us?' It's Zak again. 'Why not just pack up and go home. Or if you feel so badly about it, why not report it to the authorities?'

Ingrida's reply was immediate. 'I came into nursing

to ease suffering and to save lives. I was proud to get a job at Aurora New Dawn. But it is an organisation that is built on lies. Some people are healed, certainly, but these are people who are wealthy, and for this others suffer. More happens at the clinic than people realise. I do not like it. I can't just pack up and go home as you say. I want to stop it. I can report it and I will, but would the authorities take any notice? Of me, an East European immigrant? A woman who steals the jobs of people who live here? And how long would it take them to do something? I think the first thing I must do is to help Beth's friend.'

Beth looked at Jeannie. She was still standing and she didn't look at all comfortable. Can we trust her? she wondered. But then, what choice did they have?

Zak asked the question directly. He looked hard at Jeannie and said, 'And what about you?'

There was a slight pause before the reply. Then Jeannie said, 'I should be at the clinic now but I swapped my shift so I could come here with Ingrida. I'll do what she thinks is best.'

Is this true? Beth thought. Had Jeannie come to help them, or just so she could keep an eye on what they were doing, and maybe alert the clinic? After all, she worked in security, and she had been there longer than Ingrida.

Zak got up and held out his hand to Jeannie, who took it.

'Welcome aboard,' he said.

The two of them stood facing each other and to

Beth it looked as though they were weighing each other up. Zak's offer of his hand seemed an artificial gesture, but she supposed he did it to try to draw Jeannie into their team. And maybe Jeannie took it because it was part of an act she was putting on. But that was only her guess. She didn't know Jeannie. She didn't know Ingrida either, but she did feel closer to her. There was something about her that gave reassurance and invited trust. Beth thought she must be an excellent nurse.

But time was passing. 'We have to save Cameron before it's too late,' she said. 'Ingrida, can you get us into the clinic?'

There followed half an hour of questions. What time are the operations scheduled for? When will they start to prep Cameron? How many people will be involved? Who? What part will Ingrida be expected to play? What can Jeannie do? ...and so on. Ingrida had to go on duty at twelve, Jeannie's shift would begin at two. Two nurses would already have begun the prep by the time Ingrida arrived. She would be the senior and would take over supervision of the final arrangements. The other nurses would expect this. Dr Salamar was likely to be in and out all the time. Ingrida gave a brief sketch of Salamar: cold, businesslike, and very sharp. She was in overall charge and would be present at both the removal and the transplant, which would be carried out by two of the staff surgeons. The whole procedure would be under the strict gaze of the clinic's security team and monitored through cameras.

Then Beth asked the question that had been

gnawing at her insides since they arrived in Scotland. She spoke so quietly it was difficult for the others to hear her. 'How is Cameron?' she said. 'How bad is he?'

Ingrida shook her head and looked grave. 'He's lost a kidney. It was done properly. It was done well, the surgeons here are good. If he had been a voluntary donor and that was all he was giving you would say the operation had been a success and he could soon go home. But they've kept him heavily sedated and he's very weak.'

'Can he walk?' said Zak.

Ingrida shook her head and looked at the carpet.

Zak thought for a long time, leaning forward in his chair, his legs crossed, his chin resting on the heel of his hand. Then he got up and stood in front of them. 'Right,' he said, 'here's what we'll do.'

29

'WE HAVE to get into the clinic, and once we're in there we have to be able to move about without anyone taking any notice of us. So first things first. Jeannie, how do we get inside the building?'

It was Ingrida who answered. 'I can do that,' she said. 'I'll go in, sign on for my shift, and check that everything on the coast is clear. When it is I'll let the rest of you in behind me.'

'It won't be all of us,' said Zak. 'Just Beth, Archy and me to start with. We'll need ID of some sort.'

'Jeannie can do that,' said Ingrida.

'Can you?' said Zak to Jeannie.

'Yes, sure,' said Jeannie.

The reply had come readily enough, but to Beth it didn't ring true. Zak caught her eye. He wasn't convinced either.

'Good,' said Zak. 'Now, if we're to pass more or less unnoticed we'll need uniforms.'

'I can get those,' said Ingrida. 'There are plenty of sets of scrubs. While I get them Jeannie can do the IDs.'

'Sounds good,' said Zak. 'Okay, the next step is to deal with the security system. That's your department, Archy. What do you think?'

'It's probably fairly standard but I won't know for sure until I can take a look at it.'

'It's a system made by a firm called Shroud,' Jeannie answered. 'I don't know much about it but the user name and password are easy: "admin" and "ABC123" followed by the dollar sign.'

'That sounds too simple,' Zak said. 'I'd have expected something much more elaborate for a place as sensitive as this.'

'It's the default the engineers left when they installed the system,' Jeannie explained. 'They said we could change it for something harder to get into but nobody's bothered to do that.'

'Right,' said Zak. 'What then, Archy?'

'I think the key thing is to get the first floor cameras fixed so that they don't track us as we move Cameron out of his room and into the lift. I'll need to get into the system to do that. While we're getting ready I'll look up this Shroud stuff online and see what I can find out. It'll just be the first floor. There's no point interfering with the cameras in the rest of the building.'

'You need to watch out for Salamar,' said Jeannie. 'She's like Folken but with more balls, and she's around a lot. Folken stays in his office all the time and doesn't see much but Salamar is everywhere.'

'Thanks for the tip,' said Zak. 'Solomon is going to make sure that Folken is kept busy and he might be able to draw in this woman too.'

'I'll try,' said Solomon. 'Me and Draven have plenty to put on scumbag Folken's plate. When he's eaten what we're gonna give him he won't be in any state to interfere with anybody.'

'What are you going to do with the cameras?' said Beth. 'You can't turn them off or whoever's job it is to keep an eye on them will see straight away that there's something wrong.'

'I'll fix them so that they replay random sequences from what they've recorded over the last few hours. That way if somebody just glances at the monitors they'll look as if they're working. It's cheap and dirty because the time stamps will be all over the place and that will be a dead giveaway, but it should be enough. It would take more time than we've got to do anything better.'

'It is what it is,' said Zak. 'Next is what we do when you've fixed the system. When you, Beth, and me are all kitted out with uniforms and ID, Ingrida will take us up to Cameron's room. Jeannie, we're relying on you to get a message to the porters who have been assigned to move Cameron to the theatre. Tell them they're not needed after all. Their replacements will be Archy and me.'

'There may be a guard on Cameron's room,' said Ingrida.

'You'll have to get rid of him,' said Zak. 'Tell him to go.'

'What if he won't go?' Ingrida said.

Zak shrugged. 'He'll go. Will there be anyone else?'

'There'll be the nurses preparing him for the theatre. I will tell them that Beth is the client's own nurse who's come with her, and that she and I will take over and they're not wanted.'

'Will they go along with that?' said Archy.

Ingrida nodded. 'I think that given the chance of a couple of hours off they will run away very fast.'

Zak smiled. 'Good. In that case it's best if once we're in Cameron's room nobody talks. You've got a sweet voice, young Beth, but your accent is north of England, not Buenos Aires. While you're dealing with Cameron, Gunner will be collecting an ambulance from where they park them at the back of the building and bringing it round to the front so we can load Cameron straight in. Our job – Beth, Archy, Ingrida and me – is to get him in there with whatever gubbins he needs to keep him alive until we can get him to a proper hospital.'

There was a long silence while they digested the plan they'd worked out. It was rough and ready. There was so much that could go wrong. The genuine porters might not obey the message from Jeannie to stand down. She wasn't, after all, their direct boss. Archy might not be able to fix the surveillance cameras and all their movements would be relayed to McIntyre in the main security office. Zak and Archy might be challenged. Salamar or one of the other medics might come in to check on Cameron in the middle of what they were doing. There might not be an ambulance conveniently parked in the yard at the rear for Gunner to take. But Beth was relieved. Things were happening and her friend might soon be safe. She felt a slight lifting of the sense of dread that had swamped her ever since he was taken. Hang on in there, she said in her head to him, we're coming to get you. She concentrated hard on the message, willing Cameron to receive it and be comforted.

'What about Jonas?' said Archy.

'He'd better keep well clear in case somebody recognises him,' said Zak.

'I need him for my meeting with Folken,' said Solomon. 'When I'm done with him there he can join Gunner.'

'It will be good to have someone else at the door in case there's trouble. By that time it won't matter if he's seen,' said Zak.

'Looks like we have a plan,' said Solomon.

30

Dr Hans Folken was going through his emails. 'At last,' he said, clicking to open the one he'd been waiting for. It was from 'FO' and told him that the month's accounts were ready for him to review. The FO – Finance Officer – did the grunt work of day-to-day entering and overseeing the company's financial dealings, but Folken insisted on receiving regular updates. Naturally he was interested in the health of the business, but it was also because he didn't trust anyone.

He was pleased with the figures he saw. Six months ago he had renegotiated the NHGD contract on the grounds that the population had grown and that meant more work. The Department of Health and the Treasury had been difficult but he'd insisted and in the end they'd had no choice but to agree. That was because although the contract clearly stated that the data belonged to the government and not to Aurora, it didn't take a genius to figure out that it would be simple to make copies, and that these could be sold for a great deal of money. After all, the undersecretary who'd been conducting the negotiations for the government had said, that's what he would do. The directors had been pleased at the news of the improved arrangements, and Folken had been awarded a bonus.

He was looking forward to updating Anita when they talked that evening. Not that she was interested in the money he made. She liked spending it, though. She loved the designer clothes and the jewellery, the beach house and the 5 star hotels, the executive travel and all the other perks that being with him brought. However, she considered it vulgar to discuss money and told Folken as much whenever he raised the subject of their assets. It was the same attitude that had squandered the fortune that her aristocratic family had once possessed. But she was his wife, and Folken insisted that she had a right to know so he persevered. Another reason was that he was proud of the financial empire he was building, and he wanted her to admire it, and him.

He made a clicking noise with his tongue, a mannerism that indicated he was irritated by these thoughts, and he navigated to another place, to accounts that his Finance Officer didn't know about. They were dark and anonymous, and he'd been assured that they were impossible to hack into; they were where the real money was.

Yes, Aurora was doing well but Folken was not yet

rich in the way that many of his clients were. People like Ivanovitch were in the Premier League, whereas he was still in a lower division. But he was getting there. Soon after he'd bought his house on Grand Cayman he'd joined a golf club, the one that people told him had the highest prestige. He'd chosen the Cayman Islands in preference to some of the other sunny places where he might have purchased property because of the Cayman Government's encouragement of the financial industry and its relaxed approach to taxation. He reckoned that the golf club was the right place for meeting people it would be useful to know, and he was right. Several of those he met were in finance and their main, no, their only topic of conversation was making money.

He got to know one of them in particular who enthused about the advantages of investing with his bank. To open an account required an eye-watering initial deposit. The only way Folken could raise enough was by transferring every single one of his assets, and even then he'd had to raise a loan on his London house. He'd hesitated about entrusting all his money to this one company but it had turned out to be a spectacularly successful decision. The rate of return had been phenomenal. All he had to do was structure the fees charged by Aurora so that only a portion went to the company and the substantial remainder was paid directly into his own Cayman account. It was an easy enough matter to arrange, given the type of client that Aurora attracted.

As well as that, since meeting his Cayman friend Folken had been slowly unloading his shareholding in Aurora, a little at a time so as not to attract any notice.

The worldwide monopoly on linking transplants to a huge genome databank, which had been the exclusive province of Aurora, was changing. There was a set-up in China that was operating in a very similar way. It had rapidly outgrown Aurora and had been so successful that the procession of Chinese clients that had once made a great deal of work for the Aberdeen clinic had totally dried up. It was only a matter of time before the Chinese extended their reach and established themselves in other places, and that would take more traffic away from Aurora.

That wasn't the only issue. The organ transplant scene itself was changing. There was still a huge demand but it was becoming possible to meet it in other ways. Not long ago a team in the USA had implanted a man with a heart taken from a pig. On another front, a lab in Israel had been working on 3D printing a heart. At first they hadn't been able to produce one that would actually beat – 'A fairly important requirement of a heart, don't you think?' Salamar had said in a rare burst of humour. However, six months ago they'd managed it, and the printed heart had been implanted in a chimpanzee; so far the animal was doing well. A machine, or a room full of them, which could manufacture not only hearts, but lungs, livers, kidneys, and perhaps even eyes, ears, noses, bones, whole limbs... the vision was mind-boggling. Sooner or later, and Folken thought probably sooner, Aurora's business model would become obsolete. It was time to get out, and he was doing just that.

As he said to Anita, 'It's amazing how easy it is to make highly profitable investments when you have a lot to start with. That's why the poor stay poor and why, on the whole, the rich stay rich.' Anita hadn't been interested but told him that the regular transfer to her private account was inadequate; he'd increased it.

The buzz on the intercom on his desk was an unwelcome intrusion. He jabbed the button.

'Yes.'

'I have Mr Adebayo here to see you, Director.'

Was it really time for that already? He looked at his gold Patek Philippe wristwatch. Eleven o'clock. The computer clock confirmed it. Where had the time gone? Part of him regretted that he'd allowed this appointment to go ahead. But money was money, and according to his enquiries Mr Adebayo had a lot of it.

'Thank you, Julie. Show him in.'

A moment later the door opened and Julie stood back for the visitors. Solomon and Draven entered the room. Folken was startled. The two men didn't so much enter his office as take possession of it. It was a large room but they seemed to fill it.

'Joshua Adebayo,' said Solomon, gripping Folken's hand tightly. 'This is my personal assistant, Mr Patience Alibi.' Draven didn't offer his hand but bowed his head towards the Director. Even with his head bent he was considerably taller than Folken, who was wondering what they fed them on in Nigeria.

'Please, be seated,' he said to his guests. Solomon/Joshua chose the chair that had its back to the sunlight streaming through the office window. Draven/Patience sat beside him and got out a notepad. Folken was forced to take the position looking into the light. That was inconvenient and not the way he'd wanted to arrange it, but he assumed it was accidental. These two men wouldn't have the sophistication to engineer him into a position which favoured them at his expense.

'Gentlemen,' said Folken, 'welcome to Aurora. Will you accept refreshment of some kind? Coffee? Tea? A glass of one of our excellent highland whiskies?'

Solomon declined. Draven too, although he'd brightened at the mention of whisky and looked as though he would have liked to accept.

Solomon had arranged the meeting before they left Leeds. His intention was to get into the same room as Folken and confront him with what he'd done to Jonas. Punishment was required, and Zak had given him some priceless information and told him how to use it. He had no doubt that what he was going to do to Mr Director Folken would prove to be life-changing.

Casually he glanced at the security monitor on the side wall of the room. It was flicking between the cameras in the clinic, staying a few seconds with each. White coats here and there, someone mopping a floor, everything looked as you'd expect. He glanced at his watch, making sure Folken noticed the glint of gold. If all was going well the others should be in the building by now. He hoped they succeeded in getting Cameron out, but whether they did or not he was determined that the day would not end without Folken being very sorry indeed for what had been done to Solomon's son.

31

THE FIRST PART of Zak's plan was going well. Nobody was around when they approached the staff entrance to the clinic and Ingrida got them inside without any problems. Beth, Zak and Archy huddled in a cupboard while she found uniforms for them. All three changed together in the tight little closet into blue scrubs, caps and plastic aprons. Ingrida inspected Beth and told her to take out her ear studs and remove her rings.

'Perfect,' she said. 'You look very convincing.'

'Made for it,' said a Scottish voice behind her. It was Jeannie with their ID tags. They were labelled *Temporary Staff*. 'They should really have photos and proper labels but they're better than nothing. What's next?'

'Archy needs to fix the security cameras,' said Ingrida.

'Okay, come with me.' Jeannie led Archy away. Zak couldn't suppress a feeling of suspicion as he watched them go. Ingrida had said that Jeannie had worked at the clinic since it opened. What had made her now turn against her employer?

'Zak, please stay here until Archy gets back,' said Ingrida. 'Then you can come up with him and be the porters who are collecting Cameron. Beth, follow me.'

Beth's heart was racing as she followed Ingrida up the stairs to floor one. She was expecting at any moment to be confronted by the Salamar woman, who according to the description Ingrida had given was a cross between Cruella de Vil and a Gorgon, but they met no one.

As they got to the landing Beth was dizzy with dread. Cameron was close. She didn't feel his pain but she could sense his fear, and her whole body was shaking as she followed Ingrida towards room 5. She was always nervous before a big game but she would be all right as soon as she ran out onto the pitch. She hoped the same thing would happen here. She clenched her teeth and told herself to get a grip.

Ingrida was right about the differences between the two sections of the clinic. The donor area was clean and there was a strong smell of disinfectant, but it was also stark and cold. As they passed the other wing a door opened and Beth glimpsed a softly lit passage, plush and carpeted, which wouldn't have been out of place in a top hotel. The nurse who came out acknowledged Ingrida with a smile and looked curiously at Beth. Ingrida smiled back and paused for a moment.

'How are things going in there?' she asked the nurse.

'Salamar is supervising the final prep now and the theatre staff are scrubbing up.'

'Good. I'm on my way to room 5 to check that the donor is ready.'

'We must hurry,' Ingrida said to Beth when the nurse had gone. 'It sounds as though Salamar is busy at the moment but when she's done she'll come to get Cameron. We don't have long.'

The corridor Ingrida led Beth to was blinding white, with a row of numbered doors on one side and opposite them an entrance headed *Operating Theatres*, words which triggered in Beth all sorts of gruesome imaginings of what she thought went on in them.

Ingrida stopped outside a door labelled with a large figure 5. 'Ready?' she said.

Beth nodded, although she was by no means ready. She was a tangle of emotions: desperate to see Cameron, fearful of what she might find behind the door, in knots at the possibility that their mission might fail.

'Try not to look at him,' Ingrida whispered. 'Keep your face out of sight. I know it will be hard, but if he's at all conscious and he recognises you we don't know how he might react. It could make problems for us. Here, put this on.'

She handed Beth a face mask, and put one on herself. I may hide my face, thought Beth, but he'll know I'm here. She took a deep breath. Ingrida opened the door and she followed her into the room.

Two nurses were beside the bed, hiding the figure on it. Beth registered a sharp, antiseptic smell, tubes, screens, a soft electronic purring. She was desperate to see Cameron, to see how well – or ill – he was, but she turned away and made herself busy, fiddling with something at the sink. Out of the corner of her eye she saw Ingrida take a datapad from its cradle at the foot of the bed and study it for a moment. Then she spoke to the nurses.

'He's ready?'

'Aye, just about,' one of them replied.

'Has he been assessed?'

'Dr Bryce has been in about the anaesthetic,' the other nurse said. 'He's a bit worried about the patient's blood pressure. It's all over the place.'

'He shouldn't bother,' said the first nurse. 'In a couple of hours he won't have any blood pressure to worry about.'

The second nurse laughed uncertainly and Ingrida gave them both a sharp look. Beth felt such a mixture of horror, fear and despair that she almost choked. She wanted to scratch out the eyes of the nurse who had spoken so casually about what they were planning to do to Cameron. She couldn't help gulping noisily, and had to hide it by turning it into a cough.

'You two can go now,' said Ingrida. 'This is Stella, the recipient's personal carer. We'll take over the rest of it.'

'But Dr Salamar said we were to stay until she came back with the porters,' the second nurse, the one who'd made the crack about Cameron's blood pressure, protested.

'Dr Salamar is on her way. So are the porters. Stella and I will wait for them. You may go,' Ingrida said firmly.

The first nurse was keen to leave but the second one hesitated. Just then they heard noises in the corridor, the door opened and Zak and Archy came in. They were in full surgical scrubs, including face masks. They nodded to Beth and Ingrida but gave no sign of recognition.

There were now six people plus the bedridden Cameron in the small room. 'Off you go,' said Ingrida to the nurses. 'It's getting crowded in here and I need room to move.'

'As you like,' said nurse one.

'I know when I'm not wanted,' said nurse two, and they both left.

Only then did Beth turn to see Cameron. She almost fainted at the sight and Zak had to steady her. Her friend was unconscious. He looked awful: his face was the colour of milk and he was on his back. His eyes were closed and he was breathing slowly through a tube into his mouth. A screen showed the rhythmic spikes of his heartbeat, and on the far side of the bed some sort of electronic machine whirred and clicked. Ingrida put her hand on Cameron's forehead and brushed the hair away from his eyes. Beth was trying hard not to cry.

'How is he?' Zak asked, putting his arm around Beth's shoulder and giving her a gentle squeeze.

'He's not good,' said Ingrida. 'We need to get him to a hospital where he can be cared for properly.'

'Will he be all right?' said Beth, dreading what she thought might be the answer.

'There's no reason why he won't recover if he gets the right treatment. For the next few days he'll need plenty of fluids, and he'll have to be monitored for the possibility of infection.'

Zak released Beth's shoulder. 'We'd best get him out of here, then,' he said.

32

FOLKEN WAS PLEASED with the way the meeting was going, although it was taking longer than he would have liked. Adebeyo seemed to have endless questions, and his assistant must have been told to write down every answer because he frequently interrupted to clarify a term, a figure or some other detail. Folken wondered why he didn't simply record the meeting on his phone so he could go over it afterwards. Despite this annoyance he gave his usual polished presentation, larded with smooth assurances, and the client seemed impressed. It was time to move on, time to close the deal.

'Of course,' the Director said, 'I am unable to confirm the exact fee for the procedure until my people have had the opportunity to examine your wife and determine the treatment necessary. That will involve her spending a little time here so we can assess her needs and establish in detail what must be done. When do you think it would be convenient to you to arrange this?'

Mr Adebeyo, or Solomon, looked puzzled and his assistant looked up from his scribbling. 'Pardon?'

Folken sighed inwardly. What he was saying wasn't that difficult. 'Before we can go any further my staff will need to review your wife's medical condition and carry out tests so that we can identify a suitable donor. That must be done here, in our clinic. To get things started it would be helpful to have access to her medical records.'

'My wife?' said Solomon, looking even more perplexed.

'Yes, Mr Adebeyo, your wife' said Folken. 'He was becoming irritated and starting to wonder if Adebeyo was in fact all there.

'Oh, it's not my wife who has the problem,' said Solomon. 'It's my son.'

Folken frowned. Surely not. He looked at the information he'd taken down during his initial conversation with Adebeyo. He'd definitely written 'wife', and noted a history of ongoing problems with her liver and pancreas. He readjusted himself in his chair. 'Forgive me, Mr Adebeyo, I am sure it was your wife we discussed. I have it here.' He held up his note, although Solomon couldn't have read it from where he was sitting.

'No, no, no, no, no,' said Solomon, shaking his head. 'The problem concerns my son.'

There was a long silence. Folken couldn't

290

understand what was going on. He looked at his papers again. Had he got the wrong client? No, of course not, he didn't make mistakes like that. He was aware of Adebeyo and his assistant watching him. He'd had a funny feeling about the man from the beginning. Although he couldn't put his finger on it there had been something from the very start that hadn't seemed quite right. But he'd searched for Adebayo online and he'd checked out. Joseph Adebayo, founder and owner of Tiger Oil, Nigeria. Wife Melissa. Homes in Lagos, Cape Town and Miami. He looked at the print out of what he'd learnt, a brief biography and a photograph of a distinguished looking black man. Was the individual sitting opposite him the same? He certainly looked it. What Folken didn't know was that after Solomon had created the character of Joseph Adebayo, his friend Zak had spent most of one night planting seeds in nooks and crannies all over the internet in locations where Google would be sure to find them.

Solomon spoke again. 'I'll tell you what, Dr Folken' he said, and Folken thought he detected a sneer in his tone, 'I think it would be best if you met my son. Then you can see for yourself the problem we have here. In fact I think you should meet him right now.' He slipped a minipad from his pocket and stroked the screen.

A moment later Folken's door opened and a young man came in. 'This is my son,' said Solomon. 'His name is Jonas Eze. But of course, you already know him.'

Folken's head spun and his colour left him. He looked down and dropped a trembling hand beside the chair towards the concealed button that would summon security, but before he could touch it Draven sprang forward and seized his wrist. It felt like a metal claw. Folken looked at the young man who had just come in and now stood before him. He should be dead. If Salamar had done her job properly he would be. If McIntyre's disposal crew hadn't been so hopeless, he would be. But he was very much alive, and looking at him with an expression of pure hatred.

Solomon leant forward in his chair and fixed Folken with a steady gaze. His voice was chillingly calm. 'Now, Mr Director Folken, I want you to take a good look at my son, Jonas, here. You have done him wrong, great wrong. How are we going to put that right?'

There was a long pause. Folken couldn't meet Solomon's eye, or Jonas's. He looked at the carpet, trying to ignore the pain of Draven's grip. If he could only reach the panic button he could get help, but it was impossible to move.

You don't know?' said Solomon. 'Well I can think of several ways. Let's start now.'

Folken began to tremble.

33

IN THE END Jeannie supposed it came down to who was likely to be her best bet for her future.

She liked Solomon. He seemed a nice guy and he was certainly well off. Helping him might be a good move, but could she rely on him? She had only known him a couple of days. If he managed to get this young man out of the clinic and it was all over he might be briefly appreciative of what Jeannie had done, but what form would that take? And how long would it last?

Then there was the boy's girlfriend, Beth. She liked her too, and she felt sorry for her because she was clearly ripped up by what was happening to her man. But apart from feeling good from helping her there was nothing to be gained there.

Archy – was that his name – was a nothing, but Zak was a different story. He looked like a burnt out rock star yet he was clearly very sharp. More than that, there was something about him. It was as if he had access to a whole load of secrets, things that only he knew about and that could bring rewards; but it was all so vague, nothing definite. Besides, she was pretty sure he didn't like her.

She was on the payroll of Aurora and she'd done well with them. The company was successful and it seemed to her that it was likely to carry on being so. There was an apparently endless procession of clients, business stretching way into the future. There never had been a time when there were enough organ donors, and despite things improving following setting up the NHGD, demand still exceeded supply. So those who could afford it jumped the queue; that's what anyone with any sense and enough money would do, and Aurora used its unique position to target donors for them.

In the dark recesses of the night Jeannie sometimes had misgivings about the part she played in snatching young people from various parts of the country and bringing them here against their will to have nameless things done to them. It was completely at odds with the values she'd been brought up with. These youthful donors were innocents. The young man they'd extracted last week, Jonas had seemed pleasant, friendly, and he was good-looking in a chubby sort of way. Her evangelical mother would have called what she was doing Satan's work. She could hear her now: 'Jeannie Wallace, you're blazing yourself a path straight to Hell.' Yet working for Aurora was a good job, and she didn't believe in the afterlife. For most of the time she succeeded in thinking of the targets as objects, commodities with a price tag attached.

Her job was a good one. She knew Folken rated her, and he was a successful man. He drove – or rather was driven in – a Bentley. He had a big house near Inverurie and, they said, an even bigger one in London. Vernon, another of the clinic's security team, had once driven him down there and he said it was a massive place defended like Fort Knox. Folken went on foreign holidays; he was tanned; he wore a flash wristwatch and gold rings; his wife looked like a screen star. Jeannie liked him. He took care of his people, he didn't bother them, and when he did leave his office to walk around the clinic it wasn't an inspection; it was like being visited by your uncle. Only the other day he'd taken her aside and hinted that he might have a new job for her. She'd hoped he'd been thinking about her boss, McIntyre, who was getting close to retirement. Instead he'd asked her if she liked children. That had been a surprise, and odd because he didn't have any children. She knew there was a branch of Aurora that dealt with surrogacy, but surely it couldn't be that. Whatever, Folken clearly thought highly of her and had in mind something which would be to her advantage.

The only problem at work was Salamar, who was a different proposition. She was everywhere and into everything, and if things weren't to her liking she could be a real bitch. Still, it wasn't too difficult to keep out of her way.

There was one complication that trumped all the others, and it was a recent one: Ingrida and her crazy impulse to save the boy Jonas. She ought to report the whole affair to McIntyre, but that would definitely mean an end to the relationship with Ingrida. Would she mind that? Ingrida was a great girl. She was good fun, terrific looking, sexy, and they shared many interests, but there were lots more fish in the sea, male as well as female.

It would be best to stick with the devil she knew. Now would be a good time to earn a bit of gratitude from the powers that be. Jeannie Wallace, Head of Security. It sounded good. It could be.

She picked up the internal phone and dabbed McIntyre's number.

'Oh, hi boss. It's Jeannie. Have you got a minute? Yes, it's very important. Yes, it is urgent.'

34

FOLKEN FROZE IN HIS SEAT. He couldn't have moved anyway. The steel claw on his arm was excruciating. There was a second panic button under the edge of his desk. If he could just reach that...

The hand tightened even more, and at the same time he was jerked back. He let out a yelp of pain. The man he had been told was called Adebayo rose and crossed the room to him. He bent down, his face uncomfortably close.

'Well my-oh-my, Mr Folken. You look like a man who has seen a ghost. Anybody would think you were looking at a dead man.'

Folken felt as though his bones were being crushed. He could hardly speak. 'I don't know what you mean,' he said in a voice that sounded feeble even to him.

'Oh, I think you do, Mr Director. I really think you do.' Solomon took a chair and placed it directly in front of Folken. He nodded to Draven, who released his grip.

The Director grimaced and rubbed his arm, trying to massage some feeling back.

'You and me,' Solomon went on, 'we've got some settling up to do. You tried to kill my boy. So how are we going to deal with that?'

Folken licked his lips. His mouth was dry and he felt sick. 'I'm sorry. It was an error. My staff mistook your son for someone else. We meant him no harm. As soon as we found out he wasn't who we thought we let him go.'

Solomon's jaw tightened and his fists clenched. When he spoke his voice was taut, as if he was fighting hard to control his anger.

'Meant him no harm? You filled him full of drugs and threw him out on a freezing night. Meant him no harm? I don't think so.' He bent forward again. 'We know what you do here, Mr Director Folken. We know all about your business.' He looked at Jonas, who was still standing just inside the door, where he had been since he first came in. 'How do you think we should settle this score, son?'

Jonas took a couple of steps forward. 'I think we should call Zak's friend, Molly.'

At the mention of the name Folken looked startled, then puzzled, then horrified. He couldn't mean *that* Molly. How could they know?

'Call Molly,' Solomon echoed thoughtfully. 'Yes, I think we should do that very thing.' He went back to the chair he'd been sitting in and took a datapad from his brief case. He flipped up the screen and stood it on

Folken's desk where the Director could see it. He dabbed the control pad and there she was. Folken's heart sank as he recognised Molly Hunter.

'Molly, my lady. How are you doing?' said Solomon to the screen.

'I'm fine, thank you Solomon. Just fine.'

'Zak has told you about the little problem we have here and he said you would help us.'

'I'll be very pleased to do that.'

'Thank you. Now, Zak gave you something. Would you hold it up?' The screen was small, but it was easy to see what she had in her hand. It was a hypodermic syringe. 'Excellent,' said Solomon. 'Now please tell Mr Director Folken what you've got in that little spike you have there.'

'Certainly Solomon. It's filled with Aphthamilase.'

Folken's expression turned to one of horror.

'Aphthamilase, you say. And what is that?'

'I'm not a scientist myself,' Molly said, 'but Zak told me that it's a mixture of an induction agent and a cytotoxin.'

Solomon nodded. 'Now, my sweet Molly, tell me and tell the Director here what it is that this mixture does.'

Folken was looking sick. He knew very well what Aphthamilase was.

Molly smiled. She'd been preparing for this, looking forward to it. 'Induction agents are used to bring on labour, perhaps when a mother is late and her doctors want to deliver her baby. In

Aphthamilase the agent is combined with a special cytotoxin. Cytotoxins kill cells. This one targets the foetus.'

'So if you inject yourself with that stuff, what will it do?'

'It's used for abortions. If I take it, within twenty four hours I'll have a miscarriage. My womb will contract and the baby will be born, but the cytotoxins will by then have killed him. He will be dead.'

Solomon allowed a silence for the impact of what Molly was saying to sink in.

Folken was as white as the sheet of paper on his desk. 'You wouldn't do it,' he whispered. 'I know this drug. It's used for abortions, yes, but it's also used for sterilisations. If you take it you'll never be able to conceive again. Your life as a surrogate mother will be over.' His voice was growing stronger as he spoke. There was no way she would do what she was threatening. It would be the end of her livelihood. She could do nothing else, and without the surrogacy payments how would she live? 'You won't do it,' he concluded.

Molly leaned towards the datapad at her end so that her face filled the screen on Folken's desk. 'Oh yes I will. This baby, your son, was going to be my last one anyway. If I'm sterile the temptation to host yet another will be gone. It will be a relief to be off the treadmill.'

'So you see,' said Solomon, 'we got us a situation here. You aimed to kill my boy. Now I'm aiming to kill yours. I think that's fair, don't you? Question is, what happens next? My boy was saved by a third party, a pretty nurse. Who've you got to save your boy?'

So that was it, thought Folken. It wasn't a slip up by Salamar or the Undertaker that had led to the Eze boy being still alive. It was the nurse, that Lithuanian whore. She probably fancied him and that was all it took. Well, she'll be sorry, he'll make sure of that. But first he must avert the present threat. He would buy Molly off. She'd already had a large sum from him and was due more when the baby was delivered. Was there no end to the greed of these people? Aloud he said, 'All right, you win. I'll pay.'

Solomon laughed. 'Oh yes, you'll certainly do that. You'll pay a great deal, but there's something else too. Tell him, Molly.'

Molly made him wait, as if she was working something out, weighing things up. Then she said. 'You have a young man in your clinic, no more than a boy really. His name is Cameron. Is that right?'

'What about him?'

'Well, this will come as a surprise. The Cameron you have there is my son.'

Folken felt as though some inner part of him had just fallen away. How could this be?

'I'll do a trade,' said Molly. 'You let my son go, and I'll bring your unborn son to term.'

'A boy for a boy for a boy,' said Solomon. 'Kinda neat, huh?'

'Oh my God.' Folken felt as though everything of any substance had been snatched away from him and he was in free fall. He shook his head. 'But he's lost a kidney, he's not fit to be moved.'

Without speaking Solomon took the phone from its cradle on the desk and handed it to him. Solomon's look said it all. It told him that he must make one call and one call only. It also told him to be careful what he said. On the datapad screen Molly raised her shirt and held the hypodermic poised over the dome of her belly.

In a daze Folken took the phone and dabbed the image of Salamar. He tried to sound as natural as he could but his voice was thin.

'Dr Salamar? We have a change of plan. I want you to prepare the boy in room 5 for discharge. I have some data that suggests he's not suitable for any further donations. We'll send him to the Royal Infirmary for recovery.'

Folken paused and there was silence in the room. Solomon could hear the distant voice of Salamar. She was obviously raising objections but he couldn't hear her words. He watched Folken carefully, on the lookout for any tricks. Draven stood behind Folken, his hand resting on the man's shoulder. It could snatch away the phone in an instant. It could lock on the Director's throat.

'Yes, I know,' said Folken into the phone. 'You'll have to delay the procedure. We'll find an alternative donor. Yes, well stand them down. Something unexpected has cropped up. I'll explain it all later... I know... Yes, I know it will, but it has to be done now.'

Solomon held out his hand and meekly Folken

handed the phone back to him. He returned it to the cradle.

Folken looked at the screen. Molly still held the needle. 'I've done what you wanted,' he said, weakly. 'You can put that away now.'

There was a long pause while Molly held Folken's gaze. Then she said, 'I'll put this away when I hear that Cameron is out of your cesspit and safely in the local hospital. Until then it stays right here at my side.'

Folken looked to Solomon, but if he was hoping for support he was disappointed.

'Okay,' said Solomon. 'Now for the paying bit.'

35

McIntyre had been expecting Jeannie Wallace and had been looking forward to it because he had a soft spot for her, so he was both surprised and disappointed when it was Salamar who came through his door.

'My God, woman, you look like thunder. What's the matter?'

Salamar pushed past him and flopped down on a chair, brushing the hair out of her eyes. McIntyre wanted her out. He didn't know what Jeannie wanted to see him about but he certainly didn't want Salamar there when she arrived. She'd told him she had something important to say, important and urgent. Salamar was far too fond of pushing her nose into security matters and he didn't want her involved in this, whatever it was.

She seemed determined to stay. From her body language McIntyre could see that this was one of those rare occasions when they would have to suppress their dislike of each other in the face of something bigger.

'It's Folken,' she said. 'I think he's gone out of his mind.'

'The Director? Why?'

'He's just phoned through. He wants the boy in room 5 discharged, the one whose kidney we harvested last night. The one whose lung we're taking today. He wants him transferred to the Royal Infirmary.'

McIntyre shrugged. It didn't seem a big deal to him. His job was to stop those who were on the donor side leaving and to safeguard those in the clients' suites. That, and to organise the teams which snatched new donors and, when they'd served their purpose and the Undertaker had done her work, dispose of them. He was irked that if Folken had decided to get rid of the Cameron boy he hadn't been called, it was his job, but these things happen.

'It's ridiculous,' Salamar continued. 'The woman scheduled to receive his lung has been prepared for surgery. And he was telling me only this morning that we have clients for the liver and heart and that there would be a further harvest. Now he wants to get rid of him. Why?'

McIntyre shrugged again. 'Plans change,' he said. 'Maybe something has cropped up to make this donor unsuitable, like the last one. Or maybe these new clients have taken a look at what the fees are and had a rethink.'

Salamar regarded him sceptically. 'Really? You

know as well as I do that donor targets are never released alive. Either we take all their usable organs, which kills them, or we terminate them, dispose of the bodies, and delete the public records.' Her expression hardened. 'Always assuming that can be managed.'

'Now look, if you're referring to the Eze boy that was nothing to do with security. If the medical side had made sure he was properly dead before he was handed over to us there would have been no problem.'

This was a row that would simmer for a long time, but for now Salamar shook her head and held up her hand in a gesture of truce. She didn't know why she had brought it up. She really didn't want to argue with McIntyre, not at this moment.

'It's complete madness,' she said. 'If the boy in room 5 is discharged he'll start talking about what's happened to him. This facility requires absolute secrecy. If word gets out about what we do here, we're finished.' She didn't need to add that there was a good chance that some of them would go to prison. She and McIntyre were among those most at risk of that; Folken would be long gone.

'I expect the Director has something in mind,' McIntyre said. 'Perhaps he'll pay this lad for his missing kidney, and give him something on top to shut him up. He can live without a kidney, and a tidy sum in the bank would probably be enough to keep him quiet.'

'Maybe.' Salamar didn't look convinced. 'He didn't say anything about any payment. Anyway, I think it would take a lot to keep this one quiet. He's a truculent young man. He's been very difficult when he's been conscious, and we've had to keep him sedated most of the time he's been here.'

'Well, can't you give him something to render him harmless?'

Salamar thought for a moment. 'The only thing I can think of that we have here would put him in a permanent coma. It would turn him into a vegetable.'

'Seems an answer to me. Did Folken say anything about doing that?'

'No,' said Salamar. 'But he didn't say we were not to do it.'

McIntyre got up from his desk. He hoped the movement would be a hint to Salamar to leave. Jeannie should have been here by now and he wanted the doctor gone. 'Sounds like that's what you should do, then. If you go and deal with that I'll get some men to shift him and organise the transport. The story for the Infirmary can be that he's a volunteer donor and never recovered from the anaesthetic.'

Salamar didn't like it. 'There'll be all sorts of questions to deal with. Who he is, where he's from, where his family are, all that sort of thing. The Infirmary will dig into his health records. And there'll have to be a full medical report detailing his adverse reaction to the operation.'

'Well can't you do that?'

'Of course I can.' Salamar said briskly, 'but... Oh well.' She shrugged and got up to leave.

'Will he die?' McIntyre asked her at the door.

'Not if we're careful. But he'll need lifelong care. He must have family somewhere, so we can expect that there will be some legal repercussions from them.'

'Well, I should think Folken will have taken all that into account. He's not a man who does things without thinking. The girl who got the boy's kidney is loaded and her dad's a pal of some big names. Perhaps he's in on keeping things quiet.'

'It might need more than money and influence,' said Salamar.

McIntyre sighed. This woman was hard work. 'You deal with the medical stuff, the reports, the records, whatever it needs, and leave the rest to me. I'll create a new identity for him. Give me a few hours to get into the National Register and sort out the documentation, and nobody will be able to tell who the fuck he really is. The background will be that he has no family, he's just a drifter, a lad off the streets who came to us and offered a kidney for money.'

Salamar was still not convinced, but Folken's orders left her no choice. She would have to make sure that the boy's brain was properly wiped, though.

As she left she passed Jeannie Wallace.

36

THEIR FIRST TASK was to disconnect the equipment that was monitoring Cameron's condition, and Ingrida set about it straight away. She didn't say anything to the others but she was worried that it could be hooked up to a security system and tampering with it would trigger a siren. She threw the switch and waited. There was no signal, no sound of other nurses or security guards rushing along the corridor, simply silence as the purring and clicking stopped.

Cameron was heavily sedated and he didn't seem to be aware of anything around him. Ingrida bent forward and very carefully removed the tube from his mouth. This was the next hurdle. How well would he manage to breath on his own? There was an anxious wait as the tube came out and she turned off the valve on the wall. All was well. There was no interruption in the rise and fall of his chest.

Beth stood beside Ingrida. She wanted to help but

she didn't know what to do. She couldn't take her eyes off the drawn face on the bed. Zak and Archy waited in the background.

'So far, so good,' said Ingrida.

Next she reached down and unhooked a bag of urine, disconnected it from the tube emerging from under the bedcover, sealed it and placed it in the sink. She took a new bag from the cupboard, attached it to the end of the tube and nudged it under the covers. She stripped off her latex gloves and dropped them in the bin, then put on a new pair. Finally she turned the clamp to seal off the drip connected to Cameron's hand, grasped his wrist, gently peeled off the plaster and withdrew the needle.

Cameron opened his eyes. His pupils were dilated and they scanned the room sluggishly, searching for meaning. 'Where am I?' he croaked.

Beth jumped forward and took his hand. She kissed his forehead and her eyes welled up. 'Oh Cam,' she said, 'Cam, Cam.'

'Beth?' He smiled weakly up at her, trying to work out what was going on, why his girlfriend was dressed as a nurse, why he felt so awful. For a few moments he looked confused. Then it seemed to flood in on him, where he was, what had happened. He made an effort to sit up but there was no way he could make it.

Beth bent over and hugged him, her cheek wet against his.

'Come on, lovebirds,' said Zak, gently putting a hand on her shoulder and easing her away. He put his face close to Cameron's. 'You're not well, son. Some vile people have done some horrible things to you, but we've fixed them and you're going to be all right. Trust us and hang on in there.' He turned to Archy. 'Come on buddy, time to do your hospital portering thing.' He tapped the brake on the wheel of the bed and eased it away from the wall.

Archy came round to the head of the bed and gave Cameron the gentlest play punch on the shoulder. 'We're going to get you out of here, matey.'

Ingrida opened the door and looked out into the corridor.

'All clear,' she said. 'No one about.'

She held open the door while Zak and Archy manoeuvred the bed out of the room. Beth walked alongside, holding Cameron's hand.

'You shouldn't do that,' Ingrida said.

'Shouldn't do what?' said Beth.

'Hold his hand. If anyone sees you it will look odd, a nurse holding a patient's hand.'

'Surely not. Nurses do that all the time.'

'Not here. Not in the donor wing.'

Beth let go of Cameron's hand.

Zak said, 'If we're seen we're probably screwed anyway.'

Beth took the hand again. She hoped that Jeannie had done her stuff and managed to distract the other security people, and that no one had noticed that the cameras on this floor had been sabotaged.

They reached the end of the corridor and Zak

pressed the button to summon the lift. 'So far so good,' he said.

None of the others said anything. Cameron's eyes had closed and it looked as though he might have lost consciousness again. Ingrida felt his pulse and put her ear to his mouth to listen to his breathing. Beth's face conveyed enquiry and concern.

'He's all right at the moment,' said Ingrida. 'He's strong and he's coping well but the sooner we get him to a proper hospital the better. He needs drugs. The ambulance will be a start; once in that we can connect up his drip again and monitor his heart rate and blood pressure.

The lift seemed to take an age to arrive but at last it did and the doors hissed open. Zak gave the bed a push and Archy guided it in. Ingrida pressed the button for the ground floor and with a gentle hiss the doors slid closed.

'Right, now for the tricky bit,' said Zak.

The lift descended impossibly slowly. They were all tense. Archy was gripping the rail at the head of the bed so tightly that his knuckles had gone white. Beth was alternately biting her lip and gnawing a nail. Ingrida put a hand on her arm and she managed a smile.

'What's going to happen when they find out that Cameron's gone and you helped us? Beth asked.

Ingrida shrugged. 'I'll be gone before they can find me. As soon as you're safely away I'll vanish.'

'But that's your job gone.'

'I was finished here anyway. It is not what I thought it was when I came.'

'And Jeannie?'

Ingrida hesitated. She wasn't sure of Jeannie. She was surprised she'd agreed so readily to help, it hadn't seemed like her. 'Jeannie must do what she will do,' she said. 'I shall go home and marry my boyfriend.'

Everyone held their breath as the lift came to a gentle stop. Suppose the doors parted and they found a security detail waiting for them? But they opened onto an empty space with no one there. They manoeuvred the bed out of the lift and steered it towards the glass doors that gave onto the foyer. On the other side of the foyer, just outside, Beth could see an ambulance backed up to the front entrance. Its rear doors were open and Gunner was standing beside them. Beth breathed a sigh of relief; they were almost there, but still her heart was pounding.

Jeannie had given Zak a card which she said he was to present to the door reader so that they could get out. He held it there now, and that was when things started to unravel. Nothing happened. He slid the card about on the reader. Still nothing. He rubbed it on his overall and offered it to the reader again. The doors remained stubbornly shut.

Beth looked at Zak in panic. 'Something's wrong. What do we do?'

'Smash the fuckers down,' said Archy.

Zak shook his head. 'Not a chance, it's toughened glass. We'll have to find another way out.'

Just then one of the internal doors to the foyer opened and two figures came through. McIntyre was in front, Jeannie behind him. They approached the glass doors and stood on the other side facing them.

McIntyre had a smug smile on his face, and in his hand was a gun.

37

'WHAT DO YOU WANT?' said Folken nervously. 'I'm not a wealthy man. I mean, I have money,' he added in response to Solomon's look of scepticism, 'but I'm not in the same league as most of Aurora's clients.'

'Well let's see,' said Solomon cheerfully. 'Let's see just how rich you are. Jonas, come over here my boy.'

Jonas crossed the room, pulled up a chair beside Folken and swung the computer around to that they could all see it. Solomon took a notebook from his pocket and opened it at a page of information that Zak had given to him. He knew it had taken Zak a long time to prepare it and he had no idea how he'd obtained it; he also knew that if it was correct it was the skewer that would finish the pathetic, red faced, sweating creature who sat facing him.

'Now where shall we start?' Solomon mused. 'How about the Grand Cayman First Bank?'

Folken's colour had returned a little but now it

drained completely. How did this man who had barged into his life only half an hour ago know about that?

Jonas pulled the keyboard towards him and the computer screen came to life. He clicked a few keys and moved the mouse. Then he sat back and looked at his father. 'Ready,' he said.

Folken examined the screen. It was showing the log-in page for the bank's private clients. How had they managed to locate that? It was exclusive. It wasn't listed on the bank's main website. Most people didn't even know it existed, and even if they did come across it access was only obtained by entering biometric data from the account holder.

'Now we come to you,' said Solomon.

Jonas moved aside. Draven seized Folken's chair and pushed it and him into the space which Jonas had vacated. Solomon picked up a tiny box plugged into the computer and held it in front of Folken's face. It was a retina scanner. The Director clamped his eyes closed.

'Oh dear oh dear oh dear,' said Solomon, wearily. 'You've disappointed me, Mr Director.'

'It's all right,' said Draven. 'With his eyes shut like that he won't be able to see Molly inject herself with that stuff.'

Folken blinked involuntarily, he couldn't help it, but it was enough. Solomon was holding the scanner ready and it took only a millisecond to register the pattern of Folken's retina.

'Now for the finger print,' said Solomon.

Folken shook his head and clenched his fists. The

blink had been a reflex, a mistake, but there was no way he was going to provide the print which was the last barrier to getting into his account. Almost all his money was there. Let that stupid woman inject herself if that was what she wanted. He would find another surrogate mother, fertilise another embryo. And if Anita wouldn't provide one he would find another woman who would.

Solomon sighed wearily. He bent down till his face was no more than a hand's-breadth from Folken's. 'Listen, Mr Director,' he said quietly. 'We're going to take your fingerprint. Whether or not your finger is joined onto the rest of your hand when we do that is up to you.'

He suddenly moved very quickly, snatching something from his inside pocket and bringing his arm round in an arc towards the desk. There was a thwack, and Folken saw the thin blade of a wicked looking knife quivering in the highly polished surface. It was such a shock, such an act of barbarism, such a demonstration of this man's power and his willingness to commit violence that Folken let out a cry.

'Now,' said Solomon, 'what will it be? Your finger with your hand? Or just your finger on its own?'

Folken swallowed, and held out his hand. Draven took his wrist to steady the trembling and pressed the print reader to his forefinger.

'We're in,' said Jonas.

'Good,' said Solomon. 'Very, very good. Now that didn't hurt too much, did it?' He looked at the screen.

'My oh my. And here's you saying you're not a rich man.' He gave Folken an elbow nudge which could have been playful but was too rough for that. He opened his brief case and drew out two sheets of paper. One he gave to Jonas, the other he held up to Folken. 'Here in my hand is a list of five charities. Very worthy causes, all of them. They'll be grateful for your generosity, Director Folken, sir. Time to start, don't you think, Jonas?'

The boy nodded, put a sheet of paper in front of Folken on the desk and started to work on the datapad.

Folken was strained and drained, his normally ruddy complexion bloodless. 'But this is a press release,' he said, reading the sheet.

'Yes, isn't it?' said Solomon. 'Jonas is even now sending it to media outlets.'

'But it says I've given five million pounds to each of these five charities.'

'It sure does. What a generous gesture that it. As soon as he's sent the press releases Jonas will make the transfers.'

Folken was horrified. 'But that's twenty-five million pounds!'

Solomon pretended to count on his fingers. 'Uh huh. That's what I make it too.' He looked at Folken pityingly. 'Nothing gets past you, does it Mr Director.'

Folken felt sick. It was the bulk of what was in his accounts. 'You can't do that. I'll tell the police. You'll never get away with it.'

Solomon looked at Draven. 'Well, I guess if

Director Folken is going to tell the police, that finishes it. He obviously doesn't mind that the authorities will then start to ask questions about where such a lot of money has come from. But I expect that all his finances are squeaky clean, so a full frontal forensic tax enquiry won't be a problem for him. And of course, there's the little matter of what you've been doing here. I'm sure the police will be interested in that.'

Folken started to speak but his voice wouldn't work. He cleared his throat, then he said, 'I'll demand the money back.'

'Oh, I don't think you will,' said Solomon. 'You see, this press release has gone to the major dailies and weeklies in England, Wales, Northern Ireland and Scotland, the BBC, ITV, Sky news, Bloomberg, Associated Press and Reuters. We think there'll be international interest in such a generous act, so it's gone to some other agencies in mainland Europe and North America too. You're going to be a hero, Mr Director. Now how's it going to look if these same charities have to go to all those agencies and say, "Hey, you know the dude who gave us all that money? Well he's gone and asked for it back!" How do you think that would play, huh? Especially as they'll all be receiving about now a letter signed by you and witnessed by a solicitor announcing the donations and confirming that they're irrevocable.'

'But I never signed such a letter!'

Solomon looked at Folken sadly. 'You underestimate me, Mr Director.'

'But it's all my money,' said Folken, plaintively. 'It's everything I have.'

'Not quite,' said Solomon. 'What's he got left, Jonas?'

Jonas consulted the screen. 'Just over five million.'

'Awesome!' said Solomon. 'That's two million for Cameron, two for Molly, and one million for that nice nurse who saved you, my boy. I reckon that will about do it, don't you?' Solomon bent down to Folken and playfully chucked him under the chin. 'Don't look so miserable, Mr Director. You've still got your comfortable pad in London, the one up here, the Paris apartment, your beach house on Grand Cayman. Oh, and your cars, your art, your personal effects. This here, what we're dealing with now, is just the stuff that the taxman doesn't know about. I think you'll get by on what's left.' He turned to Draven. 'I can't see Director Folken turning up at the homeless shelter anytime soon, can you?'

'No,' said Draven. 'I don't think I can.'

Folken slumped forward, his head in his hands. Just then there was the sound of a distant alarm.

38

'RUN!' shouted Zak, and gave the bed a powerful push so that it started to roll along the corridor away from the doors.

Ingrida leapt out of the way, Archy grabbed Beth's arm with one hand and pushed the bed with the other. The four of them were running, Cameron in the bed suddenly awake and alert.

'Where's this go?' Zak yelled, pointing to a corridor.

'Double doors at the end open onto a loading bay and then the staff car park,' Ingrida shouted.

'Right, go for it!' Zak leant against the bed to turn it in the right direction.

Just into the corridor a bell started to sound, a deafening clangour almost too loud to bear. Behind them they heard the muffled crack of a gunshot and a din like a car smash as the glass doors shattered.

Archy looked back and saw Jeannie jumping over

the broken glass and coming after them. McIntyre was just behind her and he still had the gun.

'Keep going,' Archy yelled. 'I'll hold them here.'

There were three or four drip stands in an alcove. Archy grabbed two and sent them spinning on their small wheels towards the pursuers. It wasn't much but it was enough to make Jeannie and McIntyre slow down to dodge. Archy took a third stand and stood in the middle of the corridor facing the two, holding the stand like a staff. He gave it an experimental swing. The base was heavy and it made a good weapon but it was no match for the gun. If he could delay the chase for just a few seconds it might give the others enough time to get away. He was scared, but surely McIntyre wouldn't shoot him, not here, not in Scotland, not in a hospital.

'Come on then, wankers!' he shouted, and swung the stand again.

Jeannie and McIntyre stopped, just out of range of the stand. There was a moment's stand-off, then McIntyre grinned and pointed towards the end of the corridor over Archy's shoulder. Archy didn't turn; he wasn't going to fall for that old trick. McIntyre realised that.

'All right then,' he said. He smiled, and levelled the gun at Archy's chest.

Suddenly the bell stopped and everything became eerily still, although Archy's ears still rang from the din. McIntyre made a gesture to Archy to raise his hands, and a little circular motion of the gun to say he was to turn around. He was still smiling. Cautiously, Archy looked behind him. Beth, Ingrida, Zak and the bed had stopped a couple of meters from the rear doors. Standing in front of them was a woman in a white coat.

'Well ain't this just cosy,' came a booming voice from the other end of the corridor. Solomon was standing among the broken glass. Behind him was Jonas, and next to him Draven, his fingers tight around Folken's upper arm. The Director looked shrunken and weak beside his captors.

McIntyre's gaze was flicking from Solomon to Archy, to Folken, to the others, and back again. He now had two targets to watch, one hundred and eighty degrees apart. He flattened his back to the wall.

Jeannie stood beside him. 'You're a fucking two-faced bitch,' she shouted at Ingrida. 'And I'm going to make you sorry.'

Solomon took a pace or two forward, Draven with him, dragging Folken.

'Stop it right there,' called the woman in white. It was Salamar.

'Now why should I do that?' asked Solomon, continuing to walk.

'Because my colleague has a gun and you don't.'

Solomon stopped. 'Well, I guess you're right about that,' he laughed.

Beth was standing beside Cameron's head. His eyes had closed again and his breathing had become laboured. The woman in the white coat was looking directly at her. There was something in her hand too. Beth recognised it as an epipen, its purple top protruding from her clenched fist.

'I suppose,' said Zak, 'that this is what you might call a stand off.'

'I suppose it is,' said Solomon. 'You see,' he called to Salamar, 'my friend here has a knife at your boss's back. He's standing right behind him, so you can't shoot him without hitting the Director. And if you hit one of the rest of us that knife goes in.'

'This is stupid,' said Salamar. 'You think you're in some TV cop drama. We're in charge, McIntyre and I. You can't get out, and meanwhile this boy you came here to save is dying. Now back away from the bed.'

'No, I don't think we're going to do that,' Solomon said. Beth choked back a cry but he ignored it. 'In fact,' he continued, 'we're going to take the boy in this bed away, out of this shit hole. Tell her, Mr Director.'

Draven's arm straightened and Folken was jerked forward, his face twisted in pain.

'He has to go,' said Folken, only just able to speak. 'Release him.'

McIntyre's head was flicking from side to side between Salamar at one end of the corridor and Solomon at the other, like a frantic tennis umpire.

Salamar appeared to consider this for a moment. She had managed to move closer to the bed and now was standing near it, opposite Beth.

'All right, if those are your orders, Director, he can go like this.'

Beth saw what Salamar was doing a fraction ahead of the action, and as the epipen was raised she dived towards Cameron. She had no plan, everything happened too quickly for her to think about it. It was a reflex, protecting her friend just as he had protected her when they were children and the runaway tyre had come bouncing down the hill.

It was done in an instant. She made to grab Salamar's arm but the bed was too wide and her opponent too quick. In one fluid move Salamar seized Cameron's hair, pulled his head round and jabbed the epipen into his neck.

Beth felt the world lurch and a red mist swirled before her eyes. Then everything went black and she slumped onto the bed like an unstrung puppet.

Zak leapt forward and seized Salamar in a head lock, twisting her in front of him. She dropped the epipen and Ingrida kicked it away. McIntyre was distracted and Archy dived for the gun. He got a grip on McIntyre's wrist and tried to twist it but the man was strong. They struggled and Archy could feel the weapon being turned towards him. He jerked it back with all his strength and there was an ear-bursting crack as the gun went off. The bullet hit McIntyre's knee. He screamed and collapsed.

'You bitch,' shouted Jeannie and ran at Ingrida. Ingrida dodged past Zak and hurled herself through the double doors at the end of the corridor. Jeannie charged after her, straight into the arms of Gunner who was waiting outside.

Cameron lay on the bed, Beth over and across him. McIntyre was keening through clenched teeth and gripping his leg. There was a lot of blood. Folken had slithered to the floor and was leaning against the wall, Jonas standing over him. He looked to be sobbing.

39

If any of them had been asked later to list in order the things that occurred next they would have been hard pressed to do it; there was so much going on, so many people, and everything happened at a frantic pace.

Gunner strapped Salamar's arms with gaffer tape, pushed a cloth in her mouth and shoved her into a cupboard.

Ingrida gave McIntyre a sterile wad. 'It looks like the bullet's nicked your patella tendon but it doesn't seem to have lodged there. You'll be all right. Hold this on it and clamp it as tight as you can bear. It will stop the bleeding.'

McIntyre groaned. He retched but nothing came up. Ingrida looked for Jeannie but she'd vanished. So had Folken.

Medical and security staff were emerging from other parts of the building. Zak took charge.

'There's been a ram raid,' he said. 'It's all over now, everything is under control. See to the patients, keep them calm.'

Some of the staff obeyed at once but a couple of men in security uniforms hesitated.

'Who are you?' said one of them.

Zak thought fast. Who was he? 'I'm one of Signor Salvatore's special detail.' It was a risk, relying on the hope that the two men wouldn't necessarily know the names of all the wealthy clients so wouldn't know that this one was made up. It seemed to work because they looked as though they believed him. 'The police have been called,' he added quickly. 'You two secure the building and don't let anyone in or out until they arrive.'

The police hadn't been summoned, at least not as far as Zak knew, but that would stop the men calling them and keep the pair busy. Meanwhile Gunner had brought the ambulance to the rear of the building. Ingrida was attending to Beth and Cameron. Beth had slipped from the bed onto the floor where she lay limp. Cameron too was still as a corpse.

'We need to get both of them to the hospital,' she said, 'and quickly. God knows what Salamar gave them.'

With Ingrida supervising and Archy helping, Gunner and Draven lifted Beth onto a stretcher, slid Cameron onto another and loaded them both into the ambulance. Zak, Solomon and Jonas guarded the doors to the foyer, turning back curious staff who came to enquire and assuring them that the incident was over and they should go back to their duties. It was getting riskier to do that because although some of them looked frightened and left at once, others were suspicious.

Gunner, Draven and Zak went with Ingrida and the two casualties in the ambulance. The rest followed in Solomon's car.

'What do you reckon?' said Zak above the wail of the siren as Draven hurled the ambulance into a corner.

'I can't say,' said Ingrida. 'They're both breathing but their pulses are way down.' She raised Cameron's eyelid and shone her pen torch into his pupil. 'They're both of them in a grade V coma. They're not responding to anything. I don't think they have any idea what's happening.'

'Will they be all right?'

Ingrida gave him a pitying look. Zak knew it was a stupid question – how could she know?

'They need to be in hospital,' she said. 'When we arrive at the Infirmary we'll get them in and you tell the others to make themselves scarce.'

'Don't you want Gunner and Draven to help?'

'No. The hospital staff will see to everything. You need to agree on a story to explain why they're like this. It will be best if just you does the talking, so send everybody else away. There'll be a lot of questions.'

There were, and as they went on Zak realised the

wisdom of Ingrida's advice. To have had half a dozen people each giving a version of the story would have been disastrous. So he and Archy stayed with Ingrida while Solomon and the other three left.

'You've never been here,' Zak said to Solomon as he prepared to drive away.

'Suits me,' Solomon said. 'Except I'd like to have torched that clinic.'

'So would I, but as soon as Beth and Cameron are checked in I'm going to talk to the police.'

'Well good luck with that. I hope they do more than they did when our boys went missing.'

The procedure at the Royal Infirmary worked smoothly. Ingrida went in with the gurneys, by-passed the queue and told the triage staff what the situation was. From then on the medical establishment took over. It was like launching Beth and Cameron on a production line with a team of specialists contributing at each stage as they passed along. Zak handed over their ID cards and their life cards with their medical records and wondered what to do next.

'There'll be a wait while they diagnose what's wrong.' said Ingrida. 'It may take a while. Go get a coffee and come back to check in an hour.'

They faced each other.

'I don't know how to thank you for what you've done,' Zak said. 'You've been a complete angel.'

He was going to hug her, but just then another gurney came in at speed, bearing someone who appeared to be losing a lot of blood. Zak and Ingrida parted to let the gurney pass between them and when Zak turned to talk to her again, maybe to complete the hug, there was no sign of her.

Archy had been waiting in the background.

'Did you see where Ingrida went?' Zak asked.

'Probably through that door,' said Archy, pointing. It was marked *Staff Only*.

'Right. I expect she's gone to talk to the doctors. Let's find that cafeteria and get something to eat, I'm starving. And while we do that we can agree what the story is, what we're going to say about all this.' He made a mental note to get in touch with Molly and with Beth's gran, but not yet; he'd wait until he had a prognosis for them. 'We'll catch up with Ingrida later.'

In fact he never saw her again. He did get a text from her sometime later to say that she was in Lithuania and soon to be married. He texted her back to wish her luck, and that was it.

The prognosis was protracted, and as Ingrida had forecast there were many questions. The story Zak concocted with Archy's help over their coffee and sandwiches was that Cameron had volunteered to donate a kidney, and they could refer to the New Dawn TV show to support this. Zak and Archy, as family, had come with him together with Beth, his girlfriend.

The operation had been a success, and Beth and Archy had gone to a pub to celebrate. While Archy was in the gents somebody must have spiked Beth's drink, because soon after they left the pub she collapsed. They were near the Aurora clinic and Archy ran into it for help just as Cameron was being made ready to transfer to the hospital because there'd been a complication with the operation. Beth was put in the same ambulance. It was a weak story but it was the best they could do with the material available to them.

The lead consultant was certainly unconvinced. 'A complication with the operation, you say? The kidney removal has been expertly done, a first class job. That doesn't seem to me to be the reason he's gone into a coma.'

'What is it then, doctor? What's the problem with both of them?'

The doctor thought for a moment before replying. 'Let's begin with the young man, Cameron, your son.'

'Stepson.'

'Right. Well as I was saying, the issue isn't his kidney. The surgeon who did that knew his, or her, stuff. However, he's received an injection with a preparation that appears to have caused axonal neuropathy. It's something we've not come across before. If he'd been out and about I'd say someone had attacked him with a nerve agent, but I can't see how that can have happened in a medical facility. Unless, of course, someone has deliberately poisoned him.' He looked enquiringly at Zak as if he expected him to furnish details.

'And what about Beth?'

'The young woman, yes.' The consultant became even more thoughtful. 'She is a complete mystery. We can find nothing wrong with her at all. All her vital organs are tip top. Her blood is clean. She has no infections. Her brain scans show normal function.'

'Except that she's in a coma.'

'Yes. Except for that.'

'So you don't know what's causing her to be that way.'

'I'm afraid not. All I can tell you is that it seems to be some sort of psychosomatic condition, perhaps as a result of stress. Maybe she saw something that brought it on. But take a look at this.' The consultant crossed to Beth's bedside screen, turned it so Zak could see it, and pointed to Cameron's. 'This line is brain activity,' he said, 'this one is heart rate, this one is blood pressure, this one is the respiratory rate – how many breaths they're taking per minute – this one is core body temperature, and this one is oxygen saturation. Look at them carefully. Notice anything?'

'The two screens look the same,' said Zak.

'Yes they do. They are the same. In fact they're identical, in total sync, absolute harmony.'

'What's that all about?' said Zak.

The consultant shook his head. 'I have no idea. I've never seen anything like it before. It's as if they're somehow connected, a single being. They've been like this since they came in.'

'What does it mean?'

'Well, what I guess it means, and it is only a guess,

is that when one of them wakes up, the other will wake up too. However, there's another thing we must consider.'

'And what's that?'

'It's that neither of them will.'

40

DARKNESS thicker than she's ever known. It's the quality of blackness you might experience if you were shut inside a box; or a coffin.

Silence too. Complete noiselessness. A total hush. She can't even hear the faint, high pitched in-ear hiss of the tinnitus that sometimes troubles her. It's the quiet of the grave. The quiet beneath six feet of earth. The quiet of the crematorium furnace after the fire has been extinguished.

And stillness. Stillness beyond everything. Nothing moves. Her world is so without motion it's as if the earth itself has ceased to turn and hangs like a bauble on a string.

She's floating but she has no feeling. No touch. No sensation. She can't locate any of her limbs. She can't see them and she can't move to find them by touch. Are they actually there? Are they still connected to her? Is she even breathing?

But she knows who she is and she can think. She wonders how she got to be here. She remembers a wound; a redness redder than red; then black. She wonders if she has become the subject of some sensory deprivation experiment, another malign venture of Aurora. Even though she is alone she is not frightened. She is curious about what has happened to everyone else, but the isolation and the tranquility that comes with it are not unpleasant.

How long does this last? A second? A minute? An hour? A day? A year? There is no way of knowing and the question is meaningless. Time does not exist. With no motion to mark its passage everything is now. There is no past, no future, only the present. Everything is as it always has been, and as it always will be.

But not always. There comes a change, a spark in the velvet backcloth of her consciousness. Or is it a blemish on her retina as she struggles to penetrate the void?

No, it is a light. It's no more than a pinprick, no more than a glowworm at the end of a mile long tunnel. She feels it's a threat and she wants to look away from it but she can't move her head. She stares, and stares, and stares, and the light begins to move. It breaks from its terminal stasis and rocks. It's a tiny motion, so subtle she doubts it's happening at all. It must be a fault in her perception brought on by her ataraxy.

But the movement increases, and she realises that it's not the light that's rocking, it's her. Whatever it is that's bearing her has begun a gentle undulation.

The light widens, assuming the shape of a letter box. It starts to grow, and as it does fingers of radiance reach out to her. They show that she is in a vast cave. She can see that she is on some sort of raft, floating on an underground stream that flows towards the rectangle of daylight ahead of her.

There are other people around her. All of them are on rafts like hers. She scans the faces, but there's no one she can identify. They are like zombies. Each of them is sitting bolt upright and holds a rope attached to the bow of their raft. The ropes do nothing, they're useless, hanging limply in their hands. Every face looks firmly ahead, fixated like her on the quickly expanding rectangle of brilliance at the mouth of the cave.

She can hear a noise. It's distant at first, but as she gets closer to the light it grows louder. It's rushing water. A cascade. A waterfall! At the same time that she realises this she registers in her chest the rumbling thunder of the tumbling river. Many of the rafts are ahead of her and as they approach the precipice she sees them accelerate towards the edge. She watches horrified as they upend like ducks and plunge over the rim.

She is near the side of the stream, away from the main flow and near the rock wall of the cave. Here the movement of the water is less fierce than in the centre. She paddles with her hands to try to escape the force that's drawing her towards the brink. It's hopeless. However hard she works she cannot slow the raft.

Then she sees a rope. It's fixed through hoops along the side of the cave. It's close, only a few feet away. She paddles. She grabs. She misses. She grabs again. The energy of her movement has pushed her away from the wall and out towards the mainstream again. She scoops frantically, spooning handfuls of water. She's still heading for the cataclysmic drop but her paddling and the current have changed her line and she hits the cave wall further along. There's a bump, hard enough to dislodge her, but she has the wit to grab the rope. It's wet and rough and it skins her fingers so she nearly lets go, but she manages to hold on to it.

The river pulls, reluctant to surrender its prey. It wrenches her arms and she has to cling on. How long can she remain like this? She realises that time must have begun again because the water flows in time. That means that there has been a past and so there must be a future. What does this new future hold for her? She has her back to the light and is facing up river, looking back into the cave. Face after face after face after face sweeps past her, all of them focussed ahead, oblivious to what awaits when they reach the lip and the fall.

She struggles to keep hold of the rope. The strain is unbearable but she knows she mustn't let go. Then she hears a cry. It's her name, Beth! It rises above the roar of the water. She hears it again, a cry of entreaty, a cry of despair. She looks up and sees Cameron. He's on one of the rafts and he's coming towards her. He can't be the one who called. He's just like the others, looking straight ahead, his expressionless face lit by the glow from the cave mouth. His raft is travelling fast, and with a choking horror she sees that in a few seconds he will be past her and gone, into the abyss like the others. In an instant he will be lost.

Then he's upon her, beside her. She lunges for his rope. It's almost too far but at full stretch she reaches it and snatches it from his hands. There's a jerk that sickens her and almost tears her apart. With one hand she holds Cameron's raft and with the other the rope attached to the cave wall. The strain is unbearable. She is wracked. She can hear her joints cracking, feel her arm sockets being pulled apart.

She hooks one elbow over the rope at the cave edge, and that frees her hand to tie the two rafts together. Praying that her hurried knot will hold, she hangs on with both hands. The pressure eases, but only a little.

Cameron is aware of none of this. He looks at her but there's no recognition.

She works the rope along the cave wall, heaving on it to drag the two rafts away from the waterfall, away from the light which promises hope but delivers death. It's back-breaking work. They move slowly, but they do move. Back, back, back into the dark. The river fights her. Every heave is a struggle against the insistence of the current. She clenches her teeth so hard that her lip splits and bleeds. She licks the wound. It tastes of iron.

She pulls and pulls, arm over arm, one arm and then the next, one arm and then the next, away from the roaring and the drop and towards safety.

The river is broader now and less frantic. They're approaching a fork where the cavern divides into two. She reaches behind her to find Cameron's hand. She *squeezes it, and she feels an answering pressure. Then her knot gives and the rafts slip apart, drawn invisibly in different directions, Cameron's one way, hers the other. As his raft slips away he turns and his eyes capture hers. They say, 'Thank you.'*

41

A nurse had said that when Beth or Cameron regained consciousness they would be confused and disorientated, and it would be helpful if they could wake up to a face they knew. So Archy and Zak took turns to sit with them, leaving only while bedding was changed, or the patients were turned, washed, and made comfortable.

Although, Archy wondered, was comfort a relevant concept? Could either of them feel anything at all? Or were they, as they seemed, dead to the world? They were like figures on a medieval tomb, a knight and his lady side by side, calm and still as they gazed expressionlessly at the ceiling. Except that Beth and Cameron weren't gazing at anything. Their eyes were closed, as they had been ever since they'd been speared by Salamar's epipen in the foyer of the clinic.

It was two days before Zak went to the police. He reckoned that seeing Beth and Cameron looked after was the top priority, and that there was plenty of time to catch up with Folken and his crew later. At first what he had to report was treated with scepticism, but Zak insisted and the receiving officer passed him up the line to a superior, who then elevated it to someone else. At last, and having related his story four times, a search was authorised. Then there was a delay while the warrant was obtained.

A little later a pair of officers came to see Zak at his hotel, where he was taking a break while Archy kept watch on the patients.

'What made you think that something illegal was going on at Aurora Wellbeing?' one of them asked.

Zak rehearsed the story they'd prepared, that Cameron had volunteered a kidney and while at the clinic he'd learnt that most of the donors were there against their will.'

'We'd like to interview this Cameron,' said the officer.

'I wish you could,' said Zak, 'but he's still unconscious.'

'And you maintain that's because someone at the clinic injected him with some sort of poison.'

'Yes, I do. What did you find there?'

'Nothing. Well, nothing that shouldn't have been going on. You told us that what they did were organ transplants. Well we interviewed the boss,' he glanced at his datapad, 'Dr Salamar, and she told us that transplants were very rare. In fact she can't remember when they last did one. They mostly do joint

344

replacements, body shaping, cosmetic surgery of various sorts for private clients. It checks out, she showed us their records to prove it. And they've never heard of your Cameron.'

'You got the wrong person,' said Zak, marvelling at their incompetence. 'The top dog at the clinic is called Folken. Dr Hans Folken.'

The two police officers looked questioningly at each other. 'No,' said one. 'Dr Salamar is certainly the one in charge. We'll ask about this Dr Folken though.'

Zak shook his head in disbelief. Had Folken run? If he had it didn't surprise him. It was also credible that the clinic had constructed fake records. Maybe they'd prepared them in advance just in case they might someday be required; all they'd have to do would be to insert the right dates. Every procedure they listed could of course be checked, but given the police resources that would take a long time. He wanted to ask about the smashed plate glass door and McIntyre's injured knee, but he didn't want to for fear of alerting them to his knowledge of those things.

The police officers were looking at him with intense disapproval.

'We found nothing at the clinic that was untoward,' said one.

'Do you know how much a search like that costs?' said the other. 'Obtaining a warrant, staff time, compiling records, use of vehicles, the whole thing. Any idea how much? Well it's a quite a lot. Wasting police resources is a serious matter.' They got up to leave. 'You'll be hearing from us.'

Meanwhile the hospital care continued, expert and diligent. Members of the nursing staff came in every half hour or so, and a consultant several times a day. Tablets and information screens were considered and notes made. There were murmured questions and exchanges while Archy or Zak, whichever of them was there, was sent out to patrol the corridors.

On day five the consultant spoke to Zak again. 'We've managed to remove the last of the poison from the boy's system and his brain is now taking over his bodily functions, but it's as if it's having to learn to do this all over again. We don't know how long that will take but it's going reasonably well. The news about higher brain function is not so good. There's a very low level of cerebral activity. We're having a meeting tomorrow to see what we might do to stimulate more.'

The consultant left and Archy looked at Beth, studying her face. He bent to see around the tube which hid her mouth

'She's got a split lip,' he said. 'Look. I don't remember her having that before.'

Zak came over to inspect it. 'I expect she did it when she fell in the foyer,' he said.

Archy shook his head. 'That was ages ago. If she'd done it then it would have healed by now. Why haven't we seen it before?'

'Perhaps one of the nurses was careless with her feeding tube.'

Archy looked at Cameron, only a foot away. He took one of Beth's hands in one of his, and one of Cameron's in the other. Gently he squeezed them both. They were warm, but as lifeless as dead animals. Then he felt something, at first so faint he thought he must be imagining it. He squeezed the hands again, and this time there was no mistaking.

'Oh my God.' He turned to where Zak was looking at him in amazement. 'It's both of them. They're moving. They're waking up.'

42

THEY WERE THE SAME, but they were not the same. They had been to hidden places, places from which few people return. They might have remained there but they had come back, and instead of it all being over they had to pick up the untidy strands of their lives. However, first there were repairs.

Beth recovered first; she was the one who had not been poisoned, and she had both her kidneys. Zak and Archy had been sure that Salamar had got her too with the epipen but it seemed not. Beth herself didn't know. All she could remember was the white coated figure lunging at Cameron, herself diving, and a scarlet flash followed by emptiness. An emptiness that had lasted until now.

Her tubes were removed and she had her first meal. It was a mush that looked like baby food and, Archy thought, probably tasted like it too. Typical Beth, she wanted to feed herself, but she was too weak to manage it properly and Archy helped her.

She was frail, and she was sore where tubes and catheters had entered her, but the medical staff insisted she get out of bed. She walked along the ward, at first with help and then on her own. The effort exhausted her. Zak and Archy watched her with a mixture of relief and joy. Zak took photos and messaged them to her gran.

A staff nurse spoke to both of them. 'She's had a long time in bed,' she said. 'Her muscles will have weakened, but she's a strong girl and we're confident she'll recover quickly. Set your phone to a silent alarm every hour. When it goes off, one of you walk her up and down the ward. Go with her but encourage her to do it on her own. Don't overdo it, don't wear her out. As she improves you can take her out of the ward and walk her around a bit out there.'

Beth was moved into her own room, away from Cameron. She continued to improve, and was soon feeling better. She walked further each day and she began to do a few exercises, press-ups, goblet squats, sit-ups, things she'd done in her soccer training.

'Very well done, young lady,' the consultant said. 'We'll be ready to go home soon.'

'Patronising prick,' Beth mouthed behind his back, even though she was grateful for his help.

'She's back to normal,' Zak said.

Cameron recovered more slowly. All the bedside paraphernalia that had sustained Beth was taken away, but some of Cameron's remained. The site of his missing kidney was healing well but he had developed an infection in the one that was left and that took time to treat.

At first he was very fuzzy. He kept trying to move but having to stop because he couldn't remember what he'd set out to do. He would talk a little but often would begin a sentence only to lose where it was going, and the thought would fizzle out leaving him looking bewildered and helpless. Beth spent the time when she wasn't exercising or walking sitting beside his bed, watching his resting face, the curve of his cheek, the planes of his jaw, his forehead, his hair. She watched his chest gently rising and falling. She thought she knew his body but there were things about him that she'd never noticed before. It wasn't that he looked a stranger, but he was not as familiar as he had been.

Zak said. 'He's bound to be affected by what happened, you both are. You nearly died. But you feel all right, don't you?'

'Yes, I'm okay. I'm not up to running around on the soccer pitch yet but I'm improving all the time.'

'Cameron's getting better too,' said Zak. 'His kidney problem is under control and the doc thinks he'll be up and about soon. I was with him just now and I asked him how his kidney was. He said "offal".' Zak laughed. '

'Offal?'

'Offal. Awful. Get it?'

'Oh. Right.' Beth didn't laugh.

'That sounds like the same old Cameron to me,' said Zak.

Beth was discharged from the hospital as the consultant had predicted. She wanted to stay around to be near Cameron but she felt she must see Gran, and besides Cameron didn't need her. She took a train south and Archy went with her. Zak stayed in Aberdeen.

Cameron continued to make headway and followed the same routine as Beth, although as yet without the squats, jumps, and sit-ups. He progressed slowly but progress he did, until eventually he too was ready to go home. Zak texted Archy, Beth and Molly to say that they would be heading south the next day.

Most of the morning was spent in sorting out Cameron's papers and waiting for his medication to come from the pharmacy. Zak had heard nothing from the police and wondered if he ought to tell them he was leaving, but he dismissed the thought.

They walked out of the hospital into a bright, spring day, and were astonished to be met by Jonas driving his father's huge car. Beth and Archy were with him and on the journey they told Zak and Cameron what had been happening.

'Aurora's gone,' said Jonas. 'My dad made a full statement to Police Scotland. He told them about Cameron and I swore a statement about what they'd done to me. There was the video footage too that showed me being snatched outside the club, and the false plates on the car, and the phone company's record of where I'd been. My dad threatened to bring a civil case against them for dereliction of duty if they didn't do anything. It worked. They shut down the Aberdeen clinic and that was just the start. The government in England has pulled the plug on the Genome Database contract. Your friend Archy here was able to get into the Aurora systems and he found all sorts of weevils in the woodwork, stuff that the financial authorities were very interested in. He's a computer genius.'

'Aw shucks,' said Archy, smiling coyly. 'Too kind, guys, too kind. Seriously, their security protocols were crap. A five-year-old could have got past them.'

'Anyway,' said Jonas, 'Aurora's in administration, and Salamar and McIntyre have been arrested.'

'About time,' said Zak. 'What about Folken?'

'He's flown. He's not been seen either at his place in Scotland or the one in England. Rumour has it that he's in the Cayman Islands and both the houses over here are up for sale, so if you have a few million you could get yourself a bargain.'

Cameron has, thought Zak, although he doesn't know it yet.

Beth took over. 'Folken's wife is some hotshot lawyer and there was a thing in one of the papers that she's divorcing him.'

'My mum is hosting their baby,' said Cameron, 'and she's going to keep it. She wants to bring it up as her own. She told me on the phone.'

'So you'll have a brother,' said Jonas. Cameron didn't answer.

'The best news, though, is about Jeannie,' said Beth.

'Jeannie?'

'Yes. You know she vanished when we were getting Cameron out of the clinic. Well she's turned up again. She's been holed up somewhere but she's coming to England.'

'What for?' said Zak.

'Star witness for the prosecution,' said Jonas. 'She's agreed to fill in any blanks left in the stuff you, me and my dad provided, in return for immunity from prosecution.

'And there've been texts from Ingrida,' said Beth. 'She's back in Lithuania and sends her love to everyone. She's getting married and says she wants us all to go to the wedding. She wanted to know if Cameron was okay and I said he was.'

43

OKAY WAS A RELATIVE TERM. Cameron was getting better physically every day but he didn't feel right. He couldn't connect with anything. It was as if other people, everything that happened to and around him, was on the other side side of a misted screen. It was hard to make things out clearly; colours were dulled, movements blurred, sounds muffled. Keeping in touch exhausted him and he would often have to drop out, to retreat inwards so that he was merely an observer.

Beth was worried. 'He's different,' she said to Archy.

'Is he? How?'

'I can't really say. It's something inside him. I think I'm different too but not in the same way.' She'd tried telling herself she was imagining it, but deep down she knew that something fundamental had changed in both of them.

Archy didn't reply. They both seemed to be the

same to him. Cameron was a bit quieter maybe, but he'd get over it.

Beth wasn't convinced. It was hard to put her finger on exactly what had changed. The best way she could describe it was that somehow the signals between them had become contaminated by interference. Or impaired by intermittent drop out, like a poor phone connection. She didn't feel as close to him as she had. It seemed astonishing because after what they'd both been through she thought the link between them would have become even stronger. That amazing episode on the rafts in the river. Had it been a dream? Was it a metaphor for something in their past? A premonition of the future? Or perhaps it had been a vision of death. Whatever it was, it should surely have cemented them closer together. Had Cameron experienced it too? Had he seen and heard the water? Had he felt the rocking of the raft as they were propelled towards oblivion? She was afraid to ask; suppose he said no. Then she truly would be on her own.

At the beginning of their last year in school they'd been thinking about what they would do when they finished. Cameron said he wanted to go to art college; Beth loved drama and wanted to act. They'd co-ordinated their applications so that although they were aiming for different courses, sometimes at different institutions, they'd be in the same city. London had seemed the obvious choice and they'd both secured places, then they'd decided to take a year off. They'd meant it to be a time to gather some new experiences. Well, Beth told herself, they'd certainly done that.

Now she was looking forward to moving on, and she was enjoying the summer. She'd started running again and was feeling fitter. She'd been doing some reading for her drama course. She was working part-time in a florists ('With a name like Beth Flowers I have to give you the job,' the owner had said when she applied). She was spending a lot of time with Molly and her new baby. Gran had got over the demise of the New Dawn show and was now into Celebrity Skydive instead. Things were going well. The only thing that wasn't good was her relationship with Cameron. They still spent time together, he still told her he loved her, but – and it was hard to admit this even to herself – he was no fun any more. It was ages since they'd last spent a night together, and even then it hadn't amounted to much.

They were in a coffee shop near Revolution Easy, where they sometimes met Jonas. Cameron had been staring at his coffee and watching it go cold when he came out with it.

'I'm not going to art college,' he said.

It was a bombshell, yet at the same time not totally unexpected.

'Why ever not?'

'I don't want to. Anyway, they'd sling me out. My work's crap.'

'But your drawings are amazing! And the way you use colour. It's fantastic.' She thought about his portfolio stuffed down beside her bed. He'd not touched it since they'd got back from Aberdeen but the work in it was wonderful. She'd always thought so. 'You must go. It's what you've always wanted.'

Cameron shook his head.

'Is it the money Solomon syphoned off for you from Folken? It may seem a lot now but it won't last for ever, you know.'

'No, I'm not bothered about the money. Anyway Zak said I shouldn't spend it in case the police trace it when they go through Folken's affairs and it has to be paid back.'

She knew from experience that there was no point going on at him. The more she did the more stubborn he would get.

'What will you do?' she said.

'I don't know.'

And that was it. He didn't know; and saddest of all, he didn't care.

The summer ended and Beth went to London. Cameron remained at home. They spoke occasionally on the phone but there was often more silence than sound.

'What are you doing?' she'd say.

'Nothing much.'

He never asked her what she was doing so she found it hard to talk about her course, her new friends, about landing the title role in the first year's studio production of Hedda Gabler. She talked to Molly, who was also worried but really too tied up in looking after her newborn to be able to give much thought to anything else. She talked to Zak.

'He's okay,' Zak said. 'He's quieter than he was, but that's not surprising when you consider what's happened to him. Anyway, there are signs that he's coming out of it. Yesterday he was sitting at his computer and singing?'

'Singing?' She'd never known Cameron sing since they left primary school.

'Yes, and it was a classical piece too.'

'He doesn't listen to classical music. He doesn't know any classical pieces.'

'Well he knew this one. Dvorak's Cello Concerto. The slow movement, note for note.'

There had been other examples of uncharacteristic behaviour. A few days before that Cameron had been driving Zak's car and had stopped in a line of traffic. When the other vehicles moved Cameron stayed put, staring straight ahead as if in a trance. The traffic behind started to sound their horns and a flame red Audi made an exaggerated sweep around them, accompanied by V-signs from the driver. Zak had turned on the hazard flashers and flipped the bonnet to give the idea of a breakdown, then he'd got Cameron out of the driver's seat and into the back. By the time they got home he seemed normal, but Zak told him that he mustn't drive again until he'd had a medical check-up. When he'd asked Cameron to say what he was looking at he said it had been a huge room full of people, all in rows and all looking at him. Zak didn't share any of this with Beth.

Two days after the driving incident Archy found Cameron on the sofa with his head in his hands. His eyes were wet, as if he'd been crying.

'Hey, what's up?' Archy said.

'I think I'm losing it,' Cameron said. 'I'm a fruit loop.'

'Why?'

'I keep seeing things.'

'What sort of things?'

'Like I'm on a long street with these huge buildings on both sides. Big, white ones, with loads of windows.'

'What's wrong with that?'

'But it happens all the time. When I'm sitting here, or walking back from Molly's. Suddenly I'll be somewhere else, and I can't get back.'

'But everybody has daydreams,' Archy said.

'Not like this. Then I get a craze for these weird foods, beetroot, cabbage, stuff I've never bothered with before.'

Archy told Zak about this, and then Zak got some evidence which persuaded him that the explanation he'd been thinking about was right. He needed to tell Cameron about it, and the opportunity came the next day.

Archy was working on one of his computer games and Cameron was drawing something. Zak was interested. This was the first graphic work he'd seen Cameron do since before the operation and he wanted to see what was engrossing him so. He went to look over his shoulder.

It was an elaborate doodle, intricate lines in black ink, with lettering in the middle, except it wasn't English. The characters were cyrillic: мир и дружба.

'What's that?'

'It's Russian. Meer y droojva. It means peace and friendship.'

Zak was surprised. 'How do you know?'

Cameron shrugged. 'I don't know. It just came into my head.'

Zak put his hand on Cameron's shoulder. 'There's something I should share with you,' he said. 'We need to talk.'

Half an hour later Cameron sat back and tried to take in what Zak had said to him.

'So you think these ideas and mind pictures I'm getting are from somebody else. Who?'

'I think they're from the young woman who's got your kidney.'

'What?' Cameron's jaw fell open. 'I've no idea who she is. I've never met her. I didn't even know it was a woman that got it until you told me. It's you that's the fruit loop, not me.'

Zak smiled. 'Yes, it's upsetting, but what's happening to you is quite well written up. It's called cellular memory theory, and what it says is that the mechanism for recollecting sights, thoughts, feelings and some skills resides not just in the brain but in other parts of the body too. When I was digging into Hans Folken's records for Solomon I decided out of curiosity to find out who it was who received your kidney. It turns out she's Russian. She's called Alexandra Christina Ivanovitch. She lives in Moscow, when she's not in London. And get this: she's a cellist. She's quite well thought of in Russia and she's made a prize-winning recording. It's of the Cello Concerto by Dvorak.'

'It's the piece you said I was humming the other day. I can't remember a note of it now.'

'That's not surprising. Things like that come and go. As I say, unexplained connections between the donors of organs and those who've received them are unusual but not rare. The thing that's odd about what's happening to you is that if there is some sort of memory built into cells, as this theory says, then it should be this woman who's remembering things that have happened to you, not the other way round.'

Cameron looked puzzled.

'She has some of your cells in her body, which should connect your memories with hers, but you don't have any of her cells in you. You shouldn't be seeing Moscow streets, concert hall audiences, Russian phrases. She should be seeing Leeds, Revolution Easy, this house.'

'Do you think she is?'

'We could ask her and find out. Take a look at this.'

Zak pushed a laptop towards him. The screen showed a young woman bent over a cello, her hair falling forward and hiding her face. 'That's her. Look her up and listen to her play. Then when you've done that Google "memory transference in organ transplant recipients".' Zak took Cameron's hand. 'If anyone can accept the notion of two minds being able to share, it's you.'

When Beth had left Cameron for London it had felt like a bereavement. He had always been there, but now he wasn't. Something that had been a part of her had been taken away. However, over the months her grief lessened and she accepted that there was no way back and she would have to let go.

There were other things coming into her life. Molly had her baby and asked Beth to be his godmother. She made some new friends, and towards the end of her first year she agreed to flat share with a boy on her course who she'd been talking to for a few months.

As time went on Beth had some modest acting success with work in the provinces, a couple of cameo appearances in the West End, a few commercials, and some minor roles on TV.

Cameron didn't contact Alexandra Christina. He had no trouble believing what Zak said and what he found on the internet, but would she? And in any case he didn't want to see her. After all, what would they say to each other? She could hardly offer to give him his kidney back. Besides, the random ideas, visions, feelings became less of a problem now he knew what they were and realised he was not going mad. So he left it. It was a corner turned, and he began to feel more like his old self.

Eventually he started to work with Archy on creating video games. One of those he devised involved struggling in a raging torrent that threatened to sweep players over a waterfall. It was vivid and dramatic, so much so that it won an award at a games convention in Los Angeles.

Throughout their lives Cameron and Beth remained good friends. They would often talk, either meeting in person or chatting on the phone. However, they were never again able to say to each other, 'I know what you're thinking.'

CAN YOU HELP?

Thank you for reading *I Know What You're Thinking*. If you enjoyed it would you leave a review on Amazon – and Goodreads too if you can? Reviews mean a lot to an author because they introduce new readers.

A social media post would be great too – something like, "I've just read 'I Know What You're Thinking' by Phill Featherstone. If you like character driven young adult thrillers you'll enjoy this. You can find it at mybook.to/Iknow."

Please visit my website - www. phillfeatherstone.net - where you can download a **free copy** of my book of short stories, *Undiscovered Countries*. You can also join my email list to get news of my writing and more freebies.

Finally, would you also follow me on social media?

Facebook - @phillfeatherstoneauthor

Instagram - phillfeathers

Twitter - @PhillFeathers

I know how busy readers often are, so if you can find time to do any of these things I would be truly grateful.

ACKNOWLEDGMENTS

I am indebted to those of my friends and family who read my work. I would like to thank Peter Lane, Deirdre Carr, Theresa Anafi, Jackie Tansky, Rod and Helen Collett, Justin Ingham, Jane Growcott, and Emma Dunmore. I am grateful to them all. My book is better for their help

My children, John and Sarah, and their partners, Kathy and Jeff always give me their unstinting interest and support. Thank you once again, folks.

Promoting Yorkshire Authors, Book Connectors, and Indie BRAG provide writers' forums and I want to put on record my appreciation of the opportunities they provide to link with other authors. I should also like to thank Chill With a Book for encouragement and support.

As always, Sally, my wife and partner of many years has been an unfailing source of creative ideas, priceless advice, encouragement, love and support. 'Thank you' is nowhere near enough recognition of how much I owe to her.

Phill Featherstone

March 2022, Sheffield, United Kingdom

Now you've read *I Know What You're Thinking* you might like to try another of my books.

What Dreams We Had begins with a group of young people on the verge of leaving school. They are in a band which plays at the school prom. It turns out to be a disaster but they're given another chance. Everything depends on how they respond.

Chapter 1

Elena was the first in the band to realise that things were going wrong. The number was called California Rock Chick. The lyrics were hers and the tune was by DJ, but that hadn't stopped Alex introducing it as his own. Joey started a driving 2/4 beat on the drums and Alex shouted the words.

> Cool house, big pool, and her own hot car
> She don't give a shit about who you are
> She turns all the heads when she walks on the
>   beach
> She's a queen, she's a dream and she's outa your
>   reach
> She's a California rock chick rock chick rock
>   chick
> California rock chick
> Rock chick

Because it was a school prom, they'd changed 'don't

give a shit' to 'couldn't care less'. It didn't matter; what was coming was far worse.

The school banned alcohol, but Alex had managed to smuggle in a water bottle full of vodka. That and the weed he smoked at the break were enough to do it. At the end of the first chorus he stood up, clapping his hands, and began to chant.

A group of lads at the front who had been told off by a teacher for moshing couldn't believe their luck. This was payback time. They took up what Alex was yelling with gusto, more at the back of the hall joined in, and the noise grew until it seemed that the entire school was shouting as one.

California cock chick
Cock chick cock chick
California cock chick
Cock chick cock chick

The teachers went berserk, although some of the younger ones found it hard not to laugh. DJ had the presence of mind to kill the mics and Joey stopped drumming.

Steve Sutton, the Deputy Head teacher, leapt on to the stage. He was furious, scarlet with rage. He snatched Elena's microphone and jabbed a finger at DJ to turn it up.

'Silence!' he bellowed into it. 'Silence!' Raggedly and slowly the racket ebbed. 'You've had your fun. Now it's over,' he yelled, glaring at the boys at the front.

'This prom is done. Finished. You're all to leave. Those who need transport, call your parents and wait in the foyer. I want this hall cleared in two minutes.'

The students began to file from the room. Some were gleeful, many looked crestfallen, and from one quarter there was subdued booing. Several of the girls were in tears because the opportunity to get the most out of the outfits they'd worked so hard on had been snatched from them. Eventually the teachers managed to herd everyone out, but it took longer than the two minutes Sutton had demanded.

As the last few left through the rear doors, he turned to the band. 'You too,' he said. 'Out.' Joey started to undo the cymbals. 'Leave it,' he snapped. 'Leave the stuff here. You can sort it out tomorrow. I want all of you in my office at 8.30 in the morning. I hope you're pleased with yourselves.' He stamped off to supervise the rest of the evacuation.

'You idiot!' DJ snarled at Alex, advancing on him. 'What the fuck were you thinking?' Elena thought he was going to thump him.

Alex didn't answer. He'd sunk on to a chair and he looked greasily white, as if he was about to throw up. Joey hooked Alex's arm over his shoulders and helped him down from the stage. Elena followed.

———

It wasn't the Deputy Head they saw next morning. They were outside his office in good time, but he immediately led them to the room of Gina Meredith, the Head teacher. She sat behind an enormous desk and the four of them lined up in front of it. Sutton sat on a chair to the side. On the wall behind him was a large, illuminated copy of the school's crest. DJ read the motto beneath it: *A pure mind served by a pure heart.* Oh shit, he thought.

They'd decided on their story the night before. Or rather Elena, DJ and Joey had; Alex had been completely out of it. The line they'd agreed was simple: the chanting had come not from the band but from a group of boys. Sorry, they hadn't seen exactly who started it and couldn't name them. It was a lie but, as Elena pointed out, it was justified for self-preservation and it was morally acceptable because it didn't hurt anyone else.

Meredith appeared sceptical. 'Is that your reading of what happened, Mr Sutton?' she said, turning to him.

He thought for a moment. 'I honestly can't say, Head. The band may not have started the obscene chant but my impression is that Alex at least joined in.'

Alex was about to say something, but Elena gave him a warning nudge and the four waited in silence.

The school had a problem. The incident could be seen as the deliberate promotion of disorder, an attempt to sabotage one of the major events in the calendar. It had resulted in the prom, which many students looked forward to, being cut short. Already there had been complaints from parents. Suspension would be the obvious punishment. On the other hand, three of the band–Alex, DJ and Elena–were A* students, almost certain to do very well in their exams next year. Besides that, Alex's father had only recently made a substantial donation to the school fund. Finally, because it was so nearly the end of term suspension would be pointless.

At last Meredith spoke. 'Your explanation doesn't convince me,' she said. 'If I was certain that one of you was the instigator of this appalling behaviour I would have no hesitation in punishing you severely. However, you assure me that it was none of you and we have no one who can say it was, so I must give you the benefit of the doubt.'

Despite this exoneration they were in disgrace. However, less than a week later the school closed for the summer break, and by the time DJ, Alex, Joey and Elena returned to begin the new term the occasion seemed to have been forgotten. Except that the band wasn't invited again to play at school events. Instead, another group from a year below who called themselves Vampire Slaves took over. They wore black and were heavily into fangs and fake blood, but worse than that was their music: repetitive covers badly played, with no original material at all.

Not long afterwards, the band lost its name; or rather, it lost them. They used to call themselves The Green Men. That was after The Green Man pub that Elena's parents run, where they had their first few gigs and the only ones for which they were paid. They'd needed a name quickly, jumped on that and it had stuck, but it had never been right. Elena, for one, had never been happy with it.

'We're not all men,' she'd grumbled. 'I'm a girl.'

Joey had suggested Green People, but Alex thought that sounded as if they were aliens. 'Green has other associations too,' he'd said. 'Like unripe. Or immature. Or green with envy. It's just not cool.'

'It's cool when it's to do with conservation,' Elena had said.

'And what's belting out rock to a roomful of people got to do with conservation?'

The discussion had got nowhere, but now they have to come up with a new name because Alex had found the others that lunchtime and given them some astonishing news.

'The Head just sent for me,' he told them. 'Guess what. She wants us to play at the end of term awards.'

'Never!'

'What?'

'Really?'

'Yes, really. She said she's taking a risk. She said that in a few days we'll be leaving. She said we could,' and he made air quotes with his fingers, '"repeat the anarchy of last year", or we could put on a great show and ensure everybody has a good time and we leave in a blaze of glory. She said I was to talk to you all about it.'

'Why did she send for you?' DJ said.

'She assumed I'm the band leader.'

'You?' DJ was irritated. 'We don't have a leader. We're a democracy.'

'Democracies have leaders,' said Alex.

'Well it's not you,' said DJ.

'Okay, okay,' said Alex, shrugging. 'Whatever. But don't you see what this means. She's giving us another chance. We're going to play again.'

When they do play again they receive an amazing invitation from a celebrity to perform at his wedding. All their expenses will be paid and they will live in his luxury villa in Tuscany. Too good to be true? Read on to find out.

What Dreams We Had *is available as an ebook and paperback from Amazon and the usual retailers. In case of difficulty please go to* https://www.opitus.net/ contact *and send a message.*

Printed in Great Britain
by Amazon

78177886R00220